T0124204

Deceit from Beyond

Beyond

from

ELIZABETH KLEIN

authorHOUSE®

AuthorHouse™
1663 Liberty Drive
Bloomington, IN 47403
www.authorhouse.com
Phone: 1 (800) 839-8640

© 2016 Elizabeth Klein. All rights reserved.

No part of this book may be reproduced, stored in a retrieval system, or transmitted by any means without the written permission of the author.

Published by AuthorHouse 07/22/2016

ISBN: 978-1-5246-0623-7 (sc)
ISBN: 978-1-5246-0621-3 (hc)
ISBN: 978-1-5246-0622-0 (e)

Library of Congress Control Number: 2016906908

Print information available on the last page.

Any people depicted in stock imagery provided by Thinkstock are models, and such images are being used for illustrative purposes only. Certain stock imagery © Thinkstock.

This book is printed on acid-free paper.

Because of the dynamic nature of the Internet, any web addresses or links contained in this book may have changed since publication and may no longer be valid. The views expressed in this work are solely those of the author and do not necessarily reflect the views of the publisher, and the publisher hereby disclaims any responsibility for them.

Friendship

*I*T WAS A time in my life where I had started dating after being on my own for over10 years. And with the few dates I had, I must admit the prospects looked pretty bad for me finding someone compatible. I was left with the impression that maybe it was the wrong time to think I could be with anyone of the opposite sex. I know being on my own has spoiled me in many ways, but I did not think I was asking too much for that special someone.

My co-worker and longtime friend tried to help out. She had been single for many years and two years ago she had finally found her true love.

One day at work, she said she really wanted me to meet someone. He was a very good friend of her husband's, as they were both involved in a lot of community organizations. If her husband said he was a great guy, then she felt I needed to meet him, but there was a small problem.

"Okay, I imagine this guy is probably going through a divorce or maybe was in a relationship that just ended. Which is it?" I asked.

"No, it is kind of sad, he lost his wife six months ago in an automobile accident, and Ben and I think you are probably someone who could just be his friend. Nothing serious, just a friend." She said.

"I think he would need more time Lesley. It takes more than six months to get over something that traumatic."

"But you would not believe the females that are already trying to get him to go out. They play the compassion game, someone to talk to or someone around just for company. Then they try and convince him, they really care for him. And that is the point I am trying to make, I know you and you are not really looking for a husband." She said.

"And the reason I am not looking, is because I realized I am not ready."

"Please, for me will you just meet him? We are going to the Club for the Presidential election tomorrow evening. I will have Ben introduce you to him and if he hangs around great, if not, then it is his loss."

"Just this one time and no more setting me up, promise me." I said
"I promise," she smiled.

We were going to meet at the Club at around 6:00pm, as they were having "happy hour" and we could get a bite to eat while we were watching the election.

I arrived on time and Ben and Lesley were already there.

I put my purse on the chair next to her and went over to the buffet, I was hungry. When I got back to my chair, Lesley had already ordered a glass of wine for me. We finished eating and started watching the election on the big TV that the Club had.

An hour had gone by, when Lesley nudged me. I looked at her, then followed her eyes to a man who had just come in the door.

He was not bad looking and it appeared that a lot of people knew him. He was walking along the tables shaking hands and talking mainly to the guys. Some of the women got up from their seats and gave him a hug.

I noticed as he walked, his shoulders were hunched down, like he was carrying a heavy burden. Even though he smiled, he had an overwhelming air of sadness about him. He looked our way and saw Ben and Lesley. He came over to our table and Ben introduced us. His name was Michael. He had a strong handshake and I could tell he was checking me out. He only stayed at our table for a short time and then he moved onto another table.

I cannot remember much of the conversation he had with Ben, but as he left, he said any friend of Ben and Lesley's would be a friend of his. And he hoped he would see me again soon.

Because of the sadness he emitted, I came to the conclusion then and there I was not the one who could get involved with him, even in friendship. I was the type of person who wanted to save everyone, but I could not even save myself from life's trials.

After he left, Lesley asked me my impression of him.

"He seems very nice and very distinguished, but I feel time is what he needs the most right now. Time will help him get through his loss. Not another woman." I said.

"Time is good, but so is a friend," she answered.

"Lesley, he seems to have lots of friends and especially, you and Ben."

Elizabeth Klein

"Yes, he does. But you have to realize, everyone in this room has shared his life with his wife at his side. Everyone, but you, and that is the big difference. You did not know her, therefore he is not the widower, as we know him to be, but just a man to you." She said.

"I know, but he is still suffering from his loss of her. I am not sure anyone can help him get through that right now. What about his family?" I asked.

"The only family I know he has is his two daughters and a son. They live in New Mexico. His deceased wife was his second wife and she had two daughters. They live here, but there seems to be some tension between them and Michael. I have heard it has to do with the will she left. So really it is just him."

"Maybe another time and place, we will meet again." I said.

I only stayed another half hour and then left. I saw him again as I was leaving, he was watching me.

Unknown to me was that Lesley gave him my phone number.

It was a couple of weeks before he called. At first, when he introduced himself as Michael, I could not remember him. Then he said he met me at the Club on election night. Ben and Lesley had introduced us.

He wanted us to meet, as Lesley insisted he had to get to know me better and in all honesty, he felt the same way. We talked a little then he asked if I would come over to his house.

"I would ask you to dinner, but you know my circumstances and I would not want to put any female in a situation where she would be stared at and then be on the gossip line the following day, as the strange woman I was seen with. So for now any female I want to get to know, I will have to meet privately for the time being. I hope you understand." He said.

"I do understand your position, but I hope that Lesley also told you I did not think female companionship was going to help you with your loss at this time."

"It is not the female companionship I am looking for. It is a person who has no knowledge of a life I had a few months ago. I would like a person who can help me start over again in the present tense. I am tired of living in the past. I must get on with my life. But I feel I can only start with someone who does not know me and I do not know them, at least not yet. Can you understand what I am trying to say?" He asked.

"I can and I would like to help, but you must realize that if it is something other than conversation you want, I am not that person.

Do you understand that?

"I do and I want you to know that thought would be impossible for me at this time." He said.

I was not sure this was a good idea, as I knew he was still mourning over the loss of his wife. I still had that feeling I was not the one that could help him. But I felt for him and the "Mother Teresa" over took me.

We agreed Friday would be a good day and he gave me his address.

I talked to Lesley the following day at work. She was happy we were at least going to get to know each other. I told her, I was uncomfortable going to his home but appreciated that he did not want me to be the topic of gossip.

Work was so busy on Friday and I almost forgot I was to meet with him.

On the drive to his home, I wanted to turn around and go back, but for some reason I did not. I found his house, and thought even though it was an older home it was well taken care of. There was a patio in the front with two chairs. I stared at the chairs and imagined Michael and his wife sitting there together, on that porch, watching the activity in the neighborhood and the cars go by. Never dreaming one chair would be empty forever.

I knocked on the door and it seemed like forever before he answered.

He smiled when he saw me and said he was glad I came.

I walked into a living room that looked as if no one used it. There was no light in there. I suddenly was very uncomfortable and felt I should not be there. I could make out an antique couch and a chair with an ottoman and a piano in the corner of the room.

He led me to a doorway that was into a family room and this room felt more comfortable. There was a fire in the fireplace. He sat on the love-seat and I sat on the couch.

"Lesley told me liked white wine, would you like some?" He asked.

"Yes, please." I felt I needed a drink.

He went into the kitchen and came back with a glass. He also had a glass, but I do not think it was wine he was drinking.

"I guess I will start. I am a veteran. I served in the Army and did two tours in Vietnam. I still am amazed that I made it back in one piece and still have all my body parts. I am retired from service and started working for the County, and have been working there since. My first marriage ended in divorce and my second marriage ended in the death of my wife. I have three daughters and a son. My youngest daughter lives back east. She went with her mother after our divorce. Unfortunately there is little communication between us. I was hoping that would change after her mother passed away, but it did not. My other two daughters and son live in New Mexico. Susan has two daughters that live here. I am very active in the community and with the veteran's organizations. That is what keeps me going. I guess that is the short version. Now it is your turn." He said.

My first marriage ended in divorce and I went back to school and earned a degree. I have traveled around the world with my previous job and finally settled down here. I have two sons that live about four hours from here and I visit them as often as I can. I have two sisters, one who lives in the big city and the other lives here. I also have two brothers that lived here as well. My oldest brother passed away. He had been ill for a long time. I am never bored between family, friends and work. I guess that is my short version." I said.

"You are lucky to have family here. But I do go to New Mexico for visits now and then. Matter of fact I will be going to New Mexico for Thanksgiving to visit my son. I am sure you have already made plans for Thanksgiving."

"Yes, I will be going to visit my sons."

There was an uncomfortable silence for a while and then he started talking again. I found him to be very interesting and enjoyed the conversation.

But I still had an uncomfortable feeling being in the house.

I started yawning and told him I better get home, before it gets too late. He was sorry to see me go, but understood.

"For some unknown reason I feel a comfort with you. Maybe, it is that we have already set our boundaries, so no expectations. I hope you will

accept my invitation to come again, maybe for dinner, as I have been told I am a very good cook."

"That would be nice, maybe after the holiday." I said.

He held my hand as we walked to the door. I felt as if he was trying to reach out to me.

I left telling myself, not to go back. I was not comfortable, although he was easy to talk to and seemed a gentleman. I still was very aware of his suffering. I did felt now was not a good time to get involved, even as a friend.

Thanksgiving came and went and now looking forward to Christmas. My younger brother Jim is the comedian and he decided to dress up as Santa Clause. We had a nice dinner with my sister and her husband and Jim and his girlfriend. Then Santa decided to pass out the gifts singing Christmas carols. It was a nice evening with family.

The next day I called my sons to see if they received their packages.

My youngest son Damian was the only one home. He said Daniel was out with his girlfriend Shea. My sons share rent on a home I own. I did not want the hassle of renting it out so knew my sons would take care of it. But Damian was dropping hints that maybe it was time he moved out, as Shea was spending more and more time at the house. I owned a double wide mobile home here in town and told him anytime he wanted to move, he could have the mobile. I put it up for sale but the market was bad for selling it and I sure did not want to give it away. He said he would think about it. I thought it would be nice to have one of my sons living a little closer. It was the mother in me. We talked for a while longer and I told him to have Daniel call when he had some time, then we said our goodbyes.

I looked around my apartment and thought how lonely I really was. Family was great, but they all had their own lives and our togetherness was not as frequent anymore. Some days I wished I did have someone. Just to pick up the phone and talk, then my thoughts were of Michael. Maybe I needed a friend more than he did. Maybe he was right, we had set the boundaries. Maybe I could just be a friend to him.

Elizabeth Klein

I wanted to talk to Lesley and try to find out a little more of Michael, especially what his deceased wife was like. I would talk to her the following day.

Monday morning is always our busiest day and I did not get to see Lesley until late afternoon. I went into her office for a talk.

"How was your Christmas? She asked.

"It was great, spent it with family and my brother dressed up as Santa, he was cute and funny."

"You are so lucky to have family. Ben and I just spent the day inside and watched TV, just another day."

"Lesley I would like to find out a little more of Michael and even something of his late wife. Also you told me he had two daughters, but he told me he had three daughters." I said.

"He only talked of two daughters. I never knew he had another daughter.

She seemed to be surprised at that. His home life he rarely discussed with Ben. He is active and on a lot of committees here in town. His friendship is more with Ben, as they both serve on the board of some of the same committees. I think the fact that they are both veterans, is what brought them together. Michael had only been married to his wife for six years, so that was not very long.

She quit her job right after they were married and became involved in the Youth Organizations. She did a lot of sewing and had some other hobbies, so she kept busy. Matter of fact, she was attending one of the Youth Activities in another city, when she had the car accident. I could not believe it when Ben had told me that she was not wearing a seat belt. That may have saved her life." She said.

"Was it a happy marriage?" I asked.

"We only went to dinner with them a couple of times. They seemed very happy together. I had asked them several times to come to our house for dinner, but they always had an excuse not to come. I sometimes got the feeling we were not of her social standing, if you get what I mean. I would never tell Ben that is how I felt."

"I can understand to keep work at work and home life at home. Maybe now it is just difficult for him to talk of some things. I do think I will be

hearing from him again, especially if you have anything to do with it." I laughed.

"In all honesty, I was just talking to Ben and telling him it would be nice to have you two come to our house for dinner. But he told me to give it some time, so I will.

"That was very good advice from your husband, listen to him."

It was close to New Year's and I decided to spend it in Las Vegas. My son Damian and his friend were also coming. We reserved rooms in the same hotel. It was a great New Year's, standing on the sidewalk and getting caught up in the excitement and the countdown. As it hit midnight, I saw couples kissing and hugging. I felt alone again.

I need to get a life, my New Year's resolution.

Michael called a couple of days after the New Year. He wanted to know if I enjoyed the holidays and I told him I did. He invited me to his place for dinner the following weekend and I accepted. I wanted to know a little more about this man I was to be friends with.

He called me once more, just to make sure I was coming. I told him I wanted to know just how much of a good cook he was, so I would be there.

As the evening approached, I had that uncomfortable feeling again, but was not sure why. I had made up my mind that if I was going to be a friend, it would be one step at a time.

When I arrived, the table was set and there were candles and a glass of wine for me. I hoped it was not an indication of a romantic evening.

"I do not think this is within the boundaries that we set." I said.

"I have cooked most of the day, so thought a little atmosphere would be a nice introduction to the meal I prepared."

"Fair enough, I said, and it does smell good. What exactly are we having?"

"A turkey, they went on sale after Thanksgiving, so I bought one. I hope you are not disappointed."

"I like turkey and being with my sons on Thanksgiving, there were no leftovers, so turkey is good." I said.

"Well you will certainly have plenty of leftovers now, as there is no way I can eat all of this. Have a seat in the family room and I will finish putting this together."

"Are you sure I cannot help?"

"No, just go make yourself comfortable and drink your wine. I will call you when it is ready."

"Okay," I said.

I walked in the family room and decided to look around. There was a bookshelf that contained mostly books of History. There were pictures of his kids but did not see any pictures his wife's two girls. I wondered what went wrong with his relationship with them. So many families split apart after a death, it is sad. There was nothing really feminine in the family room, this must have been more his room, or maybe he put her things away. I found a book of Scotland and wondered if he had traveled there, as that is a place I would like to go someday. I picked it up and started to go through it, when a postcard fell out. It was addressed to Michael, from his wife Susan. She had written that she was enjoying herself with her sister and she wished he was there. I put the postcard back in the book.

He called me for dinner and I walked into the dining room. He moved the chair out for me to sit down and then he sat across from me.

"I hope you do not mind, but I do say a prayer before meals. I have a lot to be thankful for and especially the attractive guest to share dinner with."

He reached for my hands while he said the prayer and I was really touched by that, as it is something that should be a ritual, but rarely done.

"Help yourself." He said.

Everything looked so good and I did not realize how hungry I was. I took some of everything and enjoyed every bit of it.

We talked mostly of work and he told me of some of the things they were planning for the community, as he was associated with the Chamber of Commerce. He seemed to care a lot about the town and wanted to do things that were good for the growth of the town and for the veteran's.

Time passed quickly and I ate more than I should have. I got up and started to help with the dishes. He packaged some of the turkey for me to take home. It would be good for sandwiches for lunch.

I no longer had that uncomfortable feeling. We talked and we laughed as we cleaned up. He poured me another glass of wine and we went to the family room again. He put another log in the fireplace and it was nice.

I sat on the couch and he sat in the love seat again, keeping a distance between us.

"I must tell you, I really have enjoyed this evening. It is nice to be with a female that does not bring up the sorrow and the loneliness I must feel. I have been asked by females to come to their homes for a meal or just to talk. I feel like now that I am a widower, I am fair game." He laughed.

"I can tell you that there is a terrible shortage of unattached males in this town. Some of my female friends have settled for affairs with married men, which I do not understand at all. There really is no future for them, as the men would rarely leave their wives. Why would men do that when they can have the best of both world." I said.

"I have also been associated with some of the men that are in those affairs and I have very little respect for them. But again it takes two or I should say three and no one wins in the end. My wife had a friend of hers that was in that type of a relationship, but she said she was happy with the arrangement, as she was not interested in marriage."

"Is it uncomfortable for you to talk about your wife?" I asked.

"Time does heal and I am able to talk of her more often than before.

We were only married six years. I figured at our age we would be together longer, but God had different plans and I never questioned Him for that, although I would have gladly traded places with her. She was so full of life and love."

"I do not see any pictures of her."

"Because this is the room I mainly stay in, I thought it best to keep them elsewhere. Would you like to see the rest of the house?"

"If you do not mind, I would like that." I said.

We walked through the dining room, then the kitchen. There was a long dark hallway and there was a door to his left.

"That is my bedroom and it is a mess, so we will skip this one."

We turned in the hallway and there were two other rooms. He opened one door and told me it was Susan's work room, as she liked to sew and make crafts. It was so cluttered and there were boxes along the wall, as if

Elizabeth Klein

he was packing some of her things to put away. The next room was made into an office they shared. She had a desk in the corner of the room and he had a large computer desk along the other wall. There were two large file cabinets that were against another wall. I noticed on her desk there were numerous envelopes and cards strewn about and my thought was they were the cards Michael had received upon Susan's death. He showed me where the guest bathroom was and then we walked into the living room that still felt uncomfortable to me. He told me most of the furniture in this room consisted of antiques that they had purchased at an Auction. With the light on I realized the furniture was much too big for the room. There were two long buffets, the couch that matched a high back chair and ottoman and then the old piano. It was a room that was not used very much. It must have been Susan's room, as well.

"Did Susan play the piano?" I asked.

"She was just learning. She had bought a lot of literature and CD's to learn to play. She was doing pretty well before she passed away."

We then walked back into the family room and sat down in our usual places.

"This was Susan's house when we married. It was in dire need of repair as she did not make enough money to keep up with everything that needed to be fixed. The first thing I did was put on a new roof, she had leaks everywhere. Then I had it painted and had new carpet put in some of the rooms. Also she had a broken wooden fence in the back and I like privacy, so I had a brick wall built around the property. She was happy with that." He said.

"Did she continue to work after you were married? I asked.

I already knew that answer.

"There was no reason for her to work and she had time to do some other things she wanted to do."

"I must admit, I really love my job and see myself working even past retirement age. I do not know what I would do with so much time on my hands." I said.

"There are always things to keep woman busy. She always said there were not enough hours in the day to finish her projects." He smiled.

"I guess some woman are like that, but do not think I am one of them.

Except maybe for traveling, I really love to do that and there are more places I want to go and see." I said

"Oh yes, I remember you said you have traveled around the world. I cannot imagine a single woman doing that by herself."

"You learn fast and you are extra cautious on the things that you do and places you go. I never felt I was in any danger at any time, including my African Safari. I rather enjoyed being on my own. I did things I wanted to do and I was on my own schedule and not somebody else's."

"You have more courage than most, I must admit. But then my first impression of you was of an independent female." He said.

I was not sure how to respond to that comment, but almost at that moment I wanted to ask him what was wrong with an independent female, but decided I probably misunderstood his tone when he said it.

We talked more of my travels and he talked of Susan's trip to Scotland and said he could not go with her because of work. But from what she had said about Scotland, he may go there one day.

Time had gone by quickly and I told him I had to go. He gave me the leftovers and he said he really enjoyed our talks and hoped there would be many more ahead. I told him as long as he remembered the boundaries we had discussed I had no problem with that.

He called several more times the following week and asked me over, but I was busy and going out of town more for business.

Lesley asked me what I was doing for my birthday coming up and I told her I had no plans as yet. So she said to come over for dinner and they would celebrate with me.

"You and who else?" I asked. I knew her to well.

"Okay, we invited Michael over, so what is the big deal? I want to evaluate you two together and then give you my impression of this new friendship you have."

"So you are going to give me your professional opinion. Are you licensed to do that?" I laughed.

"It is a female thing and you know it, so show up or I will send Ben after you."

"Well if that is what it is going to come to, I will save Ben the trip.

Elizabeth Klein

What time should I arrive?

We made the arrangements and I was not sure this was a good thing, but then again I would see how he was with Ben and Lesley.

Lesley is a good cook so the meal was great. And of course the birthday cake with one candle on it (no more than one candle, I warned her ahead of time). They sang "Happy Birthday" and Lesley gave me a card from her and Ben. Michael also gave me a card and it was very nice. We really had fun that evening and Ben had Michael laughing at some of his antics, especially while he was in service. Michael had a very nice laugh and I hoped I would hear more of his laughter as time went by. We stayed pretty late and Michael said he better be heading home. We said our good-byes and soon after he left, I headed for home. I knew I would be getting a review of the evening from Lesley, with a phone call the following day as it was the weekend and there was no way she was going to wait until Monday to give me her opinion.

I woke up to early in the morning and decided to stay in bed for a while longer, but the phone rang and I did not have to guess who it was.

"Well, do you want to know my opinion? Oh wait, you don't have a choice, so no need to answer that. I think he is moving on and I think you have been a great help in that respect. The fact that he said we should do it again made me feel he is ready to get back to living life." She said.

"I would agree with you, except he still hesitates to be seen with me in public, so I think your assessment is not a hundred percent."

"Then we will all go out to dinner together, maybe that would help."

"We should wait a couple of weeks and then bring it up. Don't want him to feel he is being pushed into doing something he does not want to do right now." I said

"I guess that is a good idea. I am sure you will be hearing from him soon. Let me know how he liked the evening and of course my dinner, that is more important. I wanted the meal to be special."

"It was very good and I do not know how many times I have already told you what a good cook you are. You make me look bad."

"You don't even cook so there is no comparison. Just let me know, okay?"

"I will and I do cook. There are a lot of frozen dinners that can be put in the microwave and they taste just fine."

I heard her laughing as she hung up the phone. I think her purpose in introducing me to Michael was more than just a friendship. Maybe I should have a talk with her and tell her to slow down.

I heard from Michael later that evening and he did say he enjoyed the meal and the company. He had a good time. He told me he was going to be out of town the following week and he would call when he returned.

It seems as if both of us were coming and going due to Business.

The days passed by quickly. Lesley said when Michael returned she was going to ask Ben to bring up the subject of us going out to dinner together, there had been enough time.

I had to agree with her on that, as it now has been over ten months since Susan's death.

Saturday evening Lesley called and asked if I had heard from Michael yet, as Ben had seen him at the Club and asked him if he wanted to go out to dinner with all of us. He told Ben he would think about it.

"No, I did not know he was back in town, but then again there is no reason for him to call me as soon as he got back." I said.

"I hate bringing this up, but Ben said maybe you should know, that sometimes Michael drinks a little too much and apparently he appeared to have had a few too many when Ben saw him."

"Has he always been like that or just since Susan's death?" I asked.

"Because we have not seen that much of him after Susan died, I am not sure. I remember when he first met Susan she used to go to the Club with him all the time and then she did not come anymore. I just chalked it up to the fact that the people who go to the Club were not up to her standards, so she stopped coming with him. We never stayed late, so always left before he did and Ben has never mentioned him having a drinking problem, so I think it must be since Susan's death." She said.

"Well that is understandable, and once he gets out more he will not need to drink that much. I am sure he will call tomorrow and I will let you know what he says about dinner."

We said our good-byes and hung up.

I really had to think about this little tad-bit of information, as I came from a family of alcoholics and my ex-husband became an alcoholic after our divorce. I just did not want to get in a situation where alcohol was an issue. But I wanted to give Michael the benefit of the doubt, that he did not have a drinking problem.

He did call the following day and he said that he had seen Ben at the Club and he suggested a dinner in a restaurant of our choice.

"I thought it would be okay, but told him I would ask you how you felt about it, and I would get back with him." He said.

"If you feel comfortable, I see no reason that the four of us should not go out."

"I am fine, especially since I have met you. I am ready to start a new phase in my life. So where would you like to go?" He asked.

"You choose, as I do not eat out much, I said. Lesley brings me a lot of her leftovers, so that keeps my refrigerator full most of the time."

"I will let Ben know tomorrow and we will set up something for maybe Friday, if that is good for you?"

"That is fine, and I am sure Lesley will let me know the time, she is looking forward to seeing you get out more." I said.

"Well this is the first step and I do appreciate the friendship I have in the three of you. I will call you again soon."

And with that he hung up.

During the week I tormented myself on this friendship as things are now surfacing about this man, like maybe the drinking. What were other aspects of his life and the life he shared with Susan? I just could not help being curious about this. Lesley had asked other women who were acquainted with Susan, what she was like. They did not know her very well, but she seemed very nice. Again it was not the people she would be with. So was she stuck-up? Did she think she was better than the people Michael had been friends with? Who was this woman? For some reason, I felt if I had some insight on her, I would know more about Michael. But I did not know where to start.

Michael called me and he asked if I would come to his place before we went to dinner, as we could take one vehicle instead of two. I was not sure if I wanted to go back to his place after dinner, but he was right about just taking one vehicle.

"Would you like a drink before we leave for dinner? He asked.

"No thank-you, I will have my glass of wine with dinner."

"Well I hope you don't mind if I have a drink, it has been a long week."

"No, I do not mind and I have to agree with you it has been a very long week." I said.

"I keep thinking I should take some time off and go somewhere, but not by myself. How would you feel about some time away, just as friends?" He asked.

"It does sound nice, but time from work would be impossible now and I will be out of town for the next two weekends. One weekend was for business and the other weekend to visit my sons. Hopefully things will slow down some when the Holidays come." I said.

"Well I am sure our friendship will still be in tact over the Holidays. Just think about it."

It was time for us to go and he finished his drink. Ben and Lesley were already there. We did have a nice dinner and the conversation between Ben and Michael was about some upcoming event that they were putting together. I noticed that Michael had two more drinks, but he seemed fine. We had coffee after dinner and talked a little more. It was getting late and time to go. Michael picked up the check and Ben said the next one would be on him. Outside the restaurant we said our "good-nights", and I got in the car with Michael.

"Well that was a nice evening and I did feel comfortable, so another new step in getting on with my life. I cannot thank you enough and Ben and Lesley. I am so lucky to have such good friends."

"I do not think we are the only ones you go out with." I said.

"No, I do have a lot of luncheons with co-workers and mostly male friends. And I attend a lot functions. Matter of fact I have one coming up in a couple of weeks and I was going to ask if you would mind going with me. Would you be interested?"

"You are starting to move on, aren't you? It would be nice, but remember I am just a friend and that is how I want to be introduced to your associates."

"We set boundaries and I have been abiding to them. I will pick you up, two weeks from today, which will be Friday evening at about 6:00. I will call you to remind you, just in case you forget or you change your mind, he smiled. Also it will help a lot if I knew where you live."

I gave him my address and told him I would not forget. Again, that uncomfortable feeling came.

As usual work was busy and the days flew by. I told Lesley that Michael was taking me to one of his functions and I will probably meet a lot of his co-workers and friends. I was not sure this was the time, but he seemed to be okay with it. I guess he is moving on." I said.

"You know that everyone will think you guys are dating, no matter how he introduces you."

"Yeah, I know, but he must know the same thing. And I do believe he will tell them that I am just a friend and no more. We set boundaries before establishing this friendship."

"So you have no feelings for him at all?" She asked.

"In all honesty, no, I like the simplicity of life. I do not honestly think I can be in his world."

"And what world would that be?"

"He is well known and he needs a socialite to be by his side."

"And you believe that Susan was that type of woman, even though no-one seems to know that much about her." Lesley said.

"Maybe there will be someone there Friday night that might say something of her." At least that was what I was hoping.

The week passed quickly and I find myself questioning if I should attend this function with Michael. But I could find no answer not to go and I was hoping to meet someone there that had some knowledge of his late wife.

Michael had no problem finding my apartment. It was a small apartment complex and I liked the security.

"Welcome to my humble home." I said, as I opened the door.

"This is nice, he said, as he walked around. I like the homey feeling it has and it is nicely decorated."

"Thank you. I think I missed my calling. I like to have things that can fit, not only in looks but comfort as well. I would have liked to have been

an interior decorator, but did not think I could do well in other people's homes, trying to work around their personalities."

"Well you did very well here. Maybe you would consider re-decorating my place, as I am starting a new life and changes have to be made. I am serious about that offer, I will need help"

"I think that would be fun, but I have to know more about you. Your likes and dislikes."

"We have plenty of time for that, but think for now we need to get going."

We arrived at the Club. All the tables had white table clothes and candles on them. I was glad he informed me ahead of time, that is was a semi-formal event. It was a fund raiser for one of the committees he was on. As soon as we appeared, all eyes were on us. Michael was gracious, and he seemed more at comfort than I was. So many people came to talk to him, even as we were trying to find our table. After he seated me, he was off to talk to someone else. When he came back he had a drink and brought me a glass of wine.

"I did not think we would be such an item, this evening. Everyone commented on how lovely you are, I agreed with them. I hope you are not uncomfortable, if you are, we will just stay for dinner and leave."

"No, I am okay." I really wasn't, but this evening was more for him than me.

Prayers were said before our meal and conversations started. Some at our table wanted to know about me and what I did for a living. There was no discussion about Susan and maybe that was out of respect for Michael. We were getting ready to go, when a gentleman came up to Michael and asked him to make a speech of the project they were trying to get funds for.

He looked at me and apologized. He said he felt obligated to speak on behalf of the committee.

I watched him go to the podium and he stood to the side until he was introduced. This was a part of him that I was experiencing for the first time. He looked very comfortable in this role he was playing. He was very much respected and very much liked and he was feeding off of it.

I was disturbed about seeing this side of him. But do not know why.

Elizabeth Klein

I am sure he had made many speeches and it was obvious from the audience that he was respected. He was truly a man who was looked up to.

When he returned to the table after an applause that filled the room, we started to make our exit. Some women came up to me to say how glad they were to meet me. I could tell it was not sincere, I could see right through it.

I was relieved when we arrived at my apartment. He walked me to the door and I invited him in.

"Just for a short time, he said. I must apologize for any discomfort you felt this evening."

"It just was not the class of people I am used to be associating with. I have never felt I had to put on airs to impress people and unfortunately I can see right through them"

"You are right about that. But if you want anything that has to do with financing, these are the people that you need to impress. There are a lot of things in this town that would not exist if it was not for these people. The funds raised from them helped the development of the parks in town, the hiking trails and the activities for the kids. Not to mention the monument that we are trying to get now in honor of the veteran's. It is just what you have to do."

"I am so sorry, I meant no disrespect and I did not know until you spoke, what this function was for. You should be commended for anything you can do for the veteran's." I really meant that.

"Next time we will have a discussion prior to attending some of these.

I would like for you to attend more functions with me, to keep the single females at bay for the time being. Do you feel up to that?

"With the boundaries." I said.

"With the boundaries," he answered. He went to the door and thanked me for the evening. He would call, so we could discuss the interior decorating.

I wanted to find out more about him and of course Susan. Eventually someone would say something about her.

Michael called a couple of days later, wanting me to come over and look through the house and get some ideas for what he called "renovations".

I told him I had to be out of town for a couple of days and hopefully would be back before the weekend, so would call him as soon as I returned.

Two straight days of meetings and I was exhausted. I guess I should not complain, but being single is not always wonderful. I am the travel person because I do not have a husband or a family. I also work some weekends for the same reason, so therefore I am more flexible with my time and my life. At least my boss thinks so.

I called Michael when I returned. I had unpacked and poured myself a glass of wine.

He asked if I could come over the next day and I said that would be fine.

Again, I had the uncomfortable feeling.

I was surprised to see all the boxes, by his door as I walked in.

"I feel it is time to pack her clothes and other stuff she had in the closets. I had no idea of all the things she purchased. I guess it is a woman's thing, shopping and all"

"I am sure it is still difficult for you though." I said.

"It is, but it has to be done. I have to continue on with my life."

"You are doing that, step by step." I said.

"Thanks to you, he said. For now, I would like you to start with her room. I have packed a lot of her things in there. What is left will probably just go to Goodwill. If there is something you see that should be kept, just put it in a box in the closet and I will go through it later. I have left some small empty boxes and tape in there. Once that is done, you can give me some ideas to the changes you would make. I will keep working in my bedroom, but I want to eventually change that as well. So it looks like your weekends will be spent with me for a while. Are you up for the job?"

"I am looking forward to it but are you sure you want me going through her things?"

"Like I said there is not much left in the room, so I am okay with it."

"Well, I guess I better get started. Do you have a pen and paper, so I can put some ideas down?" I asked.

He went towards the room that was the office and used a key to open the door. He went in and gave me a tablet and pen. I thought it odd that

Elizabeth Klein

he would lock his office. But guess he was still going through all the cards and paperwork I saw in the room.

When I opened the door to Susan's room, I noticed how cold her room was. There were still a lot of things on the floor and on a table. I saw a small dresser that was partially hidden underneath some cloth that had been piled on top of it. I folded the cloth pieces and put them in a box, then started to go through the drawers as Michael had indicated he wanted none of the furniture in the room.

There were family albums and loose pictures in the drawers. As I went through some of the pictures, I did not see Michael in any of them so it must have been of Susan's family. I started to go through the albums, hoping I could get maybe a feeling of Susan and her life. She was average looking, but she had a warmth to her, in her smile and eyes.

Her two daughters were adorable. These were lots of pictures when they were younger. I thought these should be with her daughters. It is hard for me to believe they would not want them. I packed them in a separate box and I would put them in the closet. When I opened the closet door there was a rush of cold air. I looked up to see if there was a vent opened. I did not see anything, but there were some plastic containers on the shelves. I thought these were probably things he was going to keep for now. I closed the closet door and started to put another box together, when I heard the bedroom door close. I opened the door to see if Michael had walked by, but I did not see him. It was probably just the draft I felt when I opened the closet doors. I finished packing three more boxes of just "stuff", when Michael walked in.

"Thought we would take a break and get something to eat." He said.

"That sounds good. I will finish this box and meet you in the kitchen."

I taped up the box and set it on top of a couple of other boxes and I started for the door. I heard that box fall to the floor. This is getting weird I thought. Maybe it was too heavy to be put on top. I decided I did need a break.

Michael had made us some grilled cheese sandwiches. As we were eating I asked him why Susan's room was colder than the other rooms in the house.

"It has always been like that. I have searched everywhere for maybe a break in the wall or a roof leak, but nothing. It does not get much sun, so I attribute it to that. I can get you a jacket, if you would like?"

"No, I am fine. I think I will do a couple of more hours then head out. I have neglected my own housekeeping and laundry."

"I was hoping you would stay the evening, as you wanted to know my likes and dislikes." He said.

"There is plenty time for that, as I can see this is going to be a big job.

If you can move the furniture and the boxes during the week, I can start tearing down the wallpaper next weekend. That has to go."

"I was hoping you would say that, the pink flowers do not work for me and I know I have to get rid of the pink carpet. She would never change it, after her youngest daughter moved out. I guess it was a mother thing."

"We will make it neutral, so you can use the room for anything you would like."

"Well, it will have to be a spare bedroom, as I already have my office and every now and then one of my kids force themselves to come and visit me."

"You are lucky they do not live near. No matter how hard you try not to get involved in their lives, you seem to be right in the middle. My youngest son, Damien, will be moving in my mobile home in a couple of weeks, as his brother and his girlfriend are making it extremely uncomfortable for him to stay in the house. But he is a big help to me, so I am looking forward to his move."

"What of his job? Can he just quit like that? There are not many job opportunities here."

"He has some physically disabilities. He does part time and odd jobs now and then. Although he is a good painter, so I could have him do some painting, if it is okay with you." I said.

"That will work for me as I am not into painting."

"I am not either, so he will be a big help."

I got up and helped with the dishes. Michael went into his bedroom and shut the door. I walked to Susan's room and the door was closed. I do not remember shutting it, but felt maybe the door was defective. The room was still cold. I started packing the "stuff" and the time went by. Nothing more happened while I was in the room and I was thankful for that, as my imagination was scaring me.

I finished packing, so knocked on Michael's door to tell him I was ready to leave. He opened the door and came out, shutting the door after him.

"I wish you would stay, but know you have things to do. We do need to talk about your compensation for all this work you will be doing."

"Why don't we wait and if you like what you see, I will let you determine its worth."

"That sounds good and I will need you with me to pick out paint, new carpet and furniture."

"I can do that with you. I think it will be fun. Anyway, will call you and let you know when I can come over." I said.

He walked me to the door and waved goodbye as I drove away.

I was excited to do something I really enjoyed doing, but I did not like Susan's room. Hopefully once the renovation was over it would have a different feel to it.

My sister Lily called and wanted to have lunch. It had been a couple of weeks since I heard from her, so wanted to catch up on the gossip.

"So how are things going with Michael?" She asked.

"He is doing well and I am helping him with some interior decorating. I felt uncomfortable when he asked if I could start in Susan's sewing room. There was some weird stuff going on in that room."

"Like what?" She asked.

"It is the coldest room in the house and when I went to put a box in the closet a rush of cold air hit me. I thought it was air coming from a vent, but there was no vent in there. Then the door would just close and it was not me closing it. I just felt I was not alone in that room."

"You watch too much TV, especially the Sy Fy channel. Does Michael have the same feelings when he is in the room?"

"He wasn't in the room with me and he would think I was crazy, like you do." I laughed.

"Well I think your friendship with him is an illusion. Every time you are seen together people think of you as a couple and not just friends, so hopefully you will get used to that." She said.

"Look, I do not really care what people think. I have no feelings for Michael other than friendship. There are so many women waiting for me to disappear, so they can have a chance with him. He says he is not ready for any kind of relationship. But when he is ready he will not have a problem finding someone whom he feels he can connect with. And it will not be me."

"Well there is no way I could disagree with you as far as the females waiting to make a move, but never say never, it may come back to haunt you." She laughed.

"Did you just say haunt? I asked. I have a feeling that has already started."

We both laughed and finished our lunch. I got caught up on the family affairs. We made a promise that we would have lunch more often. Although with a husband, a job, and being a grandmother, she is always busy. I am the adopted grandmother as my sons have yet produced a grandchild. Maybe one day.

Michael called and said this weekend he would be out of town, so the following weekend we would plan on continuing the renovations.

"I did want to let you know, I had the furniture and the rest of the boxes removed from the room, so you can start on the wallpaper, if you want."

"Yes, I think it best to start on that as it will be the hardest job. I guess I will hear from you when you get back. Take care," I said.

I thought it strange he did not say where he was going. Usually if he had to go out of town on business he would tell me where he would be. Maybe, just maybe he has found someone. That would be wonderful.

My son was moving into my mobile home, so kept busy helping him. He went to school here so he wanted to look up some of his buddies. I was glad he would be out and about. We went out to eat a couple of evenings and a few times I was being starred at. I guess it was some people I met at the function that Michael took me to.

I took a couple of days off work, wanted to do some "fall cleaning", and have some time to myself. While I was doing laundry, my phone rang. I picked up the phone and said "hello", but there was no answer on the other end. It happened a few more times and I was really getting angry, so

Elizabeth Klein

decided I would not answer and let it go on the answering service. After about the fourth time, I heard a voice. Someone left a message and all it said was, "I knew Susan."

I did not recognize the voice. I could not even tell if it was a woman or a man's voice. It sounded like they were trying to disguise their voice. That really bothered me as there were very few people I told, that I wanted to know about Susan. And how did this person get my phone number, it is unlisted. Someone had to give that person my number.

But who is this person? And why would they say they knew Susan?

I called my sister and told her of the strange phone call.

"Doesn't your phone have the number that called?" She asked.

"Yes it does but it was an out of area number. Lily, do you think I should tell Michael of the phone call?"

"Wait and see if they call back, it was probably just a hoax. But if they do call back, don't you go anywhere by yourself to talk to this individual. You call me or our brother."

"I have no intentions on disappearing anytime soon, so don't worry about that." I laughed.

"Well, keep in touch. Between the haunted room and the strange phone call, I am beginning to worry about your sanity. I don't need you to be going psycho on us."

"I do not think you have to worry about that. My sanity has always been questioned, so it is normal for me. Don't worry, I will keep in touch. Bye".

I was worried though, something was going on that was beyond my comprehension.

At work, Lesley wanted to know how things were going with Michael.

"He seems to be okay. We are now doing some renovations in his house. I am working in Susan's sewing room. That is going to be a real job." I said.

"Doesn't that bother you, being in a dead person's room?"

"It does a little, but I love to do interior decorating, so I am enjoying it. I already have some plans to give to Michael and see if he likes them."

'It is funny that Michael did not mention that to Ben, as they were at the Club last night."

"Was he with someone? I asked. He went away last weekend and I was hoping he had found someone."

"Ben didn't mention it. So you still don't have any feelings for him?"

"No, I do not, and it is not going to happen. When we finish with the house, I doubt if we will be seeing a lot of each other. I really want him to find someone and it is not me."

"Well can I arrange another dinner at my place. She smiled. Then after dinner, maybe we can play cards."

"It is fine with me, but have Ben ask him, okay."

"I will and let you know." She said.

I was almost looking forward to start work again in Susan's room. I had so many ideas for decorating it.

Michael called and said to come over, so I headed to his house.

"Hi, how are you?" He asked.

"I am fine. I hope you had a nice weekend? Did you get some R & R?" I asked.

"I did, and it was nice. But now we start again, so hope you are up to it."

"I am. I purchased some supplies to remove the wallpaper, so hopefully they will work, as that is the hardest job. So better get started." I said, as I was walking down the hallway.

"Wait just a minute. First you will agree to have dinner with me, no rushing off, like you did last time. I would like to take you out, but am afraid if you went home to change out of your working clothes, you won't come back. So I will fix something here. Agreed?" He asked.

"I will stay and I will probably be hungry, so make a lot." I laughed.

I walked into the room and again it was cold. It is just a cold room, I told myself and started to get my supplies together. I was hoping that the wall paper was only from the ceiling to half the wall, but now that the furniture was removed, it was to the floor. I started soaking the wall from the floor up. After about a half hour, I thought I heard a voice. I looked out the door and Michal was not there. I re-enforced the door with a stub that I bought, to make sure the door was going to stay opened. I started to pull off some of the wallpaper. I was using the scraper and some areas of the wall paper would

Elizabeth Klein

not budge. It was like someone used super glue. I pushed down hard with the scraper and it literally flew out of my hand. I thought I might have hit a crack in the wall or something. Suddenly I was not feeling well, sick to my stomach. I walked out of the room and just stayed in the hallway for a few minutes. I went back in the room and started to soak the wallpaper in the center of the room. I thought maybe it would be better to work toward the corners. I looked for the scraper, it was gone. I did not see where it landed, but it had to be on the floor, I moved a few things, but could not find it. Where could it have gone? The closet door was opened just a little and there it was, on the floor. How in the world did it get in there? I picked it up and closed the closet doors. I did not want to think of this, I did not want to be scared. I started to scrape the wallpaper again and fortunately did not have another incident, thank goodness. After about an hour and a half, Michael came in and said it was time to eat.

I went in the bathroom to wash up and I could not find the soap. I looked under the sink and was surprised to see so many toiletries.

Shoe boxes full of them, small ones, like the ones you get in the Hotels.. I found a hand wash in one of the boxes and used that. Curiosity got the better of me and I started looking through the drawers. There were Susan's makeup and hair accessories. All her things were still there. I looked in the bathroom closet and again more of her things. I thought he had been going through her stuff and gotten rid of it. It has been almost a year now. Can he still be trying to hold onto her? He honestly said he was ready to move on. From some of the things he had said, I felt he was a man who had no intention of staying by himself any longer than he had to. He talked of finding someone, not necessarily for marriage, just companionship. But I also know out of respect for Susan, he was going to wait the full year and that would be the end of this month. Maybe in the next couple of months, he will start looking for someone who can be that companion for him.

We had a nice dinner and I stayed longer than I wanted. He put a log in the fireplace and it was nice. I sat in my usual place and had a glass of wine.

"Michael, it will soon be a year, how do you feel at this time?"

"I still think of her, not as much though. Time does heal." He said.

"You should start checking out some of your single female friends, and look for someone who is compatible. It would not hurt you to make the first move."

"Are you trying to get rid of me, my dearest friend? I cannot bring anyone in this house the way it is. So with your help we will get it to look more like a bachelor's pad, then I can start bringing females over."

"Well I can come tomorrow and work a little longer on getting that wallpaper off." I said. I suddenly wanted to change the subject.

"If you can make it in the afternoon, as I go to church in the morning."

"Just give me a call and I will come over. But for now I need to go home." I said, as I got up to leave.

"Always in a rush, I thought we were going to talk more of me, so you can make a determination of what I would like in this house."

"Okay, one more hour. So start talking."

He gave me insight of his "home" personality.

"I try to leave everything from the outside at my door step when I get home from work. I just want to relax." He said.

Some of his days were long and then he had some meetings in the evening, so comfort was a major thing with him and that is what he felt when he was in my apartment.

He was a good conversationalist, and we had some laughs. One hour passed very quickly. It would be two hours before I finally left.

When I got home, there was a message on the answering machine.

I just stared at it, not really wanting to find out what it was. There was no sound, just a long silence.

Who is this? I said to myself. Why is it important for them to tell me about Susan? It does not matter at this point. Michael will find someone and start a new life. I know he does not want to marry, but he does want companionship and I am sure there are plenty of females out there that would settle for that, even for a short time. If I get another call, I will simply say "not interested" and maybe that will finish it.

Days and weeks were passing by so fast. There were some days that Michael gave me the key to the house, when he could not be there. I was still

Elizabeth Klein

uncomfortable when I went into Susan's room, but just convinced myself it was nerves. It seemed like forever taking off the wallpaper. It was like it had a mind of its own. I had cuts and scrapes on both of my hands from the scraper, never thought I was that clumsy. I attributed it to my rush to get the room done.

Michael and I shopped together and picked out the paint and bought some curtains for the window. I also suggested getting new closet doors. My son started the painting the following day. When he came out of the room he mentioned to me how cold the room was. So thankfully I was not imagining it, as it seemed to be getting colder and colder. I usually wore a sweater in the room and I noticed my son putting on an old sweatshirt when he was painting.

Michael and my son hit it off and when Damian finished painting, Michael had some yard work he wanted done, so my son did that for him. He paid my son more than I thought he should, but he knew my son was limited on income, so I did not make a big deal about it. It was between him and my son.

The new closet doors were installed and I put up the curtains. Michael bought a couch that had a hide-a-bed in it. Then he purchased a bookcase and a TV to go in the room. The room really looked nice and comfortable. Michael had walked out of the room as I was admiring my work. The TV suddenly came on and scared me so much, I ran out of the room.

"What is the matter?" Michael asked, as I ran into his arms, shaking.

"The TV came on all by itself. I did not touch it."

He walked to the room and the TV was not on.

"It did come on, Michael, all by itself."

"It was probably a power surge, sometimes that happens. You are really shaking, let's go in the family room and I will make us some coffee."

He did not believe me.

He gave me a cup of coffee. Then wanted to know which room would be next.

"I think the living room, as everyone sees that room first." I was still shaking.

"And what would you do with the living room?" He asked.

"First, take down the paneling, as that makes the room dark and replace the dark brown carpet with maybe a beige carpet, which will make the room look larger. You have big windows, but dark curtains. I think blinds and maybe just a valance over the top. I am not sure about the furniture."

"Well the furniture that is in there will probably stay for the time being. But I do like your idea about the paneling and carpet. And I never did like the curtains, but Susan made them, so did not say anything."

"Damian can take the paneling down and paint. It might be a mess for awhile, but I can help him." I said.

"Then we will get started right away, as I would like to have it done before the holidays. I am thinking about inviting some of my office staff here for a Christmas party this year."

"We can have it done by then. I will talk to Damian this evening."

"I was hoping you might stay for dinner, I have some leftovers that I can heat up."

"I am not feeling that well, so think I will go see my son, then go home. Want to feel better so we can get to work."

"I do not expect you to push yourself so hard. After all you have your day job."

"I know, but I love seeing the results of the work. Susan's room looks so nice." I said.

"It is no longer Susan's room. It is a very nice and comfortable guest room."

"Yes, you are right, but no matter it turned out better than I expected."

I got up to leave but he was trying to get me to stay. I had to leave as I was still upset from that incident with the TV.

Damian and I were having a bite to eat, at his place. My son turned out to be a fabulous cook. I guess because my cooking was so bad, both of my sons started to cook for themselves at a very early age.

I told Damian about the TV turning on and no one was there and it really scared me.

"Mom, I did not want to say anything, but there is something very wrong with that room. When I was working in there the closet doors would open and I would get a sudden burst of very cold air. The hair on

Elizabeth Klein

my arms stood straight up. Also there was a whispering sound that came out of nowhere. I would check around and no-one was there. If that is Susan's room, I do not think she has left."

"Maybe you and I do watch too much SyFy. I have experienced the same things. I just cannot accept that there is a ghost in that room.

My common sense thinking can come up with rational explanations for the things that have happened in that room."

"Mom, the supernatural have no explanations."

"Well, we need to finish the living room and then think I will just give Michael ideas on the other rooms. I am not sure that I can be in that house any more than I have to. Although I will tell him you will do the painting, so you can earn some holiday money."

"Thanks mom, the money will help and as soon as you are ready, we will get started."

We finished eating and I helped with the dishes. I told him I would call him.

I walked to my car and there was some paper on my windshield. I took it off and almost fainted. It was a piece of the wallpaper I had taken down from Susan's room. It had the pink flowers on it. I leaned against the car and my knees were weak. I took the wallpaper and went back to see my son.

"Mom, what's wrong, you do not look to good."

"It was on my windshield." I showed him the wallpaper.

"This was in Susan's room, wasn't it?"

"Damian, what is happening? Why is this happening?" I asked.

"I don't know mom, but from now on, you do not stay in that house by yourself. Do you want me to take you home?"

"No, I will be okay. I think I will go straight home and take a sleeping pill and try and get some sleep. I will call you in the morning." I said, even though I was not okay.

When I returned to my apartment, as soon as I would open the door I would look at the phone. It had been awhile since I had that message on my phone, but I kept looking. I did not realize I brought the piece wallpaper in with me. I laid it on the kitchen counter.

"What is happening?" I asked myself. There were no answers.

It was approaching the Christmas Holidays. Lesley and Ben wanted Michael and I to attend a Christmas party they were having. We were seeing very little of each other since I started working on Susan's room. I promised her I would make it and I would ask Michael if he wanted to attend.

"How are things going with Michael these days? She asked. Ben says the only time he sees him anymore is at the meetings. He hardly goes to the Club anymore."

"He just keeps going and going. He has been real busy lately. He has more energy than the "energized bunny". I don't know how he does it."

"Do you still feel the same way about him? She asked. You have been with each other for almost a year now."

"Lesley I do not have any feelings for Michael other than friendship.
I have even stopped attending a lot of his functions. He cannot find someone if I am with him all the time."

"I don't think he is looking, he has you and he seems content."

"He has me as a friend and he knows it will not go any further."

"You obviously have not paid attention to Michael's accomplishments, if he wants something, he usually gets it." She smiled.

"Not happening, no matter how much YOU want it." I smiled back at her. She just was not getting the message.

"Okay, I was just hoping something would happen between you two by now. But if you are happy being his friend, go with it. I will send you an invitation, I bought too many. See you later." She smiled.

As she walked away, I almost wanted to tell her of the weird experiences that I have had. But she wouldn't believe me and I did not want her to think I was losing my mind, although sometimes I felt as if I was.

The following weekend, Damian and I started to take down the paneling. Michael had to go, so left the work for us.

"Are you okay, mom?"

"I am Damian. I am going to try and ignore any more distractions in this house."

"No mom, I am talking about feeling okay. You don't look well. Are you sick?"

"I have been feeling a little under the weather, but it is nothing. I just want to get this room done. Michael is going to have a Christmas party here, so we have a lot of work to do and not much time to do it in."

My son started to pull some paneling off, it was so old it broke in pieces. I brought the garbage can in and started to put the pieces in it. We had been at it for an hour, when we heard something fall in Susan's room. We both looked at each other.

"I will go and check it out mom, Damian said. You stay here."

As he got off the ladder, I was right behind him going into the hallway. The door was closed and he opened it slowly. There was a picture on the floor and when my son picked it up, it was a picture of Michael and Susan. The glass was cracked and I noticed there was an attempt to scratch over Michael's face.

"If there is anyone here, can you do something to let us know?" My son asked.

"No, don't do that, I don't want to know." I was panicking.

We both stood there, waiting for something else to happen, but I felt I needed to get out.

I left the room, still holding the picture in my hand.

Maybe I should tell Michael what happened. Maybe he could explain why his picture was almost scratched out. But I knew I wouldn't. I had one purpose and that was to finish the living room and call it quits.

Damian came out of the room a short time later, and said nothing more happened. So I took the picture back in the room and set in on the dresser that it had fallen off of.

It was getting dark by the time we finished with the paneling and cleaning up the mess. I told my son to go on home, I would wait for Michael.

"I told you mom, you are not staying in this house by yourself. I will stay."

"Okay, well let's raid his refrigerator and see if he has anything we can munch on."

We found some lunch meat and bread and made sandwiches. We did not say much to each other, but every time there was a noise, we looked toward the end of the house, where Susan's room was.

Michael came home, just when we were doing the dishes.

"I am sorry that I am late, did not think I would be gone so long, he said. I am glad you found something to eat, I did not even think about feeding you two."

"We were just leaving, so glad you came when you did."

"Well let's see how things are going," he said, as he walked into the living room.

Something was different about him. I just couldn't figure it out. It was as if his mood changed. Sometimes I was not sure if he really wanted to change things. Did he still want to hang onto things as they were with Susan?

"Removing the paneling sure made a difference. It has brightened up the room a lot, a very good job. So the painting starts tomorrow?"

"Yes, if you could come home over your lunch hour and let Damian in, he can get started right away and I will come after work." I said.

"I think I can get away, I will be sure and give you a call Damian."

We started to leave and he walked us to the door. He said goodbye and I felt as if he wanted us gone. I was just too tired to deal with anything more, I wanted to finish this part and stay away from the house.

My sister called the next day and wanted to know if I could meet her for lunch. I told her I could. I notified the receptionist that I would be out of the office and take messages for me.

When I met my sister at the restaurant, we had to wait for a table.

"I already put my name on the list. They said the wait was not too long. Damian was right, you look awful. Are you ill?" She asked.

"No, just tired. Cannot seem to get enough sleep, I wake up in the early hours of the morning and just can't get back to sleep."

"Are you sure that is what it is? Damian has told me some weird things are still going on in that house that cannot be explained rationally."

"Well you know my son and the paranormal. Anything that is out of the ordinary is ghosts to him."

"I would have believed that, but I am looking at you and I do not think you are dealing with these unexplained incidences very well." She said, with concern in her voice.

Elizabeth Klein

"Did he tell you about the piece of the wallpaper from Susan's room that showed up on my windshield? Did he tell you of the picture we found on the floor in Susan's room of Susan and Michael, but Michael's picture was almost scratched out? Please tell me there is a rational explanation, I want to hear one."

"The wallpaper could have flown out of the trash bin and got stuck in your windshield, you just did not notice it. As far as the picture, it was just a picture and obviously someone was unhappy with him, therefore the scratch marks."

"That is a possibility, but we both heard something fall, a picture does not make that much noise." I said.

"That could have been a noise outside and you just thought you heard it coming from the room."

"Lily, it could have been all those things. But explain to me why I wake up in the middle of night from dreams that I cannot recall and why I feel someone is trying to tell me something, but what?"

"Sis, promise me you will take some time off. You have saved plenty of vacation time use it. Go visit our sister. Go see Daniel and check out his new girlfriend. Just get away for a while."

'I am seriously considering it after the holidays." I said.

Just then her name was called to be seated. We had a nice lunch and did not talk anymore of the things I have heard and seen in the house.

I thought I should not say anymore of my experiences in that house. No-one will believe me.

I met Damian after work at the house. He was already starting on his second coat of paint.

"You must have been working your ass off, to already be on your second coat."

"It goes faster when you do not have to worry about the carpet. I just covered the furniture. I do remember you saying Michael was going to get new carpet. I will finish with the second coat at about the same time Michael will get home. It will take a while to dry, so we can come back Saturday and put the blinds up and the valance. When is the carpet coming?"

"I think he said the following Monday. So everything will be done in time for his Christmas party."

"Mom, I needed a marker, so I thought Michael might have one in his office. Did you know that Michael has locked the doors in the other rooms? I guess he does not trust us.

"I can't say you should not have done that as I also wanted to check on the rooms to get some ideas for decorating. I knew he locked them. Even when I was in Susan's room, he would go into his bedroom and I would hear him lock the door from inside. I guess maybe he does have a trust issue."

"Well mom you might as well go home, there is not much you can do, as I am almost done here."

"Thanks, I am a little tired. Damian has anything strange happened today?"

I immediately saw the change in his face.

"No falling objects or anything like that. But a couple of times I would get that cold sensation. I know you told me not to call out to anyone, but I did. I swear mom, I heard a voice and no-one else was here."

"Damian, we both have huge imaginations. Let's just get this done. Call me later, okay?"

"Sure thing, mom." He smiled.

It was nice to get home and away from that house. Things happened there, that had no logical explanation for. At least my son knew I was not crazy.

I had not been feeling well, so decided to make an appointment with my Doctor, maybe get some blood work done. I was having episodes of painful attacks all over my body. Just stress, I told myself.

I took a shower and then made myself something to eat. I was not hungry, but knew I had to have something in my stomach, so I can take something to help me sleep later.

I just finished dishes when Michael called.

"Hi there, Damian said you were not feeling well, I hope you are doing okay?"

"I was just tired. There is not much more we can do until Saturday then all you need is the carpet laid. The paint turned out real nice, good choice on the color."

"We picked out the paint and the carpet together. I have been thinking I want to do something nice for you, so made reservations for a candlelight dinner, at my favorite restaurant. I planned it for Saturday evening. Will you accept the invitation?" He asked.

"That would be nice and I do need an evening out, so yes I do accept the invitation, as a friend."

"I know the boundaries as I have said many times before. So I will see you during the day and in the evening. Twice in one day, I feel very privileged." He laughed.

"I will see you Saturday. Have a good night," I said, as I hung up the phone.

I finally slept through the night and felt good. I was going to cancel the Doctor appointment, but thought maybe the blood tests would be able to find something, as I was tired all the time and I did not like the painful episodes that I had been having.

It was Friday and as I sat in the Doctor's office, I thought this was silly, I already knew what was wrong with me. I was losing my mind.

The Doctor said that I had lost weight and maybe I should get Labs, just to be on the safe side. So he gave me a script.

Lesley wanted me to come over this evening to pick up my invitation, she did not want to mail it (she was to cheap).

I was going to cancel, but I had been so caught up in getting the renovations done. I felt bad for not keeping in touch.

"Hi, have you had anything to eat yet, we were just sitting down."
"I should have called, I am sorry."
"No apology, I will get an extra plate, have a seat." She said.
"Your kitchen always smells so good. Ben you got a gem."
"That I did, but the extra pounds I have put on are not helping my waistline." He smiled at Lesley.

"You look just fine. I am trying to keep you healthy. Good food and good loving, I always say." She winked at him.

"Okay, you guys. You have a single female sitting at your table. I do not have to be reminded of some things I am missing out on."

"If you would just let go of your inhibitions, you might just have someone very close by." She said.

"I thought Ben was already taken." I smiled.

"You know whom I am talking about."

"Lesley, I have no feelings other than friendship for him and I think he deserves more. I am sure he will be able to find someone after the New Year. I will make that my New Year's resolution."

"And how many of your New Year resolutions have come true?" Ben asked.

"I really try not to make them. I do not have a very good track record."

"Well it has been over a year since you two were introduced, so I will see how he is when you come to our Christmas party." Lesley said.

"I haven't talked to him yet, sorry. I will see him tomorrow and see if he wants to come." I said.

"Do not worry about it, I sent him an invitation, knowing you would wait till the last moment, as always."

"Now that is not true, I always get around to things, just on my time."

"Well let's eat before it gets cold. She held up her glass and said a toast.

To a good friend and a very good lover," she smiled, as she looked at her husband."

"Awkward," was all I could say. And I drank my wine.

I called Michael the following morning and asked him if I could come early to put the blinds up and valance. It would give me time to get ready for our dinner.

He said to come over now.

When I arrived he had some coffee for me and asked if I had something to eat.

"I had some toast it is enough to hold me over."

I started unpacking the blinds and asked if he could get me a screw driver. He said he had a charged one and he would put in the screws.

We worked together and had everything up in less than an hour.

"We make a good team," he said. I cannot tell you how much I appreciate all that you have done. This room sure has a different atmosphere to it, almost like we gave it life. I did not realize how dark and gloomy it was."

"Removing the paneling helped and eliminating the curtains. When the carpet comes in, you won't recognize it. I better get going, I have a few things to do before getting ready for dinner."

"Then I will pick you up about 6:00." He said.

As I was driving home, I did sort of pat myself on my back. It really did turn out nice. But I would need a break before making a decision to do the other rooms.

Michael was on time and I was almost ready.

"I hope you are hungry, this place has outstanding food."

"I am hungry and looking forward to the dinner." I said.

It was a very nice restaurant, one that I was not familiar with, but that is not unusual for me, as I do not eat out much.

Michael ordered drinks first and I looked at the menu. I just settled for a small steak. After the waiter left, Michael handed me an envelope.

"What is this?" I asked.

"Well open it and find out." He answered.

It was a thank-you card with a check for $5,000.

"Michael, I can't take this. It is too much." And I handed the check back to him.

"You did a wonderful job and it is worth every cent. So you will take the check and I do not want to hear any more about it." His voice was rather stern, so I took the check.

"Well thank you so much. My sisters and I always plan a vacation together once a year, so this will help."

"I am glad that you will use the money to enjoy yourself. You need time to get away."

"I am getting that statement from everyone, so I guess I better take the hints." I said.

"I do need to ask you for a few favors. I have a pile of things to do at work and time got away from me. If I can give you an idea of the food for the Christmas party can you go to the caterer and make the arrangements? I already told her to reserve the date and time, but she needs the menu. Also, I have accepted Ben and Lesley's invitation, but I would like for you to attend my Christmas dinner as well, as my friend." He smiled.

"I will help you with the caterer, but I do not think it is a good idea to attend your party." I said.

"We are going to be seen together at Ben and Lesley's. I just need some support for my dinner party. That is all I am asking for."

"It is kind of difficult, Michael. As my part of this friendship was to help you move on with your life and maybe find someone you can share a relationship with. How can you move on if I am a road- block for others?"

"It has been a little over a year since my wife's passing. I think I still have plenty of time to "play the field" as they say." He smiled.

"I know, but I still feel that the more people see us together, the more you may be missing an opportunity."

"Then let me worry about it."

"Okay, as long as you remember, I am a friend, I cannot be anything more." I said

He was silent for a while and then our food was served. He talked of the things he wanted for the party. He usually gave his staff gift cards, so that was easy enough. The others will have to settle on a good meal. He laughed.

When we arrived to my apartment, I asked him in for a drink.

"I don't think so, I am driving. But I would like you to stop by Monday and see the difference the carpet makes. Why don't we have lunch, then we will both go to the house and see it."

I really did not want to, but I would rather be in the house during the day than during the night.

"Let me make sure I can get away. You know how Mondays are."

"Yes, I do know and that is exactly why I would use any excuse to take a break. So lunch is good. I will give you a call and we can meet somewhere." He said.

I was beginning to get that uncomfortable feeling again. I was worried that those who saw us together more often will draw their own conclusions. But he has never made any advances toward me. Or have I missed them? Well after the New Year, I will not be spending as much time with him. Maybe I need to slowly move away.

I had to admit, Michael was right about Mondays and I was more than happy to take a break.

We meet at a small sandwich shop. Not many patrons there, so that was good. He wanted to talk more of his party, as Friday we would be attending Ben and Lesley's party, then Saturday was his party. He wanted to know if I could be at his house early that Saturday morning. He would leave the back door opened for me as he had a meeting that morning. He had hired a house cleaning service and he wanted to make sure everything looked okay.

"Do you think Damian would like to earn some extra cash? He asked.

"I would like him to bartend for the party."

"I am sure he would. I will ask him." I knew he would enjoy that job, he has a good sense of humor and I am sure he would not only bartend but entertain as well.

We finished lunch and went to his house. Michael had been to his house before lunch and let the carpet guys in. The owner was a good friend of his, so he said he was trustworthy. When we arrived the carpet guys had just finished laying the carpet and were putting the furniture back in place.

The room looked as if some life had just been put in it. Michael talked to the carpet people and I just walked around. I thought I would suggest to Michael if he would buy some Christmas flowers, for his party. I knew exactly where I would put them.

Michael asked if I could stay a little longer, as he had to get back to work and the guys were almost done.

"Yes, I can stay. I said. And Michael, I just came up with something that would really make the house more in the holiday season. Can you purchase some Christmas flower arrangements to set around in the dining room and this room? They would really give it that extra touch for the party."

I felt that Michael probably did not want to put up a tree and I could understand that being single. You don't want the hassle of putting it up or taking it down.

"I think that is a great idea. I have a credit account at one of the floral shops. I will call them and tell them that you will be there one day this week and you can order the flowers."

He had to go and soon the others left. I was alone in the house.

Damian said never to be alone in the house.

I was arranging some things in the living room, when I heard a noise.

I was drawn to Susan's room. I stood up and slowly walked to the door, not wanting to open it. Not wanting to feel the cold air again. But I could not stop myself. I turned the door handle slowly and felt the cold air rushing past me. Turn back, I told myself, just turn back and leave, but my feet did not move. I looked around the room. It is just a room, a room that I decorated. That is all it is. I started to walk in the room. I had no control over my movements. Once inside the room, the door closed. I felt dizzy and sick to my stomach.

"Please, if you are here, tell me what you want of me." I whispered.

There was movement by the closet door. I opened it.

A small box from the shelf in the closet fell. It opened when it hit the floor, letters came out of the box. I felt whoever was in that room wanted me to look at the letters. But I couldn't. I felt as if I was going to throw up and finally got some control and ran out of the room and into the bathroom, just in time. I washed my face, my hands shaking uncontrollably. This is real, I am not imagining it. Someone is in this house and whoever it is, wants me. I opened the bathroom door and ran from the house.

I went home and called the office and told them I had become ill after eating and I would be home the rest of the day.

What in the world was going on, I asked myself. Why is this happening to me? I knew I could not say anything, because I knew exactly what others would think. I was going crazy.

I knew that box fell to floor and I saw the letters. Were those letters on the floor meant for me to read?" If so, why?" I asked myself.

I was worried that Michael would have seen the box of letters on the floor, if he should go into that room. But he never mentioned it.

Elizabeth Klein

I went to the floral shop on Wednesday and picked out some beautiful Christmas arrangements. They would deliver them Saturday morning.

I still was not feeling well, but thinking that I was going out of my mind did not help. I decided not to tell Damian as he told me not to be in that house alone and I will make sure that does not happen again.

I told Michael that I was going to Lesley's Friday morning, as I was going to help her with setting things up for her party.

"Are you okay? She asked, as we were setting out the chips and dips. I have noticed you being distracted lately."

"I have been real tired lately. So I will enjoy the time off after the first of the year."

"Well, I think you need some time away. Christmas is such a busy time of year. Did you get Michael a gift?"

"I have not even thought about it. Do you think I should get him something?

"Even so-called friends get each other gifts. He is a veteran, so maybe something pertaining to the military." She said.

"That does help. I just hope he takes it at a friendship gift."

"What does it matter? You keep telling me you have no feelings for him, which for the life of me I just don't understand. He has status, class and is financially well off. So what is it about him that you can't get passed?

"Lesley he is very nice, and sometimes I wonder about my feelings or lack of them when it comes to him. It is something I can't explain. I know this sounds crazy, but it is like a warning I sometimes feel. That is the only way I can describe it."

"It does sound crazy. But if you feel that way, then go with your feelings. A lot of times we do things that we feel is wrong and if we do not listen, I'll be damned, we screw up every time."

We both laughed and finished with the party favors. I was glad when I left. Again I could not reveal anything about my feelings or things I have felt and seen in that house as I will be labeled as crazy.

I was late getting to the party. I was feeling sore all over, but knew I had to be there for Lesley.

She had a good turnout. I noticed a lot of the people I had met at the Club.

I saw Michael talking to a very attractive lady, someone I had not seen before. She sure seemed interested in him and I was happy to see that.

I tried to stay out of view, as I did not want to disrupt their conversation. I went in the kitchen to see if I could help Lesley with anything.

"I was worried about you. I sure did not want you to skip out on me."

"You know I would never do that. I was having a female crisis. I could not decide what to wear. After all I have another party to go to tomorrow night and you know you cannot show up wearing the same outfit."

"So true, and men wonder why we shop so much." She laughed.

Just then Michael walked in.

"I was trying to find you. I was afraid you were not going to show.

Lesley told me you were not feeling well this morning. Are you okay?

"I am fine, so do not worry about me. But you should be out there enjoying the party. I am just helping Lesley with a few things."

"I wanted to introduce you to a few people. They will be attending the party tomorrow evening." He said.

"Go, Lesley said. I am done in here and think I should be attending to my own guests."

I gave her a look which I am sure she understood, very well.

Michael introduced me to some his co-workers, who I am sure I will never remember their names. I was looking for the woman he was talking to when I came in. Finally he was leading me toward her.

"Margaret I want you to meet Beth, she is the one I was telling you about. She did a fantastic job with the interior decorating in the house."

"I am so happy to meet you. Michael has told me so much about you.

I will be anxious to see the changes in the house. I have told Michael many times, he needed to brighten up that house. It looked so gloomy."

"Well, I think you will be surprised." He said.

"Have you two known each other long? I asked.

"We have been friends for many years. We were actually introduced by Susan, his late wife." She said.

"So you were friends with Susan? I asked.

Elizabeth Klein

"We attended a lot of the same social events and once in a while we had lunch. So we were not good friends, but I enjoyed her company."

I was hoping I had finally met someone who had known Susan. I was trying to hold back on my curiosity, but I still had that underlying feeling of wanting to know more about her.

'There is someone else I would like you meet." Michael said. He excused both of us as he held onto my arm and we were off to meet more people that I would never remember.

After several more introductions, Michael went off to talk to Ben. Lesley came up to me.

"It seems like Margaret has been checking you out. You realize she is out for Michael. There were rumors at one time, that Michael and she had an affair, an extra-marital affair." Lesley said.

"What do you think, Lesley? Could he really do that to Susan?" I asked.

"I could never see Michael doing such a thing. Susan was with him at most of his functions, luncheons and some parties. They were either madly in love or she did not trust him.

"Were they madly in love? I asked

"How do you tell? She asked. Just being seen together does not necessarily mean love. Then again their private life was just that, private."

"Women can deal with a lot of things, but infidelity is the hardest. I should know. I had to deal with it." I said.

"I know, but you had me to get you through it. We both did a lot of crying, I did not want you to be alone. I saw the pain you went through. But out of all of that you became a better person." She said as she gave me a hug.

She knew every now and then I needed a hug.

"Thanks, I said."

I was getting that tired feeling again, so decided to leave early. I saw Michael and he was disappointed I was leaving so soon. But I told him I would be over in the morning.

"What time are the cleaning people going to be at the house?" I asked.

'About ten o'clock and they promised me they would be done about two in the afternoon. I should be back around then."

"Okay, I guess I will see you then." And I left.

I had to ask him what time the cleaning people were going to be there as there was no way I wanted to be in that house by myself again.

I woke up early the next morning and decided to go to Starbucks for coffee and a muffin. I was sitting outside on the patio, reading the paper when I heard someone say "Hello".

I looked up and it was Margaret. I was rather surprised as I had not seen her here before.

"Hi Margaret, I thought most of those who attended the party last night would sleep in today."

"I couldn't sleep and needed some coffee. Do you come here often?" She asked.

"Only when I cannot sleep," I smiled.

"Do you mind if I join you?

"Not at all, please sit down."

"Are you helping Michael with the party this evening?" She asked.

"Yes, but I do not feel he needs help, as the caterer will be taking care of the food and he hired my son as the bartender. So there is not much I can do."

"Can I ask a personal question?"

"If it is about Michael and myself, I already know the question and the answer is "no". I met Michael after he lost his wife. Lesley felt that he needed someone with no attachments to his life before Susan's death. I felt bad for Michael. He had such a great sadness about him. So when we first made arrangements to meet, I made him understand from the very beginning that I could only be a friend to him and nothing more. As long as we stayed within those boundaries, I would be there for him. I want Michael to find someone he can be happy with and share a life with, but that person is not me."

"I have to admit that I have had feelings for Michael for a long time, she said. I was sorry for him when Susan died, but I thought with time I might be able to attract him. I waited, and then I heard he was seeing someone. I had to find out, so asked him one day while we were at lunch. He did say he had a female friend. But of course being a woman, when a man says he has a female friend, there is a little more than that. At first he would say

Elizabeth Klein

very little about you, but when you started to do the renovations, he talked of how much he was impressed with the work you were doing. I knew I had to find out who you were. I made it a point to be friendly with Lesley in order to get an invitation to her party. When I first saw you, I pretty much figured I had no chance. And in all honesty I still feel that way, as obviously you do not notice how he looks at you. It is not a best friend look." She said.

"This meeting was not a coincidence, was it? You followed me here. Were you at my apartment?" I asked.

"I can't blame you for being upset with me. I had to know who you were. It was not difficult to get your last name and find out where you lived. I was on my way to talk to you when I saw you leaving. I followed you here."

"I am not very comfortable in someone looking for me, only to check me out. Also if it was that easy to find me, why not just a phone call?"

"I doubt seriously if you would have accepted a phone call from me inquiring about Michael. I think meeting face to face would be more helpful to me and to you."

"It is not helpful to me at all. You got what you came for. I think this conversation is over." I got up to leave.

"Please don't be angry with me. I was desperate to find out." She said.

"Then answer me this. It is rumored that Michael and you were having an extra-marital affair. Is that true?

There was a hesitation. Then she asked me to sit back down.

"I am hoping you will not disclose this conversation with anyone. You are close to Michael, maybe you need to know. Sometimes Michael drinks too much, not often, but sometimes. He was at the Club one evening and we started talking. Susan had gone to Scotland with her sister. He had a few too many and although I am ashamed to admit it, I took advantage of his weaken state. I told him I would drive him home, only I drove him to my place instead. I told him it was just to have some coffee before I took him home. After he came into my house, he knew exactly why he was there and he had no second thoughts about leaving any time soon. He came back to me several more times after that night.

He said he needed more of what I could give him. I never told anyone about us, but I guess Susan suspected it. I have to tell you, Michael seemed to have a need that Susan could not fulfill. He would never talk about it, but it was obvious to me. When the rumors started to spread, he told me we would have to end it."

"Do you have any idea at all, what the relationship was like between Michael and Susan?" I asked.

"I don't think anyone does. Their home life was very private."

"Someone knows something, as I received a phone call and the only thing I heard, was that they knew Susan. It might have been a warning, I don't know. But first the phone call and now this meeting with you, I am sure you can understand why I am a little on edge."

"I am truly sorry. I never intended to frighten you. I assure you I only wanted to know about you and Michael."

She said it with sincerity and I believed her.

"In all honesty he has never made any kind of a pass at me and I have known him for over a year now. I made it perfectly clear to him from the very beginning where I stood. I know what people have said about us, but I have felt that it was exactly what Michael intended. He wanted to put an end to the women trying to entice him."

"Thank you. I think we both have an understanding. You will keep this between us?"

"There is no reason for me to say anything to anyone about our conversation. Only next time you want to know something, don't follow me. There are other ways and I know who you are now." I said.

"Agreed." she answered.

I was very upset by that meeting. It seems since knowing Michael, I have had some disturbing things happen to me and more and more unanswered questions about the marriage between Susan and Michael.

I arrived at Michael's house at exactly ten o'clock. The cleaning people were not there. I sat in the chair on the porch. I was not going into that house by myself. They finally came 20 minutes later. I had a key and we walked in the house and I started to show them the rooms that needed cleaning. I was not surprised that Michael's bedroom door was locked and his office was locked. So guess those rooms did not need cleaning. I walked past Susan's room and just pointed at the door and told them I had already cleaned that

Elizabeth Klein

room. So they got their cleaning things and started to work. I sat down in the living room, while they were in the family room. The flowers were delivered around eleven o'clock, so I placed them where I thought they looked the best. Michael had left a box of Christmas items in a closet off the hallway. He said to go through it and see if I could use anything for decorations around the house. I opened the box and saw some handmade stockings, which I am sure Susan made. Then I found a beautiful wreath that I could use. There were some bulbs and a few strings of lights and on the bottom was a bag. I opened the bag, and it contained Christmas cards addressed to Susan and Michael. I knew I shouldn't, but I started looking through some of them, just standard Merry Christmas and New Year's. But one card was addressed to just Susan and it had a note in it. It was from one of her daughters and the letter said how she missed the times at Christmas that they used to have with family and friends. How much she knew her mom loved Christmas and family. Then the daughter asked, when and how did things change so much? Why did she no longer feel a part of the family? Why was Michael more important to her than her own children?

I thought this kind of odd. Why did she feel like she was left out? Why was she feeling that her mother had abandoned the family? The daughter felt she had to write her feelings even though it might jeopardize their relationship even more than it already had. The end of the letter, the daughter wrote: We have been with you all of our lives, are you willing to give us up for the short time you have been with this man?

The letter was heartbreaking. The daughter seemed to be making a plea to her mom. Was there a conflict between the family and Michael? I checked the address on the envelope and thought if I could get any answers for all the questions I had about Michael and Susan, maybe I can get them from the daughter. I took the envelope.

I finished going through the box and put a few things on the end tables and the coffee table. Michael came home early which was good, as the cleaners were finished, seeing as there were fewer rooms to do.

"The place looks nice and I do like the flower arrangements. It is starting to look more like Christmas." He laughed.

"Well I cannot stay. I have an appointment to get my hair done and my nails. So I will see you later."

He walked me to the door and said "Thanks". He would see me this evening.

I tried to put things out of my head. I really wanted to have a nice time this evening. I would not be seeing much of him until after the first of the year now as he was going to spending the Holidays with his son in New Mexico.

I arrived at his house early in case anything came up that he would need help with. But the caterer was there and she had brought the dishes and the silverware and even the wine glasses. So that was taken care of.

Damian was at a bar set-up that Michael had borrowed from a friend of his. I walked over to him and he said "What will it be, good-looking."

"I take it you are rehearsing for tips?" I smiled.

"Michael has always been more than generous with the money he pays me. But if there are any attractive single women, I may get lucky."

"I do not think that is something your mom should have knowledge of and anyway most of these women are a little older than you are."

"I think that is what you call "cougars" and I do like cats, especially wild cats." He laughed.

"Okay, just give me a glass of wine and I will stay clear of your territory."

There were already guests there and I saw Margaret approaching me.

"I hope you have forgiven me for this morning. I sure did not mean to upset you, like I did."

"I think I am over it. Sometimes unanswered questions drive us to do things that we normally would not do. And in a way I am glad that you are here. Margaret, this is my son, Damian. Do you want a drink?"

"It is nice to meet you, she said, with a smile. I think I will just have a glass of wine, thanks."

Michael walked over to where we were standing.

"Well, this is not good, my two favorite women, together." He smiled.

"It is not often for a man to claim he has two favorite women." Margaret said.

"Two is always a good number." Michael laughed.

I was not sure if that comment set well with Margaret, but Michael did not seem to notice.

"Your reputation is safe with us". Margaret said.

"And what aspect of that reputation would that be?" He asked

"I do not think you want me to disclose that." She laughed.

The look he gave was one that I had never seen from him.

"You will have to let me in on that one." I was trying hard to break up this discomfort that I was feeling from both of them.

He reached for my arm. "Someday, he said. Right now I need you for a few minutes. I want you to hand out the gift cards to my co-workers, as I call their names."

I went over to the table where we set up a Christmas basket, with the envelopes in. As he called out each name, he had a story to tell of each individual. I saw admiration these employees had for him. He said he could not call them employees, they were co-workers. He could not do his job without them and therefore they would always be referred to co-workers. You do not find many bosses like that anymore.

Michael and I had discussed what we were going to do with the flower arrangements and I told him to have people fill out a card with their name on it and we will draw the winners of the flower arrangements.

The last name he picked was my name, for the biggest and most beautiful floral decoration. I was surprised, as I never put my name in the drawing. I looked at him and he just smiled.

The party was late in ending. It had been a long day for me. The caterer started to get her things together and I was happy that most of the food was gone. Anything left-over, my son took. He was happy as he actually got tips for his bartending and did pretty well for the evening. Although no "cougars" but do not think he was disappointed.

I told Michael, I could come the next day and finish cleaning if he wanted. But he said I had already done enough and he would take care of the rest of it. We said our usual good-nights and I was glad to get home and go to the bed. I put the flower arrangement on my dresser as the fragrance was nice. I slept through the night and most of the day.

The phone woke me and it was my sister, wanting to know how the weekend went and I told her "exhausting."

"Are you going to be rested in time for our get away?" She asked.

We had already decided that we were going to Reno.

"I have yet to miss our getaways and I am not about to start now, so no fear of that."

"I am so looking forward to this year. I desperately need the break, far, far away from family, job and bills." She laughed.

"You are going with family. So you can only get away with two out of three." I said.

"Okay, I will suffer through it, just make it come fast."

"Don't say that. You know we will be heading home in no time and then we have to wait another year."

"Okay, I take that back. I want the day before we leave to come fast."

We both laughed and talked a little more and then I told her I would get back with her before Christmas, as we were having a large family get-together, so needed to make sure there was enough food.

The following week I received a message from my Doctors office and he wanted to see me. I called and made an appointment for later in the week, but they said they had a cancellation that afternoon and if I could come in then. I thought I might as well find out what it was he wanted.

As I sat in his office, bad things started going through my head, which I know is what everyone else thinks when their Doctor wants to see them.

I was called into one of the rooms and did not have to wait long before he came in.

"Have you been feeling any better or worse since I last saw you?" He asked.

"Just being tired and some pain every now and then."

"Where is the pain?"

"All over, I said. Some days tolerable and some days I just want to stay in bed. No get up and go."

"Some of your lab values are high. So I want the tests run again and if we get the same results, we are going to start running some other tests."

"Should I worry now or later?'

Elizabeth Klein

"There is no reason for worry now, until we can get a diagnosis. The important thing is to get you feeling better. Meanwhile get this lab work done as soon as you can. I will write you a prescription for pain, but only take it when you really need it, as it will make you drowsy."

After I left I decided to get the lab done the following day, but would definitely get the prescription filled. Drowsy I like.

Michael called me before he left for New Mexico. He said to keep an eye on my mail. Because we were hit and miss for the holidays, he sent my present to me. I had already given him his gift. It was a book. I asked Ben to help pick one out that Michael might like.

I told Michael he did not have to get me anything, as the check he gave me was more than enough.

"You have helped me so much this past year and I do not think a small gift is that much to do for you. I hope you have a good Christmas and I will call you when I get back home." He said.

"I wish the same for you and please have a safe trip. Take care."

A couple of days later there was a small package. I opened it, and it was a ring, a very expensive looking ring. I was uncomfortable in receiving a ring. Maybe it was just a friendship ring, although at our age I do not think there are friendship rings anymore. But it was something I was going bring up when I saw him again and I decided I would not wear it until then.

Christmas turned out to be a great time, but I was lucky, as I had a lot of family. For New Year's, I decided to stay home, I just wanted to rest. I told my sister we would be leaving for Reno the end of the month, so we needed to start saving money. It was like Las Vegas, as it wasn't only what happens that stays there, it is usually our money as well.

Michael called and said he decided to stay with his son and daughter-in-law until a week after the New Year. They were trying to get something together so he could see his two daughters. They lived a few hours from his son. I knew he had taken two weeks off. So was glad he was going to stay with his family.

I saw the Doctor again after the New Year and he was going to order some X-rays on my spine. I was in a head on crash five years ago and even though I broke ribs and my sternum, it was always my back that hurt. Then he was going to follow up on some more extensive lab work and do a nerve test. So I guess I was going to be a guinea pig for a while. I was glad though he was doing his best to find out what was wrong with me, as I did not want to tell him, I was having more bad days then good. I was leaving work early, more than I felt I should, due to overall body pain. I decided to keep it to myself until I found out what the tests would show.

Michael called when he returned. He said he would have called earlier but when he went back to work, it was crazy. As soon as he could arrange it we would go out again for a nice quite meal as he wanted to talk to me about more renovations to the house.

I told him I had taken some time off and my sisters and I were going to Reno. I would call him when I got back.

My sisters and I were ready for our "sister's vacation". My sister Barb lived in another city and she drove up. She had stayed overnight with me. My sister Lily said she would drive and she would pick us up about 8:00am. Of course my sister Barb and I were up early, packed and waiting for Lily.

We talked and laughed during the drive, catching up on old times and new times.

"So how is your "friendship" coming along with Michael? My sister Bard asked with a funny grin.

"It is still a friendship and I do not care what others have told you." I said, as I looked at Lily.

"Well if you can be a friend to the opposite sex and they are happy with that, then you are one in a million. Barb said. But honestly Beth, you need to find someone. I know how bad your divorce was, but that is in the past. It has been years now, let the past go."

"Barb, I said. My life is fine. I have family and friends. It is not necessary to be with someone, if that is not what you want, only what others want for you. You know that. Even though you have had boyfriends, you said you would never marry again."

"Ouch, she said. But I deserved that. I will never, ever marry again."

Elizabeth Klein

And then we both looked at Lily, who has been married over 30 years. "Marriage is work and I work very hard at mine." She laughed.

The drive was long and I was glad when we checked into the Hotel. We unpacked and went to the restaurant to get something to eat. After we ate, we checked out the Casino. We only play the penny machines. We do not feel as if we lose the money as fast. Every now and then we will share a dollar machine. We were playing the dollar machine, when all three sevens came up (they were different colors) but we won $1,000.00. We split the money and went back to our penny machines. The following day we went shopping and then we were going to a stage play later that evening. After shopping, I went back to the room and took some pain medication and laid down for a while. Hoping the pain would let up some before the play.

My sisters kept asking if I was okay and I told them I was fine. I reminded them the oldest sister always needed some rest to keep up with the other two.

The next day we walked the downtown area. We were playing in one of the Casino's, when we saw several security guards walk to the aisle behind us. Pretty soon a lot of people were walking that way. So I got up to see what was going on. I came back smiling and told my sisters we were only a few machines away from the next millionaire. A small Japanese man had hit his machine for one million dollars.

"I guess that is as close as we are ever going to get to a million dollars." My sister Barb said.

"Well at least we can tell everyone, we were that close." I laughed.

The three of us were pretty tired that evening, so we decided to rent a movie and make it an early night. For which I was grateful.

When we woke the next morning, we were wondering what to do.

"Well, my sister Lily said. I don't know about you two, but I am going to get a tattoo."

"A tattoo, I said. I never knew you wanted a tattoo."

"I have always wanted a tattoo of an angel and I am going to do it today."

"What does your husband think about that?" Barb asked.

"I will know when I show him." She laughed.

There are Tattoo parlors in most hotels, so it was not hard to find one.

My sister picked out a beautiful angel and we were told it would be a couple of hours waiting for her.

"Do you want a tattoo?" My sister Barb asked me.

"No, do you want one?"

"I don't know, it sounds rather daring and I looked at some of the tattoos there and I like the crosses."

"Well then go for it, I said. You only live once."

"Let's walk around a little bit and give me some time to talk myself out of it. I don't like pain, especially if it is self-inflicted."

She did not get one, but the one Lily had gotten was very beautiful.

We went to get something to eat and then just walked on through the downtown area.

"Do you realize we only have one more day." I said.

"Great, you have to remind us." Barb said, as she punched me in the arm.

"Why is it when you are having fun, time flies and when you are miserable it crawls, I said. It should be the other way around."

"If we figured that one out, we would eliminate the misery and just have fun. But the consequences of having all that fun would be; we would get older twice as fast." Lily said.

"That is not good, so we keep some misery." Barb laughed.

On our last day, we decided to hit as many Casinos that we could. After a few, we had to stop as the money was disappearing way to fast. It was fun though.

I was exhausted by the end of the day, so told my sisters I was going to the room after dinner.

"I think all of us are done in, so maybe another movie." Lily said.

I fell asleep and did not see the end of movie,

The next morning we were depressed, the packing and the memories began. We laughed a lot on the way home trying to keep our sense of humor, knowing our fun time together was over.

My sister Barb stayed with me a couple of more days before she had to go back home. She really wanted me to introduce her to Michael before she was to leave. But I told her I just wanted to spend my time with her and that I felt my friendship with Michael would soon be coming to an end.

　　　　　Elizabeth Klein

I was still uncomfortable about the ring and was realizing that maybe I better slowly start distancing myself from him.

Lesley wanted to know all about my Reno vacation, when I returned to work. And I had the feeling she was going to bring up having another small dinner party for my birthday.

"Lesley how about you and I go to lunch for my birthday, as I am not feeling up to anything more than that this year." I said.

"You are still not feeling well?" She asked.

"That is only part of it. Michael gave me a ring for Christmas. I am trying so hard to convince myself it is just a friendship ring, but my gut says it is not. Have I been blind about this friendship?

"I have seen how he looks at you, but still he does nothing to indicate that he wants to be any more than friends with you. He only brings up your name when someone asks about you. In all honesty, I don't know.

But maybe it is time I have Ben do a little probing. Men are more comfortable talking about relationships with other men."

"I think the same goes for the females." I laughed.

"Then lunch it is, I get to pick the place and pick up the tab."

"Okay with me." I said.

Lunch turned out to be at an ice cream parlor, she order me the "birthday special", which was a gigantic hot fudge Sunday with a sparkler on top.

It was so embarrassing but fun.

I took Friday off as I was scheduled for an MRI. It was one test after another since the New Year. I could not get any answers until all the test were completed.

Michael called later that day and apologized he missed my birthday.

"After the first of the year we have to start with our projections for the coming year at work and of course submit the budget, he said. But I would like to get together maybe this weekend for dinner."

"That would be nice but it would have to be tomorrow. I am going to be busy on Sunday and then need the evening to rest before work Monday."

"I will make reservations for tomorrow and I will pick you up around seven. See you then." He said.

I thought finally I can find out why a ring.

We were going to the same place we had been before. It did have a nice atmosphere and the service was always good as well as the food.

"I have been worried about you. Ben told me you have been going through some tests. I know it is none of my business, but is it something you can talk about?" He asked.

"Right now I know as much as anyone else, which is nothing. All the tests have to come in before I find out what is going on. I have had some pain, which I guess for my age is not all that uncommon. So, as my Doctor tells me, don't worry." I said.

"If and when you find out, will you tell me?" He asked

"I am sure it is nothing and if it is what good will it do to tell everyone."

"For support for one thing and after all we are friends and that is what friends are for." He said.

"As a friend, I would tell you," I said. Now I need to bring something else up. As much as I like the ring, I am afraid there are others who feel this was a step toward something else. I am hoping that was not you intention when you gave it to me."

"It was just to let you know how much I appreciate you. I noticed you never wore a ring and thought that would look good at least on one of your fingers. Please don't concern yourself with the gossip. People just cannot conceive the idea of a man and woman just being friends."

"You know you could stop the gossip if you would be seen with other females." I said.

"You are absolutely correct and to save your reputation, I will try harder to be seen with other females."

"Thank you." I said.

We enjoyed our meal and the conversation was more of the holidays and his family. He seemed to favor his son, Jeremy, but guess all fathers do with the only son.

"Jeremy was a surprise, a late in life baby. Michael said. His sisters were in high school when he was born, so by the time he started school his sisters

Elizabeth Klein

were married and had families of their own. He was good at practically everything he did and I am very proud of him."

"He sounds as if he is a fathers dream."

"I hope for you to meet him someday. I told him his old man is getting tired of the drive to New Mexico, so the next trip, he comes here."

"That will be nice and I would like to meet him."

After a cup of coffee, Michael noticed I was tired. It always shows in my eyes. Michael said time to get me home.

As we walked to my apartment, he said we will postpone any more renovations to the house for the time being. Which I was grateful for, as I did not think I could do anymore right now.

I called Lesley the following afternoon. I knew why Ben told Michael about my tests, I just wanted to know if Ben came up with anything in his probing.

"Hi, Lesley, I said. I went out with Michael last night and it seems he found out from Ben that I have been ill. So did Ben get any information from Michael?

"Ben told me the only thing Michael revealed was that he thought a lot of you and appreciated the friendship that you both had. You did help him through his sorrow and he has moved on and is enjoying life. That was about all. I did tell Ben not to say anything about the ring, as you were going to talk to him about that. So what did he say?" She asked.

"Basically the same thing, it was an appreciation ring and nothing more. And I am not to worry what other people think about us. Which
is easier said than done"

"Well he seems to be earnest in keeping it just a friendship, so guess I will stop hoping for anything more from you two. How did the MRI go?

"It was horrible, being stuck in that small tube, I said. I don't think I will do that again anytime soon."

"So when will you get the results?"

"I guess as soon as the Doctor receives all the reports. I am sure in the next week or two. I can wait. No news is always good news."

"Not always, Lesley said. But will hope for the best and no matter what you know I will always be by your side."

"I know and now I am going to hang up, because you are going to make me cry. Talk to you later."

The days did not pass very fast and I had to take another day off. The pain in my back was so bad I had to take more pain pills. A couple just did not help. I was getting to the point of really wanting to know what was causing it. And because I had not heard from the Doctor, I decided to call his office.

They had all the reports and would like for me to come in the following day. They would make me the last appointment of the day, as the Doctor would have more time to discuss the test results.

Good I wanted to know. The pain that I have been experiencing was not something I wanted to deal with much longer.

I made it through the next day and told Lesley I would see the Doctor later that day. She wanted me to call her as soon as I got home.

I was sitting in the waiting room, with some bad thoughts going through my head. The nurse came for me and took me to his office. I was trying to be optimistic.

He came in and sat at his desk. He was looking through my chart.

"I will get right to the point. You have chronic osteoarthritis in your neck, shoulders and spine. It is probably a result of your accident. There is an option of surgery and a brace for the back, but there is still the osteoarthritis. The other pain that you feel all over, I have consulted with another Doctor about it and after going through your test results, we are in agreement to start you on medication for fibromyalgia and see if that helps. But that is something that is long term and no cure for. I think work is going to be an issue for you. You have mentioned you have more bad days lately than good. You are eligible for disability. It might be something you want to consider. The pain is harder to control with the stress of a job. You have a lot to think about."

"I do not want surgery. I know about osteoarthritis. I also know of fibromyalgia, I have a friend who has it and she has suffered for years. She is on Social Security Disability. I have to admit this is affecting my job and I am afraid I might lose it at some point in time. So far they have been tolerant, but I know they will eventually want someone who is more

Elizabeth Klein

reliable. I just am not sure I can give up working. I have been working all my life and figured I had a few more years."

"You do have some decisions to make. But remember your health at this point is the main concern. The less stress, the less pain you will have to endure. I am going to start you on medication for both the osteoarthritis and the fibromyalgia. It is medication you will be on for some time. If you have any reactions you call my office right away."

"I will and thank you, I appreciate all that you have done." I said.

When I arrived at my apartment, so many things were going through my head. Would I be able to survive on such a fixed income? I can always move back in my mobile home, but then my son will have to look for another place. With him being on disability, it would be hard for him to find a place he could afford. What in the world would I do if I am not working? I am not a sit at home person, but then again I do not care to live the rest of my life in pain. This is crazy, these things happen to other people, not me. I decided to call my sister and talk to her.

"Lily, I just got back from the Doctors. I have chronic osteoarthritis and fibromyalgia. Both of which there is no magical cure for. I do not want to apply for Social Security Disability. I'm sure I have enough as far as income, it is just my sanity that I am worried about."

"Your health is more important and you know that. I have seen you suffer with this pain, if leaving your job helps, then you have to do it."

"I know, but I hear the Doctors words about stress increasing the symptoms. How do you not worry about such a change in your life?"

"You are fine, you get income from a home and if things get worse you can always sell." She said.

"I just have a lot of thinking to do. I guess time and lots of praying will help me find an answer." I told her I would give her a call later.

I then called Lesley as I promised her I would.

"Well it is not good news, but at least it is not the big C word." I said.

"That was my biggest worry, cancer. So what is wrong?" She asked.

"I have chronic osteoarthritis in my back and fibromyalgia which could have an effect on my ability to work. I have already missed a lot of work, but am hoping the medication will help."

"I agree start the medication and if it relieves the pain, then you can continue working. So do not stress over this, I am sure the medication will get you through."

"I do hope so, as I am not a stay at home person. I will get the medicine tomorrow. Also can we keep this between us, I think I will be fine."

"You know I am a married woman, I have to tell my husband."

"I know, I just don't want anything said to Michael right now."

"Okay, but you know he is going to ask." Lesley said.

"Then just say I am on medication and doing fine.'

"I will tell Ben. So I guess I will see you tomorrow."

I started the medication and after a few days the pain was not bad at all. The only problem was that it made me drowsy and it sure was hard to concentrate at work. I liked being in never-never land, just not at my job. So I decided to cut back on my medication and it seemed to help, but by the time I got home, I was ready for bed. It seemed I could no longer stay up past eight o'clock and my extra-curricular activities came to a stand- still.

My sister was concerned, as our luncheons came to a halt and I hardly called her anymore.

"Look Sis, I am glad that you are doing okay on the medication, but you just cannot stop going out and doing things. I think you may be suffering from depression. You told me that was one of the effects of the medication, so you need to go see someone. I hate seeing you like this."

"It is not depression. I am just tired all the time. I fall asleep watching TV and it really scares me when I get drowsy at work. I think others are noticing. Lily I may lose my job."

"Then go see a lawyer and start the process of Social Security Disability.

If you were let go at work, you must realize at this point you are no longer employable, you are a liability." She said.

"That is pretty harsh. But I know the truth hurts. Lily, I feel as if I no longer have any control over my life. This sure was not in the plans for my future."

Elizabeth Klein

"What you just said, about not having control, tells me you are getting depressed. I want you to see someone."

"Lily let me get through the next few weeks and if I still feel like this, I promise you I will see someone."

"Okay I will hold you to that. And by the way, I am having a family gathering for our brother's birthday, so you are going to attend that. No excuses. It will be Saturday and bring a dish."

"I will be there as I haven't seen him in a while. It is funny how you can live in the same town and never see each other."

"You know he is a gamer, once he gets started he cannot stop."

"How does his girlfriend deal with that?" I asked.

"I think she likes games as well. She would have to, being with him"

"Well at least I may get in a conversation with him at the party, no games at your place. So I will see you Saturday."

After we hung up, I kept thinking I was not employable. As soon as my medical condition shows up, there is no way anyone would hire me. So my sister is right, I will look for a lawyer and she was also right about another thing, I am depressed.

Michael called and apologized that he had not called me earlier.

"Ben told me you are on medication, but he did not say what it was for. Is this something serious?" He asked.

"No, it is not serious. The medication is for arthritis that has set in on my spine. The Doctor seems to think it has developed from the accident I had a few years ago. The medication really helps, so I am fine." I lied.

"Well I am glad to hear that. I was hoping we could have dinner Saturday evening."

"Saturday I am going to a birthday party for my brother."

'Then how about lunch Friday afternoon. I can break away."

"Can I call you and let you know. I have been working through some of my lunch hours." I did not want to tell him I was doing that in order to leave early on other days.

"Sure, that is fine. Just call the office. I have a few evening meetings this week, so won't be home until late. So hope to see you on Friday."

I was hoping some of those evening meetings were with someone.

But in talking to Ben he says he attends some of those meetings and Michael is always alone. Also when he is at the Club he is usually by himself, as well. Maybe he does not want to be seen with anyone at the Club. Yet I had a suspicion of someone that he may be spending a few evenings with.

I did not make lunch with Michael. It was a bad day and I was taking the afternoon off. I went home and went right to bed.

I stayed in bed most of Saturday. This is not me I told myself. My body seemed to control my every move. I called and left a message for my Doctor to call me. He called me back and wanted to know if I was having a reaction to the medication. I told him I was not, but I just wanted to stay in bed all day and that wasn't me. He said that it was the medication and anything he gives me, I will still feel tired and have some drowsiness. So any chance of an option was out the window.

I did make it to my brother's party and I really enjoyed myself. My brother and I did have a long talk. He can actually speak and make sentences when he is away from his games.

"I knew I had a brother somewhere in this town. I just don't see him that often." I punched him in the arm.

"I am now taking some classes at the Community College, so between that and work, I have very little time."

"Well it sure is nice to catch up on some things, seems like I am always the last to know." I smiled.

"Just does not seem to be enough hours in the day."

"So when are you going to get married? I asked him. You finally found someone to put with you, so I hope you know how lucky you are."

"Sis, when you get married, I will consider it."

"You know that is never going to happen." I said.

"And that is never going to happen because you were married and then you weren't. With one failure, you will not even allow the thought of getting involved with anyone. I have a very good relationship with her and will keep it that way for the time being. We are in no hurry to marry. Marriage is no longer the norm for some."

Elizabeth Klein

"That is a pretty negative view of marriage. Not all marriages fail."

"The statistics are not favorable for the married people today." He said.

"Oh, and did one of your games give you that info?"

"Could be, he said with a smile. Changing the subject, I am concerned about you. Lily said you are not doing too well and worried about your job. I say go for the disability Sis, I want you around for a few more years."

"I am considering it but there is so much to think about. It means I may have to budget and I am not really good at that, especially having my two sisters. We definitely like to have fun."

"You never have to worry about anything financial, you have family and you know you could depend on us."

"I know, I said. Just not sure I am ready to call it quits."

"Sometimes decisions are made for us and it is not maybe, it is when."

"I am afraid, soon." I said as I turned and walked away. I had tears in my eyes and I did not want him to see me.

I told my sister it was time for me to go and I said my goodbyes and left.

It was a long drive home, as the tears started again. It must have been the medication I told myself, or maybe my sister was right, as always. I need to see someone, not for my health but for my emotional state.

I received some recommendations of a couple of lawyers, so made an appointment with one. After I saw him I knew I would have to see someone for depression. I would have to be unemployed for the year that we would be filing and then I found out the amount I might receive on a monthly basis and I almost felt ill. It was really going to be a tough decision. The other alternative was that I was old enough to collect my first husbands Social Security. He passed away before he collected it, the amount on a monthly basis was a lot better and I could work part time, if I had to. So I chose the second option.

I went to the Social Security Office and filled out all the paperwork.

I then went to work and met with my Supervisor, to see if I could work part-time.

"Beth, I know you have been ill and you are really trying, but your position is a full time position. Also, if you go on to Social Security, you are only allowed a certain amount of income and once you reach that amount you are either cut off or you are liable for taxes. What I can do for you, is give you three months of severance pay if you give notice to end your employment. But because of your absence, I honestly do not know how much longer we can keep you." She said.

"I feel like I am in a chess game. Every move I make has dire consequences and I am going to lose no matter what I do. I appreciate your honesty and your offer. I just need a couple of more days to make a decision."

She said that would be fine, but to let her know as soon as I decided so she could start the paperwork.

I walked back to my office and broke down and cried.

I heard my door open and it was Lesley. She came to me and put her arms around me.

"I knew this was coming. The Supervisor was asking questions about you and I felt this was not going to turn out to be good for you. You have been through so much, I am so sorry."

"It is so much to deal with. Every time I think I am going to be okay something else happens. It is to the point that I have run out of options." The tears started once more.

"You are going to be okay, you are a strong person. You have Ben and me to get you through the bad times. We will always be with you."

"Thank you, I said. It is just so much at one time. I know I will be okay."

"Well dry your eyes and I will go get us some coffee and we will talk."

She left and I was grateful to have her as a friend. I looked around my office and figured I would have to start packing, so I better get some boxes. It was my way of escaping the moment.

When I went home, I called my sister and told her I had made my decision. She felt it was for the best, as she wanted me to relax and enjoy life and you did not need a lot of money to do that.

"The financial part is not a big concern. It is, what am I going to do?"

"You volunteer. There are so many organizations that need volunteers. You will keep busy. And if there are days you cannot be there, just let them know about your circumstances. They will understand." She said.

Elizabeth Klein

"It is something I guess I can consider, but not for a while, I have things to sort out. I looked around my office today. I have a lot of packing to do."

"See you are keeping busy right now." She said laughing.

I decided to go see Damian. I told him what I was going to do.

"Mom, you will be fine. You will find something to keep busy, you always do. Maybe Michael can get some interior decorating jobs for you, as everyone was impressed with renovations in Michael's house."

"I have not told Michael anything about this. I don't want him to feel sorry for me and try to help. I know I will think of something and I know I worry too much. What do you do, so you don't get bored?"

"I am a gamer mom, we never get bored." He laughed.

"Oh, right, I forgot. Unfortunately I do not think that is for me. I will have to think of something else."

We decided to go get something to eat. I always had a good relationship with Damian. I had to admire him, as he beat death twice, because of his illness. He still had a good sense of humor and takes one day at a time. I just felt bad that he has yet to find someone. He was in a good relationship once, his girlfriend had a miscarriage. After that the relationship was never the same and I do not think he ever got over it.

I called my other son, and told him that I had made a tough decision and I would be leaving my job.

"No sweat mom, you are going to be okay. I did not know that things were that bad, you should have called me sooner."

"Well there was not much anyone could do. The decision had to be mine as far as my job. But they were kind in offering me severance pay. They did not have to do that."

"Well, like I said you will be okay."

"How are you and Shea doing?" I asked.

"Same as any other relationship, you have some good times and some bad times."

"I hope more good times than bad, as I really like her."

"Well mom, she is still with me so that says a lot for her. You know how my moods can be at times."

"Yes I know, but she is a keeper, so take it easy on her, okay?"

"Sure thing mom. You take care and I'll call later."

Daniel never had much to say and he kept his conversations at a minimum.

I was tired and getting ready for bed when Michael called.

"I have been trying to call, but you must be a busy girl."

"I went out to eat with Damian and then when I got home, I called my other son. So it has been a busy evening."

"I was hoping that you might want to come to the house this weekend. I will cook dinner. Then we can have a relaxing evening by the fireplace and just talk."

"That really sounds good, I need some relaxing time." I said.

"Good, then I will see you Saturday evening and we can catch up."

"I take it you have had conversations with Ben. Is this the reason for the invitation?" I asked.

"Seeing as you have been avoiding me and Ben is not overly informative when it comes to you, I figured I would have to bribe you. But want it to be a quieter atmosphere rather than a crowded restaurant."

"I appreciate the thoughtfulness and I will see you Saturday."

I was not sure I wanted to tell him everything, but maybe by talking to him he might have some ideas about working on the side to keep me from going crazy.

I talked to my Supervisor and asked her if I could work one more month and then I would resign. She said a four week notice was more than sufficient and she would start the paperwork. I felt relieved that this decision was finally made. Lesley was upset, but I told her I expected a call for lunch at least once a month and of course I would stop by her house to check on her and Ben.

When I pulled up in Michael's driveway, I got that uncomfortable feeling again, but I attributed it to Susan's room and I had no intention of going near that room.

The house smelled good, it must be from the meal he was cooking. He poured me a glass of wine and we went into the family room.

Elizabeth Klein

"Dinner will be another half hour. Hope you are hungry, I always make too much." He said.

"What is on the menu this evening?"

"Baked chicken, which is always nice and tender and to go with it, I made rice and vegetables."

"That does sound good and I am hungry."

"Now let me know what is going on with you?" He asked.

"Well mainly the arthritis, which there is not much they can do. Then I am being treated for fibromyalgia, but the medications really help. The only problem is with the medications, I do get drowsy and sometimes disoriented. That has created some problems at work. I had a long talk with my Supervisor and the decision was made that I would resign at the end of the month and they were generous enough to give me a three month severance package. I am now unemployable due to my health and my main concern is trying to adjust to a forced retirement."

"I feel you should have called me and talked to me. I am a friend after all and yet you felt you could not confide in me?"

"Michael none of this has been easy for me. I had to make some tough decisions and they had to be my decisions. I know I will be okay as far as financially. Although I just found out to carry my insurance from work is not going to be an option. I can afford my prescriptions. I just hope I can hang in there until I can eventually get Medicare as now I am also uninsurable. So that sums up where I am at now."

"So what income are you getting, other than from your other home?"

"I am going to be collecting from my husband's Social Security. He died before he was sixty-five." I decided not tell him I had an IRA, I guess I felt that was just too much information.

"That still is a limited income, are you sure you are going to be okay financially?'

"I will be as long as I don't go on any crazy spending sprees." I laughed.

"Well I know how hard it is to borrow from friends, but if you ever need anything, you come to me. I can well afford to give you the money and I have an easy payment plan, if you chose to pay it back." He smiled.

"I appreciate the offer, but I do not borrow from friends."

'You are a very independent woman, but sometimes circumstances occur that not even an independent woman can handle. The offer stands.

I think dinner is ready, let's have something to eat, as I am getting hungry." He said.

I helped set the table and had another glass of wine.

I was disturbed again by his tone when he used the words "independent woman". That was twice he said it in an unfavorable tone.

The conversation at dinner was of the activities and fundraisers he had been involved with. And at a few, he was asked, where I was?

"I told them we were just friends and you had other commitments."

"They did not believe you, did they?" I smiled.

"No, their comment was "we were an attractive couple. Maybe now that you are retired, you would like to attend at least a couple of the functions with me."

"Have you ever asked Margaret to attend with you?" I asked.

"She already has and we had a nice time."

"Then you should ask her out more. She does care for you."

"Yes. I know and I also know the rumors of us having an affair, so at times it is difficult being together."

"But why would you care? You are single now, it does not matter."

"There are some things in my past that I would like to keep there."

He got up from the table so I got the indication the conversation was over.

I helped him clear the table and put the food away. He was putting the dishes in the dishwasher. Then he fixed himself another drink. He asked if I wanted another glass of wine.

"I think two is enough with the medication I am taking. At times, one is too much."

"I can drive you home, if you start to feel light-headed."

"No, it is okay. I have not taken any more medication since this afternoon, although I may have to make it a short evening."

"I was hoping for a longer evening, but I do understand."

We walked to the door and just as he opened it, his phone rang.

"I better get that, please stay here until I get back."

I shook my head yes, as he left me by the door.

There was a dim lighted lamp on the end table, so not much light in the room.

I turned to the hallway that led to Susan's room. I was not going to be pulled to that door again, but my eyes stayed focused at the hallway. I closed my eyes and opened them again, not sure of what I was seeing. It was a mist forming in the hallway. It was transparent, just floating.

I was mesmerized and I did not look away. I could not make out a shape, it was just mist.

"What do you want of me?" I heard myself say, but not in words, in my head.

I waited for an answer or movement, but there was just silence.

I jumped, as Michael had come back. I looked at him and then back at the hallway. The mist was gone.

"I am sorry. I did not mean to scare you. You seemed focused on something are you okay?"

"Michael, I saw a mist," then I stopped. He would not believe me.

"What did you see? He asked. You are shaking." He put his hands on my arms. What did you see?

"It was just my imagination, I am sorry."

"Then what did your imagination see?"

"A shadow maybe. It may have come from the lamp."

"It scared you that much?

"I watch too much SyFy." I tried to laugh.

"I will walk you to your car and I want you to call me as soon as you get home and I mean it. I am concerned for you."

"I am just tired, that is all and I will call you."

I got in my car and started driving home. "What do you want?" I kept saying to myself. "What do you want?"

I was glad to get home and I did call Michael. I did not sleep well that night. I was still shaken by that image.

I went to church the following morning. I loved going to church, as it was a peaceful time for me. But today I prayed for God to protect me because something was going on that I did not understand and I was afraid. I hated that house and I did not want to go back there. The worst is that I could not talk about it. I was sick most of the day. I knew it was just stress. I took my medication and was able to sleep in the afternoon.

The phone rang later that evening and it was Michael.

"How are you feeling? He asked.

"I am doing okay."

"I was worried after you called me last night. You sounded upset."

"I was just tired, I told you, so no need to worry." I said.

"I have a dinner I have to attend Friday evening, I would like for you to come with me. I think you need to get out."

"Michael, I never know how I am going to feel, so I cannot promise you that I will be able to go."

"I understand, so just give me a call Friday and let me know."

"As long as you understand I might not make it. I will give you call."

"You take care of yourself there are people who care about you."

I still was not feeling good when I went to work. I thought if this was going to be the rest of my life, I was not sure I was going to get through it. The days seem to get longer and at the end of the day I just want to go to bed. At least the medication helps me sleep, except for that Saturday night as I cannot get that image out of my mind. It haunts me.

When Friday arrived, it was a good day for me and I thought maybe I should get out for a while. I called Michael and told him I would go with him and he said to come to his place and we would take his car. I told him no, just to pick me up at my apartment. I did not want to go back to the house.

The evening was comfortable and people said it was nice to see me again. I saw Margaret at another table and because Michael had left to talk to someone else, I got up and went to talk to Margaret.

"It has been awhile since out last conversation. How are you?" I asked.

"I am fine and it is nice to see you again. I have been told you have been ill. I am sorry to hear that."

"I have good days and bad days. But my meds help." I laughed.

"Well it is good to see you again with Michael."

"We are still just friends. I cannot seem to get that through to others. I guess I should stop trying and just let them think what they want."

"I must admit, I am one of those, she said. It is hard to believe you have known him for almost two years and there has not been any intimacy between you two." She said.

"Margaret, you of all people know the truth, as I know you have already been spending some evenings with him. You give him what he cannot have from me."

She leaned over and whispered to me.

"That may be true, but when we are intimate, he is not with me. He is with someone else."

"If you think that someone is me, you are so wrong." I was getting upset.

"Then who else could it be? I know he associates with other women, but I can tell he is not interested in them. There is only you. But it is okay, as I will take whatever time he gives to me."

"I am sorry but I am not a threat to you." I now was angry.

I got up and walked away. Again that uncomfortable feeling came. Am I so blind, that I cannot see the truth? I just will not accept that our friendship is a lie. He has never expressed any desire for me. The times he has kissed me, it has always been on the check. He has put his arms around my shoulders a few times, but not enough to call that intimate.

No it is not me he is thinking about while being intimate with Margaret. He may be seeing someone else. He is fair game and I am sure he is not turning away invitations.

Just as I reached my chair he returned.

"I was wondering where you walked off to and then I saw you were talking to Margaret."

"We have met for coffee and I like her." I said, hoping to see a reaction. But there was not one.

He said he would get our drinks and be right back.

I wanted to go, but did not want to bring any attention to us, by leaving shortly after we just arrived.

I made it through the dinner. People talking but I was not listening.

Michael looked at me and said he would have one more drink and then we would go. He said I looked tired. It was awhile before he returned and his drink was almost gone, for which I was thankful. He finished and we got up to leave saying goodbyes as we walked in between the tables. I was glad to get outside to get some fresh air.

"You made it through another night with the money crowd. I appreciate you coming with me this evening. I would like for you to attend these dinners and functions more with me."

"Why me and not Margaret?" I asked.

"I like Margaret, but she wants more than I can give her. She thinks it is time I should think seriously about marriage. I have told her many times that I am not in any hurry to re-marry. I enjoy myself more with you and I attribute that to the boundaries that we have. I know exactly where I stand with you."

"Well I am comfortable with you, for the same reason. But I think you should be with someone you may have a future with."

He did not answer and we walked to his car.

We returned to my apartment and he walked me to the door. He thanked me once again for going with him and kissed me on the cheek and off he went.

Margaret is so wrong about Michael and me, I said to myself.

I was surprised when I checked my bank account and Social Security had already automatically deposited my check. It was going to be enough for me that I should not have to worry.

I had one more week before I was leaving work and time was going quickly. I realize now that I made the right decision, as my back had really been painful these last couple of days. It was easier to endure by lying down, which was not going to happen at work.

I called my sister for a lunch date and we made arrangements for Friday.

It was nice seeing her again. Even though she was years younger than me, she seemed to understand me better.

"I am glad you called, I did want to see you. The holidays are approaching again and I want to run away." She said.

"And where do you want to run away to?"

Elizabeth Klein

"To Vegas, what happens in Vegas stays in Vegas. Also I have some good comps for the New Year."

"You are married. You need to celebrate it with your husband." I said.

"My husband has not been able to stay up until midnight for the last ten years. So the excitement is gone."

"Well go ahead and make the arrangements, even though it is months away. You know I just cannot say "no" to you."

"I know, you have no attachments, therefore you are free to go anywhere and at any time. Oh what a life." She laughed.

"Oh yeah, it is just a wonderful life. I am thankful though, I will survive through the pain, sickness, and sometimes depression as long as I keep my faith. At least that is what my pastor says." I smiled

"Hey, if you have God on your side, you have everything."

"I truly want to believe that but sometimes it is hard." I said.

"I know, I worry about you but you are a strong woman and you will survive. You have a lot of family that cares for you."

"Oh great, now you are going to make me cry. I have been so emotional with all this medication."

"Let's get through lunch, before you make a spectacle of yourself."

We both laughed and I did make it through lunch without the tears.

The last week of work was difficult, not so much because of my health, but because I had been working for this company for ten years now and truly enjoyed my job and the staff that I worked with.

I heard the rumors that I would have a surprise party, so tried to prepare myself for that, as I have been an emotional wreck.

I went out to lunch that afternoon with Lesley and some of the girls from work. When we returned I heard the yell "surprise" and everyone was there. They had cake and ice cream and gifts. It was hard to open the gifts, I was afraid I would cry, but I did a good job in holding it back. I was only going to be there half a day. Everyone helped me pack the gifts in my car and I had some left over cake. I gave each one a hug goodbye and told them this was not going to be the last time they saw me as I would definitely come back and check on them to make sure they were doing a good job.

Going home was difficult, as the reality set in. That part of my life was over and I was going to have to start a new phase. At my age that is not easy. I was going to check into volunteering, probably after the first of the year. The holidays were coming, so knew I could keep busy through them for sure.

I carried the gifts in my apartment and laid them on the table.

I made some coffee, changed my clothes and watched some TV. This is it I thought, to myself.

Michael called me later that afternoon.

"So how was your last day?" He asked.

"It was a mixture of emotions, but in the end depression set in."

"I know it must be hard on you, but you know it is for the best. You have to take care of yourself."

"That is a line I have heard way too much lately."

"How about you come over for a nice quiet dinner tonight?" He asked.

"How about you get some take out and come here instead?"

I made up my mind I was not going back to that house.

"Sounds good to me, I will see you about six."

I had to change again as I was in pajama bottoms and a sweatshirt.

He bought some Chinese food, which I like and we had a nice meal on my small dinette set.

After dinner we watched some TV and just talked for a while.

"Will you be going to New Mexico for the holidays this year?" I asked.

"No, I made it clear to my kids it was their turn and so far no takers."

"I am sure they will re-consider and come visit with their father." I said.

"I would hope so. I would like them to meet you. I have told them if it weren't for you I am not sure I would have come through the mourning aspect of it all or at least it would have taken me a lot longer."

"I do not think that I should meet your family right now. It might give them the idea that we are more than just friends and I do not want to do that. I am not the female who is going to replace your wife."

As soon as I said that, I knew that I had chosen the wrong words.

"There is no one who can replace my wife. But why are you so dead set against relationships? Do you honestly want to spend the rest of your life getting older and being alone?"

Elizabeth Klein

"No I do not want to spend the rest of my life alone and I am not dead set against relationships. I have seen so many relationships and marriages fail because they were together for the wrong reasons.

Sometimes it is the financial insecurity, the fear of being alone or just to have someone, anyone in their life. I am hoping that there is such a thing as love out there." I said.

"There is such a thing as love, but love does not just appear out of nowhere. It becomes evident in being secure with each other, in having the same likes and dislikes and just enjoying each other's company."

"Where did you read that at?" I was laughing.

"I think I saw it on TV." He was laughing with me.

He left early for which I was grateful. It had been a long day for me.

It was just after Thanksgiving that Lesley had called me and told me that Ben had called her and said that Michael was in the hospital. She was heading over there and she wanted me to go with her.

I told her to come by and get me.

When we got there we met Ben. He said Michael had not been feeling good and finally went to ER and they were going to admit him and do some tests. He was still in ER and Ben was able to get us in to see him.

"Why didn't you call us Michael, when you were not feeling well?" Lesley asked.

I was going to ask the same question, but she beat me to it.

"I thought it was the flu, but then the chest pains started, so I thought I had better come in. I already saw my Cardiologist and he is going to do some tests. Hopefully I will be out of here soon, I hate hospitals." He said smiling.

"Why are you seeing a Cardiologist?" I asked.

"I had a stent put in about eight years ago, so he keeps an eye on me."

"Well I think all of us need to keep an eye on you from now on." Lesley said, with a smile.

"I agree with that." I said.

Ben asked if he should contact his family.

"I don't want to worry them, maybe wait until I get home."

"I think you can tell them that you are going to have some tests done." Ben said.

"Maybe after I get settled in, I will call my son."

We stayed with him a little longer and I told him I would visit with him later that evening.

"Does he have a heart condition?" I asked Ben, as we were leaving.

"It is nothing serious, the stent was working fine and he has been doing okay. I am sure it is just the flu that has been going around. But I am glad that his Cardiologist will follow up with him."

"Well, I will see him this evening." I said.

Lesley drove me back to my apartment.

"Do I see some genuine caring for this man?" She asked.

"I would care the same if you or Ben were in the hospital." I said.

"You always seem to have an answer, but I am not convinced of that answer."

"Well convinced or not, it is the truth. And as his friend I will visit him this evening."

"Okay, if that is the way you want to be, but I see it as something different." She smiled.

When I was in my apartment, I felt that I was truly worried about Michael and was hoping that this was something minor.

I bought some flowers, before I went to visit him. I know some men hate that.

"Hi, how are you doing?" I asked, as I sat the flowers on his night stand.

"I am doing fine."

"So how did your test turn out?"

"The Cardiologist wants to put in another stent. He said it was just for pre-caution. So I will have that done tomorrow and should be home the next day. So it is a very simple procedure."

"Well you have been through this before, so you should know."

"I could use a few days off anyway." He said with a smile.

"This is not the way to do it though. There are easier way of getting time off."

"Well it must work in some ways, as you are here. Lately I have not been able to get you to the house for even a short visit."

Elizabeth Klein

"I am sorry about that, but being home more, I seem to be more comfortable there and can finally get some things done."

"Are you telling me you are becoming a home bound woman?" He smiled.

"No, but I might as well tell you that I was able to get a side job and I am doing some computer work for someone."

"Can I ask who that someone might be?"

"It is Steven from work. He is taking some night classes at the college and just needs some help every now and then."

"This Steven from work, is he interested in the computer work or is he interested in you?"

"My, aren't we inquisitive. He just happens to be young, married and has two lovely small children. So do you have any more questions?"

"Sorry, I just want to make sure you are safe."

"Safe from what?" I asked.

"Safe from other men who are hunting for an easy target."

"Are we talking in the similarity of the cougars?"

"Yes we are," he said. We both started laughing.

The nurse came in to give him his medication. So I thought I better leave.

"I will come tomorrow and see how well you take this simple procedure." I said.

"Can I at least have a kiss on the cheek before you go?"

"Yes you can." I kissed him and told him to try and get some rest.

I said a prayer for him as I was leaving. I hoped that he would be fine after his simple procedure.

When I woke up I was not feeling well. It was going to be a bad day. I took my medicine and slept most of the day. By the time I got up, it was late afternoon, so took a shower, had something light to eat and headed for the hospital.

When I entered Michael's room, he was not there. But there was a younger man sitting in a chair. He looked up at me.

"Hi, my name is Jeremy, I am Michael's son. I imagine you are Beth, he told me you would be here."

"Is your father okay? I asked. I was feeling very uncomfortable.

"They were running late on the surgery schedule, so he went down a little bit ago. I talked to the Cardiologist and he said dad would be fine."

"That is good news. When did you get in?"

"Late last night, I have a key to the house. I thought I would surprise him. If I told him I was coming I knew he would try and talk me out of it, but I wanted to know for myself how he was doing."

"That is so thoughtful of you and I am sure he is happy you are here. You will be a help to him when he goes home." I said.

"Well I can only stay a couple of days, but I am glad I came. Do you want to go with me to the cafeteria and get some coffee? He will be awhile."

"That sounds nice, I would love some coffee."

We talked of him as he was growing up. He told me of his three sisters that he missed growing up with, as he was the unexpected one. When he was talking of his dad, you could tell he really loved him. I liked him.

We did not realize how long we had stayed in the cafeteria and decided we better get back to the room.

Michael was already in the room, by the time we got back. He was groggy from the sedation, so I did not stay long. I told Jeremy that I would be back in the morning to see his dad. I said how much I enjoyed his company and I was glad that he came.

I called Lesley to update her.

"I just got back from the hospital and Michael had his surgery. The Doctor said he came through it fine and he could go home tomorrow."

"Oh that is good news. Does he need some help when he gets home?" She asked.

"No, his son is here from New Mexico. It was a surprise when I walked into Michael's room and saw him. He seems so nice. We had a long conversation when we went to the cafeteria, while waiting for his dad to come back from surgery."

Elizabeth Klein

"Yes, I have met him. The first impression is deceiving though. At least that is my thought."

"Now, why in the world would you think that?" I asked.

"Just from things that Ben has told me."

"Like what?" I asked.

"Maybe, I should keep my thoughts to myself. If you like him, then that is all that matters."

"No, I want to know why you feel he is deceptive."

"From what Ben has told me, every time he gets into financial difficulties he calls his dad. His dad put him through college, his dad bought him a vehicle, and his dad has given him numerous loans to keep him out of trouble. So I just get the impression that his love comes at a price."

"But Lesley, if Michael can afford it, then it is okay to help your kids out. I have done that with my two sons."

"I know and that is why I told you that is just how I feel. I could be wrong and I hope that I am."

"Sometimes feelings are deceptive, but I am glad you told me and if you get feelings about anything else let me know."

"Even if it is about you and Michael?"

"We will avoid that conversation. I will call you in the morning after I see that Michael is okay."

"Thanks and I am sorry that I brought up how I feel about Jeremy."

"No don't be sorry. I appreciate your honesty. Talk to you tomorrow."

After our conversation I told myself first impressions are usually right. But sometimes you just have to take time to get to know a person before you judge them.

I tried to watch some TV, but was feeling tired. So took my medication and went to bed. I did set my alarm, so I could be at the hospital early.

When I arrived at Michael's room, I saw Jeremy talking to Margaret.

"Hi there." I heard Michael say.

I turned my head and he was sitting up in bed. He looked well.

"How are you doing?" I asked.

"Just fine and it is nice having all this company. Maybe I need to come to the hospital more often."

"I don't think that is a good idea, Margaret said. They have strict visiting hours and it is not the happiest place to be."

"I have to agree with her." Jeremy said.

"When are you going to be released?" I asked.

"As soon as the Doctor comes in and signs the release papers, so maybe another hour or two, although I am more than ready to leave this place now."

"Michael I really have to go, I have a job to get to. Margaret said, as she gave Michael a kiss on the cheek. I will check on you in a couple of days.

And Jeremy it was nice see you again, you take care."

"Dad, you are getting to be a real ladies man. You have two beautiful women to take care of you. I am sure you will be in good hands, after I leave."

Jeremy was wrong about that statement, there was only one woman that had been in the room that could take care of his dad and it was not me.

Margaret left, and I was getting that uncomfortable feeling again. I wanted to leave.

"Beth I am going to the cafeteria. Can I get you a cup of coffee or something else to drink?" Jeremy said.

"I would appreciate a cup of coffee, Jeremy."

He left and Michael looked up at me.

"How have you been feeling? He asked. You look tired."

"I had a bad day yesterday, but feeling better today. But you should not worry about me. Just take care of yourself."

"I intend to and I will take it easy for a long while."

"Good, you try to do too much sometimes, with your job and your meetings."

"What do you think about my son? I am very proud of him as I have already told you."

"He is sweet. And the fact that he is here shows how much he loves his father. I can understand how proud you are of him. And I am glad he will help you out today when you go home."

"Why don't you come over later and we will order a pizza?" He asked.

　　　　　　　　Elizabeth Klein

"That sounds nice, but I think you and your son should spend some quality time together."

Just then Jeremy was back with the coffee. The three of us just talked and had some laughs. The Doctor came in and said Michael did fine through the surgery and he was going to release him.

I told Michael that I would give him a call later and see how he was.

I told Jeremy if I did not see him again before he left, to have a safe trip home.

I was glad to leave. There was that uncomfortable feeling again.

I called him later that evening and he said he was happy to be home. He would probably go to bed early though, as he was feeling tired. He said Jeremy would be leaving early in the morning, so he wanted to be sure to see him off. Then he gave the phone to me so I could talk to Jeremy. I told Jeremy it was nice meeting him and hope to see him again soon. He said it was nice meeting me and to take care of his dad for him. I was set back by that and did not know how to respond, so I just said "okay".

I thought Margaret can take care of his dad for him.

I did call Michael the following day and he said he was feeling a lot better.

He said he saw Jeremy off that morning and was glad he came.

"Why don't you come over and sit with me awhile?" He asked.

"I wish I could, but today is not a good day for me." I did not want to go back to that house.

"But I will tell you what, if you are feeling up to it, I will make dinner for you on Saturday." I said.

"I am sure I will feel fine by then. Matter of fact I may go into the office Friday, just to check on things."

"That sounds like you. You just cannot stay home and relax."

"It is what keeps me going. I will see you Saturday."

I do not know how much longer I can keep up with the excuses for not going to his house. But what I saw the last time I was there, still haunts me.

Lesley called and wanted to have lunch with me. I know she feels bad about revealing to me her feelings toward Jeremy, but I was glad she did.

"Ben said he saw Michael at the Club and he looks good." She said.

"I know, he wants to go to his office Friday. I guess that surgery was not as bad as it sounded, he is doing well."

"He must be, but I do not think it wise that he should be drinking again, so soon after his surgery." She said.

"He was drinking at the Club?" I asked.

"That is what Ben said. Maybe he just needed to get out of the house for a while."

"Yes, it probably was time for him to get out."

But my thoughts were he should not have been drinking. He needed to take it easy for a few days.

She changed the subject and started to catch me up on things at work.

"Do you miss working?" She asked.

"You know I thought I would. But it is surprising how much I do to keep busy. Even cleaning the house is time consuming. In all honesty I do not miss work at all. My only problem is I don't seem to get with others because they are all working."

"I never thought of that, but it would be a disadvantage. Except for me, I will always take time to have lunch away from the office, only I hate going back once I am out."

"I remember that feeling." I laughed.

"Speaking of going back, I better get moving. Thanks for lunch and I will get with you later."

"You are welcome and next time you can pick up the check." I smiled.

I had to go grocery shopping Saturday morning, as I had very little in my refrigerator. I was going to make a meat loaf. I cannot do too much damage with a few pounds of hamburger. I thought baked potatoes would be easy as well. I bought a veggie tray, for vegetables. I knew he drank Vodka, so I purchased a small bottle of that and the condition would be that he only was allowed one drink. And also I purchased a bottle of wine.

I went home and started the meatloaf. Everything else could wait.

Michael arrived with a bouquet of flowers.

"Why the flowers?" I asked.

"If I recall, someone brought me flowers while I was in the hospital. So I am repaying kindness with kindness."

"Thank you, that was very thoughtful."

"Something smells good, what are we having this evening?"

"Meat loaf, it is the only thing I can make that I can't destroy."

"If it tastes as good as it smells, you did something well."

"I bought some Vodka, but you must promise me one drink, as I want you to have a safe drive home." I said.

"One glass will be fine."

He made his own drink and I had a glass of wine.

I had already set the table and everything was ready, so we took our drinks to the table. He reached his hands out to me and he said the prayer. I am glad he reaches for my hands, as I am always forgetting.

We had small talk at the dinner table and he was enjoying the meal, until he asked me if something was burning. I had forgotten that I had biscuits in the oven and they were definitely burnt. I was so embarrassed, but he had a good laugh.

"I am not much of a cook, but you would at least think I would remember if I had something in the oven."

He was still laughing. "It happens as we get older. But I might suggest that you invest in a fire extinguisher."

I started laughing, so we had fun at my expense.

After dinner he helped with dishes and I got some deodorizer to help get the smoke smell out. I did not dare look at him while I was spraying, as I knew he was smiling.

"That was a good dinner, so I do not believe you are that bad of a cook."

"Then you should ask my sons, as they started cooking when they were young, because they could not stand my cooking. They preferred seasoning on their food. My oldest brother had ulcers when he was eleven and my mom had ulcers, so I grew up in a "bland food" family."

"So do you like your son's cooking?" He asked.

"Yes I do, although I think sometimes they overdo the seasoning. But I have to admit, when they grill a steak, it has taste and it is tender."

"And what do you think of my cooking?" He asked

"Your cooking is good. I honestly believe men make good cooks." I said.

"My son, Jeremy, is also a good cook. But I think his wife out does him. He really found his soul mate. They have only been married a couple of years, but I see the same love between them as I saw when they first met."

"Did you find your soul mate in Susan?" I asked.

I should have never asked that, it just came out.

"I had been single for a long time when I met Susan. We had only dated a year when marriage was brought up. She wanted to get married. I told her we should take more time before we made a decision like that. I guess she did not feel that way. After I said that, she started to pull away from me and I felt like I was losing her. I guess I did feel love, as I did not want to lose her. So we married and in the end I lost her anyway."

He said with sadness.

"But you had time together as man and wife, so that was a good thing."

"You have been single for a long time, is the possibility of marriage in your future?" He asked.

"I know you should never say never, but no. I would never set myself up for a broken heart that not even super glue could put back together again. I am damaged goods both physically and mentally and I would never subject that on to another person. I know that sounds awful, but I am okay with it." I have my family and they have always been there for me and at the end of my life, they will still be there. I cannot say that much for some relationships."

"Well I do not agree that you are damaged goods. You give yourself no credit. You are a survivor and that is something you should be proud of. I have been out there in the dating scene. I have seen the broken women, who have lost everything because they feel sorry for themselves. There is nothing worse than self-pity."

"I do not like the self-pity as well and I guess I could call myself a survivor." I said. But I knew exactly what I was.

We talked a little more and I started yawning. It was no use to continue on, as I was feeling sleepy.

"I guess it is time I should leave."

"I am sorry, when I get tired, I start yawning. Nothing like giving an indication that I am done for." I smiled.

Elizabeth Klein

"I did enjoy the meal, the burnt biscuits and the conversation. You get some rest and I will call you tomorrow."

He got up and gave me a kiss on the cheek and left.

I thought of Margaret again, she was so wrong in thinking that anything more than friendship existed between us.

Christmas was fast approaching and Michael wanted to have his dinner party again this year. I did such a good job in organizing things last year that he wanted me to do it again, that is if I felt up to it. I really needed something to do, as I had so much time on my hands. I had already finished my Christmas shopping, so I told him I would. I made a promise to myself not to be in the house by myself or in the dark, ever again. Even though when I went over there, in the daytime, to talk to Michael as to how he wanted it set up, I still felt that I should not be there.

The day the cleaning people arrived, I sat on the back porch and had coffee. I knew I should not be sitting in the cold, but I was not going to even chance being pulled into that room again.

The caterer wanted to come over to see the setup, I told her it was the same as last year and I would come to her with the menu. When the flowers were to be delivered, I took Damian with me. As soon as the flowers came, I set them on the counter and left. I figured I could set them on the tables before the guests started to arrive.

I was safe or so I thought.

When I arrived at the party, there were already a few guests there. I saw Michael showing the caterer where to set up, even though I had told her it was the same. I walked up to help him as it was my fault that it was not coordinated beforehand. Fortunately Michael did not say anything to me about it, as I really did not have an excuse I could give him for not making sure it was organized. I should have been there earlier.

He went to visit with the other guests and ignored me for a while, which was okay.

I saw Margaret and went to talk to her.

"Are you still seeing Michael?" I asked.

"Should I be confiding in you?"

"Margaret I would like for us to be friends. I have not been well for some time and am not spending much time with him these days. I can assure you I am not a threat to your relationship with Michael."

"Michael has told me you were not well. I am sorry to hear that you have not been feeling any better. But you must understand that it is still hard for me to believe that you and Michael can be as close as you are and no intimacy is involved."

"Margaret, I am sure he tells you there is nothing between us but friendship. Are you saying you do not believe him?"

"You do not know him, I do. If it is not you then it would be someone else and I would have found out by now. There are no secrets in this crowd."

"Obviously not, how else would Susan have known about you and Michael?" I said.

"Be careful, you are getting close to crossing the line with me."

"I am just trying to tell you, I do not have the answers you are looking for, but it is not me. I am happy that Michael is with you. I think he does care for you. Maybe since the death of Susan, he has a difficult time with making a commitment with anyone in a relationship and in intimacy. Maybe that is where you get the feeling he is not with you."

"Don't you think I have thought of that? I have tried to be patient. I cannot believe he can be holding back his feelings because of something he had with a wife who is dead."

"I know, I have to admit it sounds ridiculous. But do not give up on him, he will come around."

"Beth, I have given him years, he will not change even if I threaten to leave him. There is more to him." She stopped. She turned to see where he was and although he was across the room, he was watching us.

I saw a look that I had seen before in him. I could not explain it, but it appeared as a threatening look.

My head started to throb, something was happening to me. It was as if what I had said next did not come from me, but another voice.

"There is more isn't there? There is something about him you won't tell me."

She turned and walked away.

I had to sit down. My head hurt, but not from pain. There was a screaming in my head with the words "know the truth." What truth, what was it I had to know? I was getting dizzy. I held my hands to my head. "Stop", I was screaming back in silence. "Stop it now."

Michael came over to me. I could barely make out what he was saying. His words came through the haze that I was feeling.

"Are you all right? Beth are you okay?

I looked up and there were a few people standing around me. I felt embarrassed, I had caused a scene.

"I am fine," I said. I had to think of something to say and quick.

"I had taken some medication and it did not mix well with the wine. I will be okay in a minute."

Everyone started to return to the party. Michael did not move.

"You don't look good. I am going to take you home."

"Michael, you cannot leave your own party."

"Then you can rest in Susan's room, on the couch."

"No, no I can't." I whispered to him. I started to shake.

There was no way I could even get close to Susan's room without making another scene. A scene that no one would want to see.

"I need to take you home, guests or no guests. You are not well."

"Please, I will just sit here and as soon as some of your guests leave, then you can take me home." I said.

But I wanted to go home. I wanted so much to go home.

It would be another hour before the guests started to leave. I stood up and apologized for my disrupting the party. They were very kind in their responses.

After they left, Michael helped me with my coat and was holding my arm as we walked to his car.

"My car." I said.

"Don't worry. I will be over your place tomorrow to check on you and we will get it then."

I did not argue. I just wanted to go home.

When we got to my place, he opened my door as my hands were shaking so bad I could not hold the key.

He came inside.

"Is there anything I can do for you? I hate just dropping you off."

"Michael, I just need rest and I will be fine. I am so sorry I made a scene at your party. I should have never had wine after I took my medication."

"That is something you do not need to concern yourself with. The party was nice, no matter what happened. Margaret stepped in and helped with the gift cards and I gave her one of the floral arrangements. So everything turned out okay. I am more worried about you."

"I will be okay. I will call you tomorrow."

He gave me a kiss on my forehead and left.

I collapsed on the couch. It's the house, it's the house and I am going crazy. I cried because I actually thought I was losing my mind.

I eventually cried myself to sleep and when I woke up it was still dark outside. It took me awhile to get oriented. I did not know where I was for a moment. I slowly got up from the couch, I felt so weak. I made to my bedroom and checked the clock and it was 3:00am. I changed into my nightgown and took some more medication. I wanted to be drowsy.

I am losing my mind, I said to myself, before I fell into a deep sleep.

The phone woke me, it was Michael.

"I did not mean to wake you, but wanted to make sure you are feeling better."

"As soon as I get up and move about, I will be able to tell. I do appreciate the call though. I probably would have slept all day."

"If I could stop by and get your car keys I can bring your car to you. Ben and I are going out this afternoon and we can stop by for the keys and when we get back, I can drive your car to you and Ben said he would take me back to my place. That way you can stay home and rest."

"That seems like a lot of trouble for you two to go through, just to get my car, but thank-you for your thoughtfulness."

"I will let you know when we are on our way for the keys. See you later this afternoon."

I thought I had better get up and get a shower to wake up. I was glad they were getting my car. Going anywhere near that house was not in my plans any time soon.

Elizabeth Klein

I called Lesley to see what the "boys" were doing today.

"I am not really sure, but I was glad Michael called Ben today, as Ben was more than happy to get out of the house. I think he does need some macho time." She was laughing.

"Lesley I need to talk to you. Do you think you can come over after they pick up the keys?"

"Sure, no problem, just give me call after they leave. Are you okay?"

"I just need to talk to someone. I'll explain when you come."

It would be two hours before Michael came for my keys. He said I looked much better and he was relieved, as he was worried.

I called Lesley when he left.

When Lesley came, I broke down and cried some more.

"What is wrong with you?"

"Lesley, I think I am losing my mind. I need to talk to someone who will help me and not tell me I am crazy."

"Tell me what has you so upset. Did Michael do something?"

"No, it is not Michael. It is his house. When Damian and I were doing the renovations, we had some experiences that we could not explain. Susan's room being so cold, doors closing, things falling on the floor, a TV turning on by itself. Then last night, at the party, I was talking to Margaret. She started to tell me something pertaining to Michael and when she saw him watching us, she stopped. She did not finish her sentence. Suddenly there was this loud voice in my head, screaming "know the truth". I heard it Lesley, I swear I heard it. I felt faint and sick. I was holding my head wanting it to stop. Michael rushed over to me. Others at the party came as well to see if I was okay. I was so embarrassed and I was frightened at the same time. I did not imagine it and yet I could not tell anyone. What is the truth, Lesley? Does this have to do with Michael?"

"I don't know. But I do know you are not going crazy. Maybe you need to put some space between you and Michael for the time being. Meanwhile I will see if there is anything more I can find about him and Susan. I have wondered about her a lot, maybe I can find some answers for you." She said as she gave me a hug.

"Thank you. I just want to be left alone, no more voices."

"Try and get some rest. I better leave before the guys get back. I will call you and don't worry we will get to the bottom of this."

After she left, I wanted so much to believe that she did not think I was losing my mind. I needed her to help me.

When Michael dropped off my car, I was glad that Ben was waiting for him outside. I just did not want him to stay.

I called my sister and asked if she had gotten the reservations for Vegas yet. I really needed to run away.

"I did and for a little more money, we have a small suite. So we are moving up."

"That sounds great, let's just hope the money will step up as well."

"Even if it doesn't, it will be nice to celebrate the New Year there."

"Did you check with Barb?" I asked.

"Yes, but she can't get the time off, so she said to send pictures."

"She will be missed, but we will make a toast to her at midnight and we definitely need a good and prosperous New Year."

"I will drink to that from the time we get there to the time we leave." She laughed. By the way, are you going to stop by for our family gathering at Christmas? I am having an open house, no more large meals. By the time I cook all day, I am so tired I don't get a chance to enjoy Christmas. So this year it is just snacks and everyone that comes can bring a dish. Now I know you don't cook, so just bring Michael. It is time he meets your family and I will talk to the others and tell them to try and behave themselves."

"You know telling them to behave, is only going to make them act up even more. But I can always tell Michael that I am adopted. Anyway, I will have to talk to him and see if he doesn't have any other plans. So I will let you know."

I told her I would call and I thanked her for suggesting to going away for the New Year. If she only knew how badly I needed to get lost.

I was not sure if I wanted to introduce Michael to my family. He kept asking me what I was doing on Christmas. I told him I always try to spend some time with family. I agreed with Lesley, that Michael and I needed some time apart, but the holidays were tough when you are alone. I finally gave in and asked him if he wanted to go with me to my sister's.

He said he would like to meet my family. So I told him the time and he said he would pick me up.

My sister had a crowd at her house. We had a hard time trying to find a place to park. Her husband was very involved in Search and Rescue, so there were a lot of the people there that I did not know. But then again Michael was well known in the community so he knew a few of them. And Damian came a little later, so Michael talked to him. All and all it was a nice evening and I forgot about the voice for the time being.

When Michael drove me home and walked me to the door, he handed me a gift box. I was surprised.

"Merry Christmas," he said.

"Michael you did not have to. I did not get you anything."

"You did give me something. I had no plans for this evening and it was a pleasure to spend it with you and your family. So thank you very much and accept this gift."

"Well thank you." I gave him a kiss on the cheek, "Merry Christmas."

He told me to open it later, so after he left, I opened it. Inside were twenty one hundred dollar bills and a note that said, "Have a good time in Vegas."

I wanted to call him and tell him I could not accept the money. But I tried that before and it did not work. I would call him tomorrow and thank him. At least it wasn't another ring.

The New Year was approaching and my sister and I were on our way to Las Vegas. We had a nice drive, but glad when we finally checked into the hotel. I could not believe the size of the room. We had a small kitchen, dining room and living area. The bedroom was huge. We had a king size bed and a spa for the tub. This was luxury.

"I could almost spend most of my time in here." I told my sister.

"It is nice but the action is downstairs and I need a drink, so let's go."

We played the machines for a while and had a couple of drinks and I told her we better get something to eat. Especially before I have one more drink or I would be up in the room.

It was an early night for me. I went back to the room and took a shower. I was watching TV, when she came in.

"I am worn out, she said. Losing just takes everything out of me."

We both started laughing.

The next day we hit the Mall. I really bought too much, as everything was on sale and with the money that Michael gave me, I really had fun.

My sister and I even treated ourselves to a manicure and a pedicure.

By the time we returned to the hotel, we were both tired. So we took a nap before we got ready to hit the streets for the New Year's celebration. Even though I had been there before, for New Year's, the excitement in the air never changes.

The streets and the sidewalks were crowded. Everyone was having a good time, laughing and even singing. Some had a little too much to drink, but what the heck, it was time for celebration.

"Where are we going?" My sister asked. She raised her voice to be heard over the crowd.

"Doesn't matter, just keep walking." I yelled back.

It was getting harder to move through the crowd. There were way too many people.

All of a sudden we heard some yelling. I thought how strange, as it was not midnight yet. The crowd was pushing my sister and I forward, as there was more and more shouting behind us. Then people started moving into the street. I looked behind us. I could see the crowd trying to move out of the way. There were some men running through the crowd toward us. As one man was coming near, I saw he had a gun. Women started screaming, there were other men running behind the first man. Maybe about three of them and they all had guns. My sister and I were against the wall of one of the Casino's, we had been pushed there. We did not dare move. We did not know which way to run. Then we heard "stop" and I could see some policemen coming behind the men that had the guns. The policemen did not draw their guns. There were just too many people. All they could do was chase the men. As one of the men was running toward my sister and me, he grabbed another man, who was trying to get out of the way. He put his arm around the guy's throat, turned the poor man towards the police and put a gun to the man's head. He was using him as a hostage. The policemen stopped and tried to talk to the man with the gun. But you could tell he was as scared as the man he was using as a hostage. He kept looking around for

Elizabeth Klein

an escape. Then he tried to turn his hostage, to continue down the sidewalk, trying to make his getaway. He tripped and his gun went off. My sister screamed as I fell to the ground. That was the last thing I remembered. Everything went black.

I felt as if I was dreaming, I could hear voices in the distance but could not make out what they were saying. My head hurt so bad, I tried to move my arm to touch my head. My arm would not move, it was being held down by something. I was scared, where was I? Why couldn't I wake up?"

"Can you hear me Beth," a strange voice was saying. Beth, try to open your eyes."

How silly, I thought, I can open my eyes. I tried but my eyelids felt as if there were weights attached to them. I wanted to rub my eyes, but again something was holding my arms down. Slowly my eyes were starting to open. Everything was hazy. I could see outlines of people, but I could not see their faces. Who were they?

Then I heard my sister's voice and I knew I was okay, she was here.

"You are going to be okay, sis, you are going to be okay."

A strange man stood above me and put some light in my eye. That hurt and I shut my eyes again.

"Beth, it is okay, open your eyes."

I did as he said. I wanted to see who he was and I wanted to see my sister.

"Lily," I said.

"I am here." She moved so I could see her better. She was crying.

"I smiled and the first thing that came to me was, "did I miss New Years?"

"Not really, she said, it came. You just decided to sleep through it."

That strange man came back into view.

"Hi, Beth, I am Doctor Stevenson. You had an accident. Do you remember what happened to you?"

"Running, people were running, a very loud noise, someone was screaming and then, I can't remember."

"It will come back to you slowly, he said. There was an accident and you had a head injury, but you are going to be okay."

I saw him turn to talk to my sister and she was nodding her head. She came back to me.

"I have to go now, but I won't be far away." She said.

"No, stay here. I was starting to panic. Stay here."

She looked over to the Doctor and he said she could stay, but just for a short time. He left and she moved the chair by my bed.

"I was shot?" I asked.

"Yes, you were. But you are going to be fine."

"Where was I shot?"

"This can wait until later, now you need some rest."

"No, where was I shot?"

"The bullet grazed the left side of you head. You are so lucky you have such a thick skull. The bullet did not penetrate. There is no brain damage that the Doctors can see as of now."

"Why can't I move my arms?"

"They have your wrists tied down, to keep you from touching your head. Even though you have a thick skull, the bullet cracked a part of it. There was some swelling and fluid. The Doctors drained the fluid and said that it will heal."

"How long have I been here?"

"Four days. They induced a semi-coma, to keep you still until they could evaluate any further damage that the bullet could have caused."

"I am okay?" I asked as my eyes started to close.

"Yes, you are okay." I could barely hear her answer as I drifted off to sleep.

When I awoke again, the lights were dim and it was dark. It must have been night time. I was trying to focus my eyes on someone in the chair in the corner. His head was bent down, he was sleeping.

"Hi," I said. Not sure my voice was loud enough to wake that person up.

He raised his head and I was surprised to see that it was Michael.

"Thank God, he said. I was hoping you would open those beautiful blue eyes, so I could see you."

"Is my sister still here?" I asked.

Elizabeth Klein

"Your whole family is here, even Ben and Lesley came, when they found out you finally decided to wake up. They are in the cafeteria. The Doctor says visitation has to be kept at a minimum for the time being."

"I want to go home." My voice was raspy.

"You will soon. The Doctor says you will probably need some therapy and as soon as you can regain some balance you will be home."

"How much longer?"

"It does not matter. You cannot go home unless the Doctor feels you are ready. Until then you are stuck here, with us."

"You miss work."

"I have taken a few days off. Your sister needs to go home for a few days. So I will be here."

"Can I have a drink?" My throat was so sore.

There was a glass of water with a straw on the table. He gave me the straw and I swallowed a few times. He then rang for the nurse to let her know I was awake. They were going to notify the Doctor.

Michael held my hand and we just looked at each other. I could not think of anything more to say. I looked up at the ceiling for a while, trying to take everything in. How could this happen?

The door opened and it was my sister, Lesley and Ben. My sister and Lesley came to the bed. Michael said he would see me in a little while. Ben waved at me, as Michael and Ben walked out the door.

"You look much better." My sister said.

"I think you look marvelous, Lesley said, with tears in her eyes. I promised myself I would not cry, so much for promises."

I smiled at her.

The nurse came in and said the Doctor was on his way and if I needed anything. I said "no".

My sister looked at me and asked, "How are you really feeling?"

"Okay, for being shot. I just want to go home."

"You will be home soon enough. They are going to be doing some therapy and once you are up and walking, you will come home."

"Knowing you, Lesley said, they will not be able to keep you here much longer."

I looked up at the ceiling again. My head did not hurt when I looked up.

My sister and Lesley left. They only stayed a few minutes. They said they would be right outside the door.

I must have drifted off, I heard someone calling my name. It was Damian.

"Hi mom, I just wanted to see you for a few minutes."

"It is so good to see you, I am glad you came."

"How are you doing mom? Do you feel okay?"

The look on his face showed how worried he was.

"Damian, I am going to be okay. You know how tough I am."

"You sure are and I know you will make it through this. You know that I will help you mom."

"I know and I do love you."

"I love you too, but I better leave, the nurse said the Doctor was on his way. So I will see you later."

"See you soon and please don't worry everything is going to be okay."

As I said that, I was hoping that was the truth.

I started thinking what was going to become of me, as I still did not know how bad I really was.

I heard the door open and it was the Doctor.

"Beth, your family says you want to go home and you will soon. We are going to get you out of bed tomorrow. The physical therapist will be with you and he is going to help you get on your feet. As soon as you get strength in your legs and walk on your own, we will release you. I will have the nurse come in and take off your restraints. You are going to be fine in no time at all." He smiled.

The nurse came in and took off the restraints. My sister and Lesley came in after she left.

"Damion and I are going to take off, my sister said. I am going to drive back home, but as soon as you are ready to leave, I will come and get you out of this place." She gave me a hug.

"I am staying over, Lesley said. So I will see you tomorrow. I think Michael wants to come in and say goodnight."

They left and Michael came in. He held my hand.

"When I heard what happened I was so angry at first, he said. I thought this could not be happening to me again. To lose someone I care so deeply

Elizabeth Klein

about. I prayed and the anger left as somehow, someway I knew that you would be okay. I needed faith and lots of it, he smiled. I wanted to see you to make sure you were all right."

He kissed me on the forehead. I could still feel his hand around mine, as I started to drift off to sleep.

The following morning I had a tray by my bed. They wanted me to eat, but it was going to be a liquid diet for today. Whatever it was it tasted awful. The IV's and tubes were removed from my body and I had a sponge bath. It was the first time I saw the side of my head. It was bandaged and I knew they cut my hair on that side. I looked awful, I wanted to cry. The physical therapist came in. He had a walker with him. I kept thinking I did not need a walker, the Doctor said I was fine.

The therapist's name was Frank. He sat me up on the side of my bed and held me there in case I was dizzy. I told him I was okay. Then he put his arm around my waist and stood me up. My legs gave way and he held on to me.

"Try again, he said. Keep your knees locked."

He moved the walker closer to me, and I held onto it tight.

"Please hold onto me. I am afraid of falling." I said.

"I have you. We are going to work on just standing for now, with the walker and as soon as you feel comfortable, I will have you move one foot, then the other. But we have time, so no hurry."

I waited for a while and then moved my left foot and I felt as if I was going to fall. I had no balance.

"It is okay. With a head injury, it may take a little longer to regain your balance. That is why we are working with the walker. You may have to use it for a while."

I was upset, but I did not say anything. I knew the only way I was going home, was to get my legs moving so I could walk, even if it was with the walker. We worked for over an hour and I was able to walk across my room. I was exhausted and he helped me back to the bed.

"Can I try again later?" I asked.

"I will come back this afternoon. Meanwhile get some rest."

I tried to stay awake, but I couldn't.

I woke up in the afternoon, and had some more fluids and a chocolate shake. I wanted to try the walker again, so I called the nurse.

Frank came up a half hour later and I was able to stand on my own. Then used the walker and I made it out to the hall. Even though I was scared as my balance was horrible. I held onto the walker and wanted to go more.

I saw Lesley and Michael walking toward me.

Frank wanted me to go back in my room and I told him "no."

"You look great, Lesley said. This is amazing."

"She wants out of here." Michael laughed.

Frank turned me around and said I did super for my first day, but not to over- do it. So he led me back to bed. A couple of times I thought I was going to fall, but just could not give in to it.

I talked to Lesley and Michael for awhile, but I did not want visitors, so pretended I was tired.

The following day, Frank worked with me in the morning and then Michael helped me that evening. I just could not stop. I wanted to go home.

The Doctor said I was doing better than he expected and as long as I was able to use the walker I could go home soon. They just had to run some more tests to make sure there was not another bleed or fluid around the incision area.

A couple days later there were two men from the police department that came. They wanted to get a recording of what I remembered that day, which was not much. I then learned I was not the only one hurt that evening. The man that was held hostage broke his hip and there were two other women who were trampled by the crowd. One was still in the hospital, the other one was not hurt that bad. Fortunately no one else was shot. They were able to apprehend the man that shot me and wanted to know if I would be able to identify him. I told them that I couldn't. I did not remember much of what happened. They said that it was an on-going investigation and they may be contacting me again.

I just wanted to forget.

I felt tired and the nurse gave me something to sleep.

I was very drowsy when Michael came to visit. He said he had to leave.

Elizabeth Klein

"It is hard for me to go. But the Doctor said you will be ready to go home in a couple of more days. Your recovery has been a lot better than expected."

"I just keep going." I smiled, but was still half asleep.

"You will be well taken care of when you return home, and I will be part of that. But I need to go for now."

He kissed me on the forehead and turned to leave.

Just as Michael opened the door, there was a man who was entering my room. He introduced himself and said he was a Lawyer. I remember Michael telling him I was still recovering and then walked him to the door. I was watching them and I vaguely remember something said about a lawsuit. Michael looked over to me and then turned to the other man. I saw Michael pull out his wallet and give the man a card. Was it Michael's business card? Michael came to my bed and said he would take care of it. I did not have to worry about being hassled by a Lawyer. He turned and said he had to go. He needed to get back home and back to work. He would call me every day and see me when I got back home.

He kissed me goodbye and he left.

I know the Lawyer was there for something, but after he left. I just could not remember why.

After another week, I was finally going to be released. I was still using the walker and was given strict instructions to keep using it until my balance had improved more. I was given a prescription to continue working with a physical therapist once I returned home and I was given medication for my headaches. They weren't constant anymore, but every now and then I would get a bad one.

My sister came to get me. I was to return in two weeks to have my stitches out. The bandage was off and my hair was shaven in that area. I was going to have to figure a way to brush my hair from one side to the other and hopefully cover my bald spot. I asked Doctor Stevenson why my Doctor could not take the stitches out, as it was over a couple of hours to travel to see him. He promised me one more visit and then the follow ups could be with my own Doctor. I did not argue.

It was so nice to be home again. It felt as if I had been away for years instead of a few weeks. My sister wanted to stay with me but I told her I was fine. I just wanted to be by myself in my own place.

But it did not last long. My son Damian came by. He bought me some flowers and wanted to make sure I was okay.

"I am fine, just a little tired, so I will lie down and rest for a while."

"Okay, mom, I know when I am being asked to split. If you need anything just call."

"I will, and thanks for the flowers."

After he left, the phone started ringing and I did not answer. I was tired and if I had to tell one more person I was fine, I would scream.

The following days were hectic, flowers started to arrive and I finally answered phone calls. My Pastor came over and I had a wonderful talk with him. I told him there was not a day that goes by that I don't realize how fortunate I am and I thank God for that.

I hated the walker but knew my limitations and sure did not want another stay in a hospital. So for the time being I was relying on my sis and friends to get me to physical therapy. Many times I would be disappointed because my balance was not improving as much as I thought it should. And always the same response, sometimes it takes longer than we expect.

Michael came over a few evenings and brought take-out for our meals.

He would always make me laugh and stop feeling sorry for myself. I enjoyed his visits more than I thought I should.

I was in bed for a couple of days, only because now that I was off the hospital drugs, I had to start taking my medication and get it in my system again. So body aches, headaches and a balance deficiency. I was in good shape and I was home.

I did get a clean bill of health from Dr. Stevenson. I asked him how much longer before I regain my balance and he said just give it some more time. Same answer.

I felt I was finally starting to get back to normal.

Michael informed me that the Lawyer had tried to call me, but could not reach me, so he gave him a call and said I did not have to appear in court if there should be a trial, which I was extremely thankful for. I kept telling everyone I just could not remember the details of that night.

So I was hoping that would be the end of anymore contact with the Lawyer as I only wanted to forget the whole incident.

Then my life took another horrible turn. The bills started to come in. The hospital alone was over two hundred thousand dollars and that did not include the testing that was done. Other Doctors I never heard of started billing me, for things I did not even know I had done. There was no way I could afford all those bills.

Lesley told me that I could file for medical bankruptcy and she gave me the number of a Lawyer to see. It was the only thing I could do.

After talking with this Lawyer, I was really depressed. She could help me, but I had too many assets, and I would have to try to eliminate some of them. One of them would have to be my home that my son and his girlfriend lived in. I felt horrible that they would have to leave. But then again it was not a seller's market, so I could not even sell it for what it was worth. I would talk to my son, maybe by having his name on the title may help.

I also would talk to Damian and tell him I might have to move in the mobile home with him. Hopefully it would be for a short time until all this could get settled. I started crying. All my things would have to be packed away and stored. Just when I got my apartment to be a comfort for me. I felt as if this burden was going to be more than I could endure.

I talked to my family and let them know what was going on. My sister said her garage had some space I could put some of my things in there. Because Damian did not have a lot of furniture, my furniture could go in the mobile. And he was happy he would have a room-mate even if it was his mom. I kept telling him it was only going to be temporary.

"Mom, my life is not all that exciting. I am a gamer, so no problem."

"I never wanted any of this to happen, but unfortunately it is out of my hands." I told him.

I never told Michael, he started to get real busy at work and we did not see much of each other on the weekends. I was hoping he was with Margaret or someone else. I did not want him to get involved in the mess of my life right now.

I gave notice at my apartment complex and Damian and my brother started packing up my things for me. I was not using my walker anymore, but had a cane now and I was more comfortable with that, plus I could drive. Some little things I could pack in my car and take over to the mobile home.

When I returned to my apartment later one evening, Michael was there.

"I feel bad because I have not been over to see you as much as I should have, but now I feel even worse that you did not even care enough about me, to let me know what the hell was going on. I finally got it out of Ben that you were moving in with your son. But he said I would have to talk to you, as to why you were doing that."

"Michael, I said, so much has happened in such a short time. Believe me when I tell you I wanted so much to call you and let you know how my world has fallen apart. But I couldn't, I had to make some decisions and make them quick and I know how at one time you said you would help, but my pride would not ask you."

"Then at least give me the decency of knowing what the hell is happening."

"The hospital and Doctor's bills started coming in and I have no insurance. The real sad thing is I knew I had to start looking for some but as luck would have it, I was too late. I feel as if my world has turned upside down.

I did have to give up my apartment and move in with Damian and I may have to sell my other home, which will make my son and his girlfriend have to find another place to live. But even then I still may owe on it, I am not sure I can get enough for it."

"I don't know why you could not come to me. I would have made your apartment payments, rather than have you move in with your son, but I was not given that option and it is a little too late."

He seemed angry, but the decision was not his.

"If given a chance, I may be able to help you save your house. Again, I only want to help you. I have a very good Lawyer. He can get all the information he needs and get this settled. There are ways that this will all be worked out. We are going to do this together, and did you notice I was using the "we". He said.

Elizabeth Klein

"If there is a way you can help with my house, than please do. I worked hard for that home and I do not want to lose it. And I am only moving in with Damian for a short while, until this mess is over." I said, as I turned away from him.

"I just want you to understand that you do have friends. It is that damn independence that you seem to want to hang onto. Even if it means you may lose everything." Again, he said that with an angry voice.

"I am not used to seeing you so angry. Maybe we can talk about this some other time, I am really tired."

"I am sorry, I care for you. And I want to take care of you. You have been through so much you do not need to be going through this on your own."

"Michael, I appreciate how you feel, but I do have family and they are always the first to step in when any of us need help. I understand where you are coming from, but try and understand how I feel as well."

"Again, I am sorry. I am being insensitive. I will leave and give you a call tomorrow." He kissed me on the forehead and left.

This was a side of him, I was not sure I wanted to see. I did not realize that he had a temper, but maybe it was my fault, I should have told him.

I had an appointment with my Doctor and just thought it was another follow-up with the physical therapy. But it wasn't.

"I received a notification from Doctor Stevenson and it has been over three months since your last CAT scan. I am going to give you a script for it and will forward the results to him. So make an appointment at the hospital as soon as you can."

"Doctor you know I do not have insurance, so I am not able to get this done right now."

"This is very important. You can make payment arrangements with the hospital. It needs to be done."

"I just need some time, I promise to get it taken care of as soon as I can."

I walked out of his office after getting a lecture. Nothing I seemed to be saying to him mattered. I should have asked him if he would pay for it.

I finally made arrangements to meet up with Lesley for lunch. She said that she had almost given up on me, as I have not been taking her calls lately.

"Well it is nice to see you now and then. I am lucky to get a phone call from you these days." She said,

"I am so sorry. The move was hard on me and I just needed to take some time just for me."

"Well how is it living with your son?"

"He is wonderful, he keeps me laughing. He has such a great sense of humor. I thought I would really be depressed going back to the mobile home, but I am not. We are doing okay."

"Are you still considering filing for bankruptcy?" She asked.

"All the bills seem to be in and Michael's Lawyer is taking care of everything. I am still concerned as to what to do with the house. I checked and there is such a thing as a short-sale. It would get me out from under the house, but my credit will be shot, but it already is so why worry about it."

"If you have to do that, you have to. And how is the physical therapy coming along?"

"I stopped going. Why keep paying when I know I am getting my balance back. Now that the walker is gone, I do just fine with the cane.

Although now my Doctor says I need another CAT scan. I just cannot afford anything else right now and I tried to tell him that, but he did not listen."

"I wish I could help you. You have been through so much and yet you seem to be holding it together. You amaze me sometimes."

"You forget I have a wonderful family and they are always there for me. My sisters seem to know when I need a phone call or just to go out every now and then. I am so fortunate." I smiled.

"I guess you are, but always remember you have some good friends as well. And this friend wants to see more of you, so don't be a stranger."

We had a nice lunch and she caught me up on a lot of things at work. She said a lot of the people I worked with have left, they found better jobs out of town and moved away.

As we left she gave me a hug, I promised her I would keep in touch.

A couple of days later Michael called and asked if I could come to his house, as he had some things to discuss with me. I was not sure I wanted to meet with him and I knew for sure I did not want to go to that house.

Elizabeth Klein

But I wanted to make amends with him, as I think the last time I talked with him we were both tired and maybe things were taken out of context.

I drove there and that old familiar feeling of turning around came upon me again.

He opened the door before I could even ring the doorbell.

"Come on in." He said with a smile.

I walked in the living room and sat on the couch.

"Can I offer you some wine?" He asked.

"No thanks. It does not go well with the medication, as you recall."

"Yes I do and I apologize."

"What is it you would like to talk to me about?"

"Are you doing okay, Beth?"

"I am doing as well as expected, under the circumstances."

"I met Ben at the Club the other night. I did have a conversation with him and coaxed him to tell me the truth of how you were." He said.

"And what truth did he tell you?"

'They are worried about you. Lesley had lunch with you and was more than concerned for your health. She was afraid this could really break you physically and mentally. If it is any comfort to you, my Lawyer told me, if you agree to have my name added on your title, then you do not have to sell your home. But we can discuss that later. As far as your tests, I will pay for them." He said.

"I will not take money. I think I made that perfectly clear already."

"Beth, it is not money that I am offering. This is really hard for me as I have crossed the boundaries that we agreed to. I want you to take me. I want you to marry me." He said.

I think the shock of that showed on my face, I never knew that was coming.

"You would marry me out of pity? I don't think so, Michael."

"You don't know do you? You have no idea. I have been in love with you since the first time I saw you at the Club. I knew if you ever found out you would run. I wanted us as friends, if I could have nothing else from you. I almost lost you when you were shot and I do not want to chance that again. I am getting older and although I have tried, I just cannot see myself

with anyone else. I love you Beth and who knows maybe you would fall in love with me one day." He laughed.

"Michael, I do not love you. It would be unfair to you to say that maybe one day I would. I have never lied to you about that. I always wanted you to find someone else."

"I have tried, it is no use, there is only you. We can work some things out. You no longer have to stay with your son. You would move here. And you would never have to worry about medical care. My insurance will cover you as my wife. You cannot take chances with your health.

Look, I know this has been a platonic relationship and I have to level with you, so many times I wanted more, but not at the chance of losing you. Please, accept this proposal, it comes from my heart."

"Michael I am honored that you want to marry me. But it is for the wrong reasons. I might be at my lowest point in life but I will get through this. And there would be another reason that I cannot consider marrying you. There is no way I could ever live in this house. This was yours and Susan's home."

I thought for sure that would put a quick end to this conversation.

"Whatever you want, you know that. And if you would allow me to be the co-owner of your other home, we can save that house and still rent it to your son and his girlfriend. We will get a place of our own. You will never have to worry. I have been thinking about a bigger place anyway, as our Christmas parties are getting larger and we need more space." He smiled.

"This is so much to think about. Michael, I appreciate all that you have done, but I am not sure marriage is the answer.

"It is the answer, the answer to us, to your health and to our future, and I think you cannot deny that"

I wanted to leave. He was beating me down. I was falling into a dark place, alone and scared, uncertain of my future.

I was agreeing with him. But his proposal, it felt wrong.

Since the accident, it seemed as if my life was over, my health, all the financial disasters, the possibility of losing my home and of course now having to live with my son. Michael had been my friend for years. He was always with me in one way or another. I started crying, maybe this was

Elizabeth Klein

another chance at life. He wanted an answer. He would not let me leave until I gave him one. He knew I would run.

He picked me up and held me in his arms. I let him hold me, he was saving me. If nothing else his arms were strong and I felt safe in them, almost liked I belonged there.

I could not stop crying, it was as if the tears had been kept silent for months. He held me tighter and in between the sobbing I said "yes.

He held me for the longest time. I moved away from him. I told him maybe it was best that I left. I had a lot to think about

He said we had a lot to talk about. We spent the rest of the evening together and he did most of the talking. With him as my husband, I did not have to worry about my health or my sanity. We were starting a new life for both of us and his love for me had no boundaries.

He wanted me to start looking for a home for us as soon as possible. The market was a buyer's market and he knew we could get a good deal on a home. He also wanted me to get the CAT scan as soon as possible and he would pay for it. He said I could not wait until the marriage. As soon as we were married, I would be on his insurance and if more tests were needed I would be covered.

The wedding I would plan and anything I wanted was fine with him.

We would not tell our families yet, because he wanted to discuss some things with his Lawyer first. But he would put me in touch with a realtor and I was to start looking for us a home. He asked what I wanted in a home and I told him it did not really matter. Then I asked him what he was going to do with this house and he said he would keep it for a while and most of everything would stay in that house. He wanted all new things in the new house, he said "for us."

"There is no turning back, he said. This is our future we are planning and it will be a good future. You will never have to worry the rest of your life. I will be here to take care of you."

"It is hard for me to comprehend someone taking care of me. I have had that responsibility for such a long time. It will be difficult to get used to."

"We will have a lot to get used to, but we will do it together." He smiled.

"The first thing I want you to do is get your test, that is important and the rest will fall in place. And remember you said "yes", there is no turning back.'

I was getting tired and he noticed.

"Go home and get some rest. We have plenty of time to work things out for our future together."

He kissed me on the lips, our first real kiss.

As I drove away, I was sick. I could not believe I said yes. Why I asked myself? Because for the first time in a very long time someone stepped in and lifted the burden I was carrying. But my thoughts were at what price? I was honest with Michael when I told him I did not love him, maybe with time I might. How much time? I thought.

When I got home, I slept through the night for the first time in a long time. It was peaceful sleep.

When I woke up, it was as if I had dreamed all that happened. But reality hit and I had told him I would marry him. I was weak with all that had happened these last few months. Could marriage to Michael really save me?

I made the appointment for the CAT scan at the end of the week. It was not for Michael, I had to be sure I was going to be okay, for us. How funny in a matter of days, I am thinking about what is good for another in my life. Did I lose my independence by saying "yes?" No I told myself, never.

The realtor called and she asked what I was looking for in a house. I told her an opened entrance way, a large kitchen and living room, three bedrooms and two baths. She said she had a lot of homes on the market, so we could look at any time it was convenient for me. So I made an appointment for the following day. Michael called me later that day. His tone was different, more loving and caring. Everything was changing. I guess I was going to change as well. He ended the phone call with "I love you."

I did tell Damian. I told him not to tell anyone for the time being.

"Mom that is great, I have always liked Michael. But mom, you cannot live in that house and I hope you are not considering that."

"It was a shock to me when he said I could move into that house. I told him I could not live there and Michael told me he understood and I am to start looking for us a place of our own. Everything is happening so fast, that I want to slow down. But am afraid if I do that, I may change my mind. Damian did you know how Michael felt about me?"

"I think everyone saw it but you, mom. I think you have always been afraid of getting involved with anyone. You just could not see what we saw."

"I am still afraid, but for the first time in a long time, I feel this is the man I need in my life and I can even say I want in my life. I just feel that the timing is bad, I have so much going on now."

"It is the timing that answered what you needed most in your life. You have someone who will give you everything you deserve."

"The problem is, I am not sure I can give him everything he deserves?"

"You have been giving him what he needed, he wanted you and you were always there for him. Now he is there for you. Don't question it mom, go with it, you have nothing to lose." He smiled.

I was questioning a lot of things and the one thing I knew I was not going to lose was my independence. I could not chance losing that, no matter what.

Michael's Lawyer had worked everything out. I had put Michael's name on the deed to my house. So any sell of the house, he would get half. But I had no intentions of selling it any time soon.

The CAT scan came back negative for any new bleed. So I was given the good news and there was not a need for anymore testing.

The house hunting was frustrating. The realtor was not very good in acknowledging what I wanted. Finally I found a good buy on a large home with a beautiful back yard, a nice patio with a fountain and a built in bar-b-cue. It was in foreclosure. When Michael saw the house he really liked it. The rooms were large for the entertaining he wanted to do. And he was very impressed with the master bedroom and the huge bathroom it had. We put in a bid for it and I really thought we were going to get it. After a couple of months of bidding and going up in price each time, we found out we were bidding against ourselves. Even though the bank insisted there was another bidder, we found out there wasn't. So Michael made the offer we made prior, if they did not accept it, it would be our last offer. They did not accept it.

I decided to take a break from the house hunting for a while. I was disappointed we did not get that house, as Michael really liked it.

Michael said it was time we made an announcement of our engagement.

I figured there were some that already knew.

"We will tell our friends first, especially Ben and Lesley." I said.

"We will. Then I am making plans to go to New Mexico as it was time I met the rest of his family, his two daughters."

I was not comfortable with that, but knew it had to happen sometime. Of course everyone was happy for us, when word got around. There were a lot of congratulations and happiness for us. All except one and that was Margaret. I had always told her I was not a threat and now I will have tell her different. I guess in a way I was truthful, I did not know how he felt about me.

I called her, as I wanted us to meet face to face. At first she did not want to talk to me at all, but I kept calling and I finally got her to agree to meet me at the coffee shop. When she showed up she looked awful and I knew she had been crying. My heart broke for her.

"I did not lie to you. I was oblivious to the feelings Michael had for me. I was not interested in a relationship with anyone. It was when I was at my worst that Michael revealed his feelings toward me. Even after I told him my feelings for him were not that of love. He told me in time, I would fall in love with him and time was all that I had left." I said.

"I knew how he felt about you, but I still thought I had a chance. I knew the truth when you had your accident. You were all he could think about and he had to get to you. Even when he returned, he told me then, there would be no more of us. I was holding onto him with the sex, it was never anything more to him. But I was in love and when you love a man as long as I have loved him, you do not give up easily. I still thought I had a chance. You did not seem to show him any kind of affection as I thought you might, especially since he was so concerned about you. But he would not take my calls and he avoided me. So many wasted years for nothing and I put up with a lot from him, things that now you are going to have to deal with."

"And why won't you tell me what I am going to have to deal with?" I asked.

"Because now it is your cross to bear, it is the price you are going pay for his love. This is the end for me and the beginning for you, but I will have the last laugh. I already know what the outcome of this marriage is going to be. I know what you are going to have to endure and I know that one day the pain I have to deal with now, will one day be yours. She got up and turned to leave, she stopped. She looked at me and said. "There is no such thing as "happily ever after." Then she walked away.

I sat there for a long time. I remembered the voice that said "know the truth." Was I blinded to something else of Michael or was it just Margaret? I never dreamed that I would be marrying Michael. I never wanted to hurt anyone.

Deception

*E*VEN THOUGH *I was troubled about the conversation I had with Margaret, I convinced myself that she was so torn about my engagement to Michael that she had to strike out at someone. I felt some guilt, as I did lead her to believe that I would never be a threat to her and Michael. It was obvious to so many others that I was the one. But I did not lie about my feelings toward Michael. None of what has happened in the last couple of weeks was my intention. From the very beginning of my involvement with Michael it was just friendship. Lies, how many more will come to surface with this marriage?*

As weeks passed Michael seemed very discouraged with me for not setting a marriage date and he felt I was taking too much time to find another suitable house. I told him that maybe he should start looking, as we were both so disappointed over the loss of the other house we wanted.

He thought that we should marry now and live in his home just until we could find another place. There was no way I could explain to him why that was not going to happen.

He then told me that he was going to take some time off of work as it was time to go to New Mexico and meet his family. I knew that time was coming and I told him I just did not feel ready for that now. But from his expression it was obvious, it was not a choice.

"I know it will be difficult for you, but you will be fine. I have talked to my daughters and they are anxious to meet you as Jeremy spoke so highly of you."

"Then Michael we will stay in a hotel, as I do not want to stay at anyone's home, it will just be too uncomfortable for me."

"My daughter Diane has said we must stay with her, she has already made arrangements for us at her home."

Elizabeth Klein

"Michael, I think you should have talked to me about that. I would never make plans without informing you first." I was becoming very upset.

Why would he allow these arrangements to be made without talking to me?

"I do not want to hurt her feelings and you will get to know my grandkids as well. I will be with you the whole time." He said, as if the decision was final.

There was not much more I could say. I knew sooner or later this was going to happen.

We left early Thursday morning and we were coming back on Sunday, so I thought I could survive a couple of days. We arrived at his daughter's house in the evening. I was so uncomfortable. I meet his daughter Diane and her husband Bob and their two children. The oldest, a girl named Michelle and her younger son Thomas. Michael and Bob went outside to get our luggage. Michelle gave up her room for us. She would sleep on the couch in the family room. Once we were settled in the bedroom, we gathered in the living room. It was a very nice home and comfortable. The kids eventually went into the family room to watch TV and Michael and his daughter were catching up. My initial feelings were this daughter was not happy with her father's decision to marry. When she would look at me, it was not with any affection. She asked what I did for a living and I told her I was not working at the time. I liked the reaction she had to that.

"So you are on unemployment?" She asked.

"No, I do have an income that I manage with."

"And what income is that?"

Michael finally stepped in and said it was really no concern of hers.

"She is to be my wife and she will not have to worry about finances."

"I am sorry, Dad. I did not mean to pry."

She then asked if we would like something to eat or drink. I asked for some water and Michael asked for a drink. She said she was prepared and had purchased some Vodka for him. He made his own drink and then he brought me some water. After I had the water, I expressed how tired I was. Michael apologized to me for not realizing the trip would be hard on me.

I said my goodnights to everyone and Michael came in the bedroom with me. I got my nightgown and robe out of my luggage. He showed me where the bathroom was, so I could change clothes. It was then it hit me that Michael and I would be sleeping together. I am so old fashioned and felt this was not a good situation because we had not engaged in any intimacy. I told myself that was such a stupid attitude to have as it was not like I was new to this scenario. It was just that it had been a long, long time since I was in bed with a man.

He laughed at me, when I told him it had been awhile since I was in this situation.

"Nothing is happening I assure you. I may reach for you, just to hold you during the night. I have to admit I have been waiting to do that for a long time. But for now I am going out to visit with my daughter and Bob for a while longer and I promise I will not disturb you if you are asleep."

He gave me a kiss and said sleep well.

I thought how lucky I was to have him. Even though I do not want to be here, I did get some comfort from him. I knew he already told his family that I had been shot, but he will probably tell them that I have other problems as well and of course his daughter will feel that I am marrying for financial gain, so I will let her think that.

I did fall asleep right away and later I awoke when I heard Michael come in, but pretended I was still asleep. I was facing toward him. The only light was from the window and I saw that he had a little too much to drink, as he was off balance when he was undressing. He was going through his luggage to find his pajamas and just pulling stuff out and it was falling to the floor. He finally found his pajama bottoms and put them on. Then he was holding himself against the wall as he went into the bathroom, it was just outside the bedroom door. Before he returned to the room, I rolled over and faced the wall. I felt him get in bed and he turned away from me for which I was grateful. Maybe all of them had a little too much to drink.

When I woke the next morning, he did have his arm around me. So I kept still. I waited for a few minutes then slowly moved out of bed trying not to wake him. His arm tightened around me and he asked where I thought I was going, I told him to the bathroom. He let go of me.

As I walked outside the room to the bathroom, I could hear the kids in the family room watching TV. I hurried and returned to the room. Michael had put on a pullover shirt and still had his pajama bottoms on.

"I am going to get a cup of coffee, you go ahead and change, then come out."

"Okay and thank you for the privacy. I appreciate it."

"Our time will come." He smiled.

I dressed and dreaded the long day ahead. The other daughter was going to show up later. I only knew she was the oldest, she was divorced and her children were grown and had families of their own. I kept wondering if I was going to survive another day here.

Michael decided we would all go out to breakfast.

Good I thought. I am more comfortable away from the house. It turned out to be nice. The kids talked to me and I enjoyed her husband Bob. He interacted with his kids so well, but Diane seemed distant.

Her conversations with her father were of all their troubles.

The kids always were on the go with school and sports, everything seemed so expensive. She said she was looking for a job, but she had been a stay at home mom for so many years and now she said no one would hire her.

Michael did not seem very sympathetic. He told her to try and get something part time and then maybe she can work into a full time position. There was more to that conversation, her voice lowered in her reply.

Before we returned to the house, Diane wanted to go to the store, there were some things she needed. As we were shopping I noticed Michael put another bottle of Vodka in the shopping cart and some beer and Diane was putting other things in the cart as well. He had paid for breakfast and now he was paying for the food she needed.

We were only back at the house for an hour when the other daughter came. Her name was Ellen. She was very likeable and had a good sense of humor, she laughed a lot. Her affection for her father was very obvious. I did not know daughters kissed their fathers on the lips, but he did not seem to mind. As the day went by the beer was passed among the daughters and Michael had his drinks. I noticed Bob did not drink much, maybe one beer. I did not have anything to drink as I wanted my medication, I liked drowsy.

Pizza was ordered for dinner, the drinking continued. Both daughters drank more than their share of beer. They were reminiscing, laughing and even dancing with each other. It was good to see the daughters this way, as I thought of my own sisters and how much fun we had together.

Then Ellen sat on her father's lap with her arm around his neck and kissed him multiple times on the cheek. He was very comfortable with this and I just had an uneasy feeling. I was looking at Michael trying to get his attention as it had been another long day and I had taken enough medicine to have that drowsy felling. I needed to call it a night and I needed him to help get me out of there. Finally, he looked at me and thank goodness, he knew.

He moved his grown daughter off his lap and told everyone it was time for me to call it a night, he saw I was done for. He helped me up and held my arm and as we were walking to the bedroom I said goodnight to everyone and I would see them in the morning.

"I am sorry, he said. I ignored you and did not see that you were not feeling well."

"You were enjoying your family, as you should. You return to them and I will be okay."

He gave me a long lingering kiss and left. I should have felt something but I did not. Am I so dead inside that I can no longer show intimacy? What is wrong with me?

I listened to the laughter outside the bedroom and I wondered what was the truth of this family and why did Ellen desperately need the attention of her father? As time goes by I am sure I will find out.

I slept soundly that night. I did not hear Michael come to bed. His arm was around me when I woke. I laid there for a while and thought this would be the rest of my life, waking up in the morning with his arm around me. The rest of my life, I would have the feeling of security in his arms. Wanting more than anything that it would be the truth.

When everyone finally got up, we had another breakfast out. There was a lot more talking and laughter. It was at breakfast that I found out Diane and Bob had invited some friends over for a bar-b-que. So now I was going to be on display for their friends. I am sure of the conversation that will take place among their friends after Michael and I leave and I doubt if it will be in my favor.

The daughters stayed close to their father. The others were at the bar-b-que with Bob as he cooked the hamburgers. Some of the women had brought some chips, salad, etc., and was putting them on the table.

After we ate, I was left alone again. I really felt like an outsider. And as an outsider, I went through the backyard gate and took a walk. I needed some fresh air. No one would miss me. I found a small park a couple of blocks away. It was still in the subdivision. I sat on a bench and tried to relax. I want to go home. I just needed to make it through this evening. I guess I stayed there longer than I thought and I saw one of the kids walking toward me.

"They are looking for you, Thomas said. You did not let anyone know where you were going."

Like I really had to, I thought to myself.

Then I saw Michael and he seemed annoyed. He was.

"If you wanted to take a walk, then at least tell someone, like me for instance. Do you know how worried I have been?

"I just took a walk. I am not lost."

"But no one knew you took a walk."

There was no use in continuing with the conversation, he was not going to listen. Of course going back was horrible, I guess I made another scene. I sat down in a lounge chair and I was good for about two hours. Then enough was enough. I walked into the house and the kids were watching a movie so I sat with them. They were easier to be with than the adults. I sat through two movies with them and knew my time was up. I told the kids that I was going to bed, I was not feeling well and if anyone should inquire where I was, please let them know.

I really wanted to sleep, so took two sleeping pills that night. I honestly think I could have slept through an earthquake.

The next morning, I did not care what happened, as I was going home.

The daughters were emotional around their father and looked at me and said it was nice to meet me. My thoughts to those words were, and nice to see you leave.

Michael apparently was still annoyed with me and did not talk much, as we were traveling home. Then we stopped for lunch.

"I know it was difficult for you, but I did not appreciate your attitude. I took you there to meet my family as I had met your family. Why was that so difficult for you?"

"Meeting my family was maybe four hours and you did not have to stay the night, a totally different scenario. I knew that it was going to be hard for them to accept me in the family and believe me I can understand. They cared about Susan a great deal, I heard that. I feel those comments were directed right at me. How do you think I was to react to it?"

"That was insensitive and I let them know that. And I did let them know that you were first and foremost in my life now."

"Maybe you should not have done that. It is not good to put me above your family. A family that has always been there compared to someone you have only known for a couple of years."

"My love for you is something my family will have to accept. I am sorry, I was a little angry with you. I apologize." He reached over and held my hand. Are we still friends?"

I had to laugh

As he was driving, he started to reveal a little more of his past. He told me his mother was an alcoholic. As young children, they lived with his aunt and uncle for many years. His mother could never hold down a job. He had a sister that was a few years older than he was. He never knew his father and the sister never knew hers. It was a difficult childhood for both of them. His aunt was his saving grace. She adored him, as she could not have children of her own. Any love he received, he got from her. As soon as he was of age, he enlisted in the Army. He had to escape the life he was living. He married his high school sweetheart and started a new life.

He tried to save his sister as she became a drug addict. She eventually died of an overdose. He tried to save his mom and she died of alcoholism. His marriage was not the best, not until his son was born and that gave him another chance of a better life. When his wife finally wanted a divorce, he agreed and with a large settlement. She gave custody of their son to him. After the divorce he had a few affairs, but he knew he could never be serious about anyone until Jeremy was out on his own.

Elizabeth Klein

That is when Susan came into his life.

"You said you tried to save your sister and your mom. Are you trying to save me?"

"If loving you means saving you, then yes."

"You cannot save people. They have to save themselves. Please do not feel that you have to save me."

"I do not feel that way and I think you know that. You accepted my proposal."

I could not tell him, I was at my lowest and weakest moments of my life. I needed someone and he was there for me. It was not the words that he wanted to hear and not the words I ever wanted to say to him.

"I have met all but one daughter. I noticed she was not mentioned at all. Is she an outcast?"

I had over- heard from some of the conversations of the other sister's, that she was not a part of the family

"She decided to cut ties with the family when she went back East with her mother." He said.

"Maybe you should try and contact her. Tell her you are getting married."

"She would not care. But it has been some time since I talked to her. Maybe it is time."

"What is her name?"

"Her name is Candice, but we called her Candy. She loved candy and of course Halloween was her favorite holiday. She could have as much as she wanted, then she would get sick." He smiled.

He became silent, as if trying to recapture memories of a happier time.

It would be midnight by the time he dropped me off at my place. Damian was asleep and Michael helped me with my things. As he was leaving, he held me tight and gave me a kiss.

"Don't question what we have. We have each other and that is enough."

"Thank you, I said. You mean more to me than you think."

We kissed again and then he left. I stayed up for a while, thinking about his family. I was not really comfortable with the daughters and I wondered what Candy was like. I did hope he would try and get in touch with her.

I was in bed for two days, just did not feel well at all. Maybe the trip took more out of me than I could endure. But it was over and I was glad. Never again, I thought.

I started the house hunting as soon as I was feeling better.

I finally found another home that I thought Michael might like. It was another foreclosure. He put a bid on it and within a couple of weeks we were told it was ours. The house was only a couple of years old. It was near some mountains and we were high enough to see some of the city lights at night. It was more than I could have ever dreamed of and it was hard to believe it was actually ours. Many days, after receiving the keys, I would walk from room to room, trying to visualize how I would decorate. I had so much of my life packed away and it would be wonderful to find places for them.

Because the previous owners took all the appliances, we were given compensation to buy new ones. Also, Michael gave me a budget of $10,000.00 to furnish the house with new furniture and I was able to do it within the budget. I decorated the house and ordered the furniture. I wanted everything in place before we moved in.

Marriage was my next project.

I wanted a small wedding and we could always have the reception in a month or two after the marriage. I did not want a lot of family there. We were married in a small chapel and had Lesley and Ben and my sister and her husband with us.

Michael had rented a cabin in the mountains for our honeymoon. It was absolutely beautiful. Our wedding night was platonic, Michael had a few one too many while celebrating. When the morning came so did our consummation of our marriage.

We were there for four marvelous days. We would take walks and hold hands. We talked of our future together. I felt the love he had for me and I only wished I could return it.

Once in our home, I felt as if God had blessed me. I had everything I ever wanted, a beautiful home and a loving and caring husband. It was going to be a good life.

Or so I thought.

Elizabeth Klein

After a couple of months, I knew the truth. Michael drank and he drank a lot. He said a drink coming home from a hard day at work was not that much. Only it was never one drink. I saw a side of him that I was not sure I could deal with. But for now I will have to.

For some reason he suddenly became insistent that we plan a reception. He had many associates asking if we were going to have one to celebrate our marriage. He decided the Club would be the best place for the reception. They would provide a buffet and he would pay for the first drink for the guests, after that they were on their own. Also, if we wanted a DJ, they could arrange that as well. He seemed to have already planned this and I did not have much say about it.

I was surprised when he told me that he had invited his son. He asked that I make sure the spare bedroom was made up, as Jeremy and his wife were coming. He just did not seem to feel I should have any prior knowledge of who he was inviting. I asked him if his daughters were coming and he was not sure. If they decide to come he would get a motel room for them, as he did not want anyone other than his son at our house.

"That does not make sense. Just your son can stay with us and not your daughters. Why?"

I have my reasons and that is the way it is going to be."

"I now have some understanding why there is animosity between your siblings. You cannot play favorites with your children."

"This discussion is over." He said as he walked out the door.

I thought we would get this reception over and then we needed to have a real serious talk. There were two of us involved in this marriage, not just him.

Jeremy and his wife showed up the evening before the reception. We went out for dinner and it was a nice evening, I really enjoyed his wife.

After we came home from dinner, Michael and Jeremy decided to go to the store. I did not have to guess what they were going to get.

Jenny and I sat in the living room

"This is a beautiful home, Jenny said. I like how you decorated it."

"Thanks, Jenny. I know some of the family was upset that their father had to buy a home for us, especially since he already had one that I could have moved into."

"I do not blame you for wanting a place of your own." She said.

"Jenny I am getting the impression that you and the sisters do not get along. Is there something they did to you?"

"It is the way they treat Jeremy. They are jealous of him. It just goes to show you their immaturity. They are grown women with lives of their own and yet because their father paid a little more attention to Jeremy when they were growing up, they see him as the favorite."

"They are right." I smiled.

"Yes they are, but he is hard working and does not need his father to support him. You will eventually see that the only time those girls call their father is when they want something and it is usually money."

"It is funny that you should say that. I know Diane was telling him how she had been looking for a job, but nobody would hire her."

"Diane has no intention of getting a job. She needs to get off her dead ass and help her husband out. She can spend money, but she does not want to earn it. When she gets herself in financial trouble, she calls her father."

"How did Susan deal with that?"

"Susan did a lot to help out Diane and her family, not so much financially but many times she would fly there and spend a week or two, to help out. And when Ellen called her father and needed to be bailed out of a jam, she knew Michael would always write a check. A short time after Susan's death, I was with the daughters one evening and we were all drinking. I was shocked when they started to put Susan down. I have never said anything, but that really bothered me and I saw how two faced they really were. They will treat you the same way, nice to your face and hating you behind your back, because you may interfere with the flow of money to them."

"Michael does what he wants with his money. If he wants to send them money, I do not think I will have much to say. So they do not have to waste their time worrying about me interfering."

"Have you and Michael talked about your financial security if anything should happen to him?" She asked.

Elizabeth Klein

"We have talked and he tells me not to worry, I will be taken care of. Of course when a man tells you that, you should worry. So we will have more discussions on that as time goes on." I smiled.

"I am so glad Michael married you. He really needed someone. He is a good man, but you have to be a strong woman with him at times."

"I am finding out what some of those times are." I said.

"He does drink. No-one says anything, but they all know. Jeremy told me his father has had a drinking problem since Jeremy could remember. It caused a lot of friction between his father and his mother and was the main cause of their divorce. She could not take it anymore."

"Do you know anything of the other sister?"

"Jeremy and Candy were close. But when she left with their mom, she did not keep in contact much. Every now and then he gets a card from her, but she never answers his phone calls. At one time I suggested we go see her. At first he wanted to and then he decided against it."

I wanted to ask her more about Candy but just then they returned from the store and told us to come into the kitchen. Michael pulled out a bottle of whiskey and Jeremy got four small glasses.

"It is not uncommon for us to make a toast to family." Jeremy said.

So four glasses were filled and Jeremy toasted to his father and his new step-mom.

I never considered myself as a step-mom and it sounded out of place, but I guess that is what I now was.

After two more toasts I said I was going to bed. It was going to be a long day tomorrow.

As I was getting ready for bed, I could hear more toasting and laughing.

I kept thinking about Michaels drinking. After our marriage, I knew, but you want everything to be so perfect you try not to think about it. I guess the many evenings he spent alone at his other house, he drank. How was I to know? Another deception, or was it a weakness in his life that he could not or would not accept the truth?

The reception turned out to be very nice. We had a big turnout. On the invitations, I requested no gifts. With two houses we had plenty of everything. Michael and I were called to have out first dance together. It was a slow dance and he held me tight and told me he loved me. After the dance, we walked to the table that had our cake on it. A woman had decorated a lot of the cakes at the Club, but this was her first wedding cake. She did a beautiful job.

I gave Michael the knife and he cut the cake. I smiled at him and whispered "don't you dare", as the piece of cake came closer to my mouth. He was good, although I could tell he was seriously thinking about it.

After everyone had their cake, I sat and visited with my family. I had not kept in touch with them as much as I should have since my marriage. I could not tell them that this marriage was far from being perfect. I did not want them to know. Know the truth, maybe this is what those words meant when I heard the voice in my head.

It was a long evening and I was exhausted. Everyone helped clean the tables. Some of the women made beautiful centerpieces for each table so I told the female guests to please take them.

When we finally returned home, I went to bed. It had been a long day but a good day. I heard the cabinet door open and glasses being clicked so I knew more toasting was going on.

Jeremy and Jenny left in the morning and I must admit I really enjoyed them and I told Jenny to call me once in a while. I wanted to know more about the family.

In the months to come I did learn more. It was approaching Christmas. Michael said it would be nice to go back to New Mexico. I told him that would be a nice idea and I hoped he enjoyed himself, because I was not going to go with him. After a few heated discussions I reminded him that we had a large house now because he wanted to entertain more. So we would make use of the house and continue on with the annual Christmas party.

I was looking for any excuse not to go see his family again.

He finally agreed. I contacted the caterer and she came over. She was thrilled with the big kitchen and said the set up would be a breeze. I gave her the menu and everything else was taken care of.

Elizabeth Klein

It seemed as if Michael invited more and more people. We never knew who would show up and this year we had a house full. They loved the house and we were complemented on how beautifully it was decorated.

I asked Michael if he invited Margaret. Our intimacy had decreased dramatically lately and I wondered if he was seeing her.

"I have not seen her and when I asked about her, someone said she moved."

I felt bad when I heard that. She had to get away and I could not blame her.

I invited my sister and her husband. My brother said he would come but only if he could wear the Santa suit. I asked him if Santa had a tux and tie, as the party was more on the formal side. He did not come.

"So now that you have settled in, how is married life?" My sister asked.

"We will have a lunch date soon and I will tell you all about it."

"That does not sound good. Do I need to bring my Kleenex?"

"Look around sis, I have everything I ever dreamed of. But when you finally get there, you find it comes at a price."

"It always does, and it all depends on how high of a price you want to pay."

"You are telling me this happens to everyone?" I smiled.

"Sometimes I think only to this family, but know there must be others."

"I will call you, I said. I am not sure what we are doing Christmas day. I hope I can get him to come over to your place for maybe an hour."

I saw Michael wave me over toward him. We did the gift cards again this year, so I helped him. It was late and everyone was saying their good-byes and they had a wonderful time. As the last person left, I started to pick up things. I had enough Christmas decorations stored away and I made my own table arrangements with them. I told Michael I could use them for next year, but he said we could always buy more and my arrangements went out the door. I finished picking up the paper plates and cups and he put those in the bag for trash.

When we finished, he reached for my hand and we sat on the couch.

"You have not told me what you want for Christmas and I only have a couple of more days to get you something."

"What do I need? I have everything. You have been very generous with me. You are my Christmas." I said

He kissed me and said, "thank you."

"I have been thinking. How would you like a new car? Your car is getting older and eventually will need work. I want to make sure you are in a safe car, so that is what I want to give you. I have been looking around, so tomorrow we look together. We can trade in your car. So what do you think?"

"I cannot ask for such a gift."

"You did not ask for it. It is something I am going to get for you."

I put my arms around him and all I could say was "thank you."

"If we get it tomorrow, you cannot drive it until Christmas. And forget about getting it wrapped." He laughed.

As I was getting ready for bed, I said a prayer for the blessing that God gave me even if he had a fault.

We did purchase an Audi. It was two years old and had very low mileage. It was luxury and comfort to the max. I loved it. We traded in my car and he did all the paperwork and wrote a check for the balance.

Of course I could not drive it home, but that was okay.

That evening he was drinking and he received a phone call from Diane. Because we had connecting recliners, I could hear the conversation,

She was telling him how bad Christmas was going to be for them this year. Her and Bob decided they would not give each other gifts. The kids were just going to get clothes that they needed, but nothing more. She was really laying the guilt on thick. He caved and said he would send her some money, but the gifts were to be from Grandpa and Beth. I got up and left the room, I did not need to hear anymore.

I took a shower and got ready for bed and he still was talking to her. I think he had a couple of more drinks during their conversation.

I went to bed.

Finally, it was Christmas and when he took me in the garage to see the car, he had put a bow on top. He handed me the keys and I took it for a drive. I drove right to my sister's.

They had just finished opening their gifts and my sister and her daughter were still in their pajamas. I listened to all the stuff they got for Christmas. Then my sister asked me what did I get?

"I can't bring it in the house, so you have to come outside."

They all got up and my niece ran outside.

"Oh my goodness, my niece said. This is yours?"

"Yes it is. This was my Christmas gift." I said.

They started opening doors and looking at all the gadgets that I will never learn to use.

After a while, I told them I had to get back, as I was only out for a test drive. I was hoping on seeing them later that day.

When I returned home he was laughing.

"Having fun, are we?"

"Yes we are." I smiled back at him.

We had a good day, he cooked a nice dinner. Damian was coming over to eat and open his gifts.

When Damian arrived, he inquired about the car outside.

I told him it was a gift from Santa because I was a very good girl this year. So good in fact that I was put to the top of Santa's list.

"I guess I had better start being good now, he said," laughing.

We had a wonderful time, a lot of laughter. Damian opened his gifts. Michael had given him a hundred dollars in five dollar bills stuffed in a stocking.

I said it was getting late and I suggested we go over my sister's for a while.

"I think it is a little too late to go over there. Anyway you were there this morning." Michael said.

"But I told her we would be over."

"Then call her and tell her we are not going to make it."

I was hurt. This had been a tradition with me for years. Something you just do not change.

"Then Damian and I will go there just for a while." I said.

"Then go and I will clean up."

I picked up my keys and told him I would see him later and left. I was angry with him. If it were his family, we would be there.

Damian and I stayed at my sister's for about an hour and then Damian went home. I knew exactly what I was going to come home to and he did not let me down. He was drunk. We did not have much to say to one another and I did try and watch a movie with him. But he was half asleep, so I went to bed. Merry Christmas, I said to myself.

And as I was drifting off to sleep, I remembered the words "know the truth." And I said to myself, "maybe I do."

The New Year, we just stayed home. He started celebrating early and was asleep before mid-night. I woke him up and told him the New Year arrived and he missed it, so he could go to bed. I made a New Year's resolution, he is an alcoholic and I can either live with it or leave. By next year, I just may be gone.

When he returned to work, it was nice to be alone. He was not a nice alcoholic. He could be very verbally abusive. Sometimes that is worse. With the verbal abuse it becomes embedded within you. You don't forget.

When he came home that evening, he gave me two dozen roses and apologized. Then he got himself a drink.

I tried so hard to get beyond this, but I did not think I could settle.

I had lunch with Lesley. I waited until after the holidays to call her.

"So how was your Christmas?" I asked her.

"We flew back east to Ohio, to see his family. It was nice, but I froze my ass off." She laughed.

"I do not think I could ever travel over the holidays. It is crazy out there."

"That it is, she said. But it was better than sitting on the couch watching TV all day, like we usually do."

"How was your Christmas?" She asked.

"Well I am driving a nice car, so Santa was good to me. But after that we had a rough few days." I said.

"Why, what happened?'

"The alcohol became an issue." I whispered

"Then it is true, he is a drinker." She said.

"I am afraid he is, but this is between us, understand?"

Elizabeth Klein

"I had a feeling he was. Remember when I told you that I would check into some things, when you were experiencing a lot of paranormal shit.

Well I found out that is why Susan no longer came with him to the Club. One night he had way too much to drink. She was trying to save him some embarrassment and she held him tight, like she was hugging him. They were walking toward the door and as they went out the door, he fell flat on his face. She had to go with him to the Emergency Room. He had five stitches over his eye. He hit the rail as he was going down.

She was so embarrassed, she told him she would never go to the Club again."

"That would do it for me as well." I said.

"Anyway he was good for a while. I guess his drinking was to be at home and if they went out, she warned him, only a couple of drinks."

"She seemed like she was such a strong woman and yet she stayed, knowing he was not going to change"

"He is doing the same thing to you that he did to her. Do you know that the car she was in at the time of her accident? It was a car he bought her for Christmas. Exact same scenario just a different woman." She said.

"If only I could talk to one of Susan's daughters. I once had an envelope with an address, but I lost it." I said.

"Don't go any further. You are married to him and it does not look like you are abused. Are you?"

"Sometimes verbally and I honestly do not know what is worse."

"I will tell you what is worse. When you have to leave that beautiful home of yours and move back with your son." She was harsh.

"Thanks for reminding me, I have nothing and nowhere to go."

"It is not that bad, is it? You can continue to be yourself, just don't let him possess you."

"Please Lesley, when I start losing myself, you will tell me, won't you?" I begged her.

"I promise you, as soon as I see a change in you. I will come and get you myself."

"Thank you so much. You are a true friend."

We finished lunch, or Lesley did. My appetite seemed to disappear after our conversation.

The evening of my birthday Michael gave me a gift. It was a small box, so knew it was jewelry. I told him I do not wear a lot of jewelry so to think of something else, next time. He told me to just open it. When I opened the small box, I actually held my breath. It was a beautiful one karat diamond ring. He said he did not like the wedding ring set I picked out. This was much better. I could not argue about that. It was absolutely beautiful.

Lesley and Ben invited us over to their house for my birthday. Michael really did not want to go. I had to remind him of who his friends were after Susan died. I did not have an argument after that.

Of course as soon as we got there, he asked me to show them what he got me for my birthday. I showed them the ring.

I had to laugh at Lesley as she really gave Ben "the look".

"I will have to do a lot of overtime to afford something like that." He said to Lesley.

She looked at him and said, "then do it."

I was hoping she was joking.

It was nice being with them again. I noticed Lesley watching Michael.

I was hoping she was not doing a psychological assessment of him. I did not want to know the results.

I was tired when we got home. I went to get ready for bed and he went for another drink. Our intimacy was non-existent. I attributed that to the alcohol and the medication for his heart. It was a dangerous combination and I told him that many times, but he still kept trying to convince himself that he did not drink that much.

My sisters were getting anxious for another getaway. I told them to pick this year's adventure. Surprisingly, it was Disneyland. That pick was from my sister Barb. We were able to get a reservation at a hotel near Disneyland and we could have the fourth night free. With that came our passes for two days at Disneyland. So we did pretty good, as far as expenses. Because I had the nicer vehicle, we would take turns driving to California. Of course I would not tell Michael that, as I knew he would not let me take the car if he knew my sisters would be driving it.

Even though Michael knew this was a tradition of ours, he was upset that I was going. I tried to ask him why and he could not give me an answer. Then he asked how I was financing this trip. I told him I had my own money from my account.

"Then I do not need to give you any money. You seem to have enough." He said in an unpleasant tone.

"Not necessarily, I said. It is going to be expensive with food and gas."

"Hopefully your sisters will help with gas and you do not eat much."

"What is the matter with you? Why is this suddenly an issue with you? I asked. We go away every year."

"It is not an issue. If you need money, all you have to do is ask?"

When hell freezes over I told myself. I have a credit card that you will never know about. I went into our room and started to pack, we were leaving in the morning.

When he left for work the following morning, there was no money offered to me and I did not even get a kiss good-bye.

Such childish behavior, I told myself. I really needed a break.

The drive was long and my sisters did all the driving. It had been awhile since I was in California and a much longer time since I had been to Disneyland. It was a long drive, I was so tired. After we checked into the hotel my sisters were hungry. I did not feel like eating, but my sister told me I was going to get something.

I think all of us had a good night's sleep. We went downstairs in the morning for our free buffet breakfast and it was good.

We went upstairs and got our passes, we hung them around our necks, which was a good idea. We would not lose them. We waited for the shuttle to take us to Disneyland. When we got off the shuttle, I could not believe we were there. I think it had been twenty years since I had last been there. It changed a lot.

We went to the new park first to see what was there. We rode a couple of rides. One ride was in a replica of an old hotel and the elevator would fall. My sister Barb did not want to go on that ride at all.

We called her chicken and other choice words. She finally gave in. It was the best ride ever and we survived. When we went to the gift shop, we were looking at our picture just as the elevator fell. My sister Barb did not like her picture, so she was going again. Lily said no way was she going on that ride again. But I was all for it. So we went again so my sister Barb could get a better picture!

It was a long day and we agreed we would make our first day there short and finish seeing everything the next day. It did not work, we were still talking we should get back to the hotel, as the fireworks were going off at nine o'clock that night. We were there for fourteen hours.

I took my medicine and collapsed in bed. My sisters took turns taking a shower. I was sound asleep when it was my turn.

I could barely make it out of bed the next morning. I took a shower while my sisters were getting ready to go downstairs for breakfast. The shower seemed to get my blood flowing again and my brain kicked in, so did the aches and pains my body felt. I had something small for breakfast, I could tell I over did it yesterday. But the kid in me kicked in as soon as we reached the gate to Disneyland. After some of the rides, we did some souvenir shopping and I tried to find Michael something nice, even though I thought he was an ass hole when I left. I found a small stuffed tiger that had the big eyes, I thought it was cute. We stayed and watched the fireworks again so another fourteen- hour day.

We spent the following day just driving around and going to the malls.

My credit card was soaring, but I did not care. The day was going well. But we were not watching the time and found ourselves on the freeway during rush hour. It was not very pretty.

The next day we were off to the beach. All of us needed a restful day at the beach, before returning home. It was so nice under the umbrella just listening to the waves and the seagulls. We watched a beautiful sunset that evening. It was also the sunset of our vacation.

I must admit I was not sure I wanted to go back. He was still at work by the time I dropped my sisters off. My sister Barb was staying with Lily, and she was leaving in the morning.

Elizabeth Klein

When I opened the door, I noticed the nice fragrance coming from everywhere. As I walked through the house, there were bouquets of flowers in every room.

All I could think of was Dr. Jekyll and Mr. Hyde syndrome.

I was fixing dinner when he came home. He must have been at the Club, when he kissed me there was alcohol on his breath.

"I hope you accept my apology. I really missed you while you were gone. I had some time to think and I should be happy that you spend time with your sisters. Sometimes I just want you all to myself."

I still was not happy about the day I left. And as far as wanting me to himself, I almost told him slavery was abolished a long time ago.

"It was a difficult time for me when I left. I said. Sometimes I do not know if you realize how much you hurt me by your attitude. If you are going to get mad at me, then get mad at me when I actually do something wrong. But not just because your feelings are hurt."

"I know, I know. I do try but I have lost one person I loved, I am afraid of losing you."

"If you lose me it is because you caused it. And love does not have strings attached."

"Is that what you think?" He asked, surprised I said that.

"Sometimes, I do feel like it. You know I do not have a lot of money. Would it really have hurt you to give me some money for the trip? Was that your punishment to me for going with my sisters?" I asked.

"No and using punishment is pretty harsh. I told you I was just upset and that was all it was. I love you and you know that."

"I do know it, but just go easy with me. I take so much of what you say to me personally and it does hurt."

"I am so sorry, that is the last thing I want. Tomorrow I am going to the bank and open an account with both our names on it and you can use the money for anything you want."

Finally, I thought maybe I got through to him. I told him to go change his work clothes and wash up for dinner. He kissed me as he went into the bedroom. I put the big eyed tiger on his pillow, he saw it.

He brought it out with him and kissed me again.

"I thought of you while I was away." I said.

"Thank you, I will keep this with me forever."

We had dinner and he wanted to know all about the trip. The atmosphere was calmer and we laughed.

The next afternoon he stopped by the house and gave me a checkbook to the account that he opened for us. He said he ordered checks so just use the bank checks for now. The money in the account was mine. There was just one thing, he was only putting five hundred in the account and I was to let him know when the account was low and he would put another five hundred in it.

Control, I thought. He has to have the control.

I had enough in my own account that I would never use that stupid checking account. But in reality I wanted to drain that account every month, but I was not like that.

There were more and more evenings when he came home late. He kept saying it was due to all the meetings he had to attend. I had Lesley ask Ben about all these late nights so I could find out if he was really at meetings. So far she said he attended most of the ones that Ben had attended. But I just felt something was wrong.

There was another function scheduled to raise money. As usual he was always involved in these things. The function was at the Club.

I was greeted by the same people that attended the Christmas dinner. Michael talked to a lot of people there, I watched him, he did look and act distinguished. He did deserve some credit, he worked hard for causes he believed in.

I looked around the room and I noticed I was being watched by another woman. I did not recognize her. She was someone I had not seen at these functions before. She walked over to me.

"I am sorry I did not mean to stare at you. I just heard that Michael had married. Congratulations." She said.

"Thank you, but do I know you?"

"No, my name is Andrea. I was a friend of Susan's."

Finally, I thought someone who knew Susan. But would she talk of Susan?

"I have heard so much about Susan. It was devastating to Michael when she died." I said.

"Yes, I was at her funeral. I had to admire him, he was emotional, but with dignity."

I thought how could you use that word at a funeral? It was a time where there should be a lot of emotion, without dignity.

"Did you know Susan?" She asked.

"No, I never met her."

"She was very outgoing after she married. Michael and Susan attended a lot of these functions together."

"I also heard she was active in the other Organizations." I said.

"She was, but after her marriage she left for a while and I was surprised to hear that she started volunteering again."

"So you were not real close friends, then?" I asked.

"There were some problems she had and we did not get together as much as I wanted to."

"Some problems, usually that is when you need your friends the most."

"These problems were of her marriage and sometimes you keep them to yourself." She smiled

I was going to ask more questions, but Michael came to the table.

"Hello Andrea, he said. It is nice to see you attending these functions again. I know how difficult your divorce was, so am glad you are getting out and about again."

I had never heard such sarcasm come from him. He definitely did not like her.

"I heard you married again. I just came over to congratulate your new wife. I did not know you were even seeing anyone, so it was a surprise."

"Time goes by quickly. He said. I felt I was ready to start my life again."

"Hopefully it will be a happy life." She said.

And again there was sarcasm in her voice as well. She walked away.

"You do not like her, why?" I asked

"She is a gossiper and she lies. She talked about everyone, behind their backs, that is until people started talking about her. She married a younger man and he tired of her and started sleeping with other women. She has money and thought she could hang on to him with that, but it did not work.

The divorce was ugly, he revealed some very personal things about her and she went into hiding."

"She said she was friends with Susan."

"She was not a friend of Susan's. Susan did not like her." He seemed a little annoyed. And you do not need to be talking to her. She uses people."

I thought to myself, I would very much like a conversation with her. Maybe she would have some answers about Michael's and Susan's relationship. I will have to find a way to contact her.

I noticed she left shortly after we talked. I watched her and I knew I would have to be careful. Maybe Lesley knew her and I wanted to know if she felt that I could trust this woman.

I called Lesley the next day and she did know Andrea.

"Can you tell me something about her? I met her last night at one of Michael's functions and Michael let me know he did not like her."

"If I remember right, she became a friend of Susan's only after their marriage. But that did not last long because as you say Michael did not like her."

"So you think Michael told Susan not to see her anymore?" I asked.

"I am sure he did."

"But why? What did she do to him that made him feel that way?"

"He dated her before he met Susan. So guess their breakup was not very pleasant."

"You would have thought he could have mentioned that, when he told me not to talk to her." Another deception, I thought.

"So are you going to contact her? Lesley asked.

"Lesley, I will need your help. Can you find out if she is involved in anything or has special places to go? Maybe I could accidently bump into her somewhere."

"I will ask around. But you better be careful. If Michael finds out you were talking to her, he may get very angry with you."

"That is the point. If we met accidently, he cannot get angry over that."

"Okay, but I am not getting a good feeling about this. I know you, once you set your mind on something you don't let it go." She was worried.

I did have to be careful, but I needed some answers.

It would be two weeks later that Lesley called and told me she found out that Andrea was a member at the Health Club in town and she was usually there Tuesday and Thursday mornings. I checked the Health Club and they had a Sauna there, which would be beneficial for me, so I joined. I told Michael that I had joined that evening at dinner and told him the Sauna would be good for me especially with the arthritis. He thought it was a good idea and I was relieved. "Finally," I said to myself.

I saw Andrea Thursday morning as she was working out and she saw me, while I was checking in.

She came toward me.

"I did not know you were a member here."

"I just joined, I heard they had a Sauna and I could use that for my aches and pains."

"I just finished my workout, the Sauna sounds good." She said.

That happened quick I thought. Was she after something from me?

I was in the sauna first and she came in about ten minutes later. We were the only ones in it.

"I was hoping to see you again, but was not sure if I should." She said.

"Andrea, Michael cannot know that I have had any association with you. He says you use people and you like to spread gossip that is false."

"I am not surprised. I often wondered if that is what he said to Susan. So what do you want from me?" She asked.

"I am looking for the truth. I know this sounds crazy and I cannot blame you for thinking that but I have had some experiences in the house that Susan and Michael lived in. I have felt the presence of Susan and I had the feeling she was trying to tell me something. I felt if I could meet someone who knew her, maybe I would know. It does not seem like anyone really knew her or at least admit to it. No one talks of her"

"It does sound crazy, but I guess if you believe in that sort of thing, it is possible. Is that why you did not move into that house?"

"Yes, but I never told Michael. I just said I would like a place of our own."

"I guess I underestimated Michael. He must really love you, to buy you a home. I was convinced he could never love anyone, he was incapable of it."

"Why would you say that?" I asked.

"I knew Michael would have never told you about us. So you had to have heard it from someone else. Did you inquire about me after that evening we met?"

"Yes, I did and again he must never know we talked."

"Are you that afraid of him?" She asked and she smiled.

"I do fear Michael. I need to know the truth about Susan and about him."

"And what will you do after you find out the truth?"

"I will face that when the time comes."

Just then two other women walked into the Sauna. I was so close in finding out, but now what do I do?

Andrea and I looked at one another.

"Thanks for inviting me, she said. Lunch at the Diner at one o'clock sounds good to me." She got up and left the sauna.

I waited awhile longer and then I left. Andrea had already gone.

I did not want to go to the Diner. We could not be seen together.

But I kept telling myself I had to go.

When I got there she was sitting in her car. She told me to get into her car. We were going to her place. She pulled up into her garage and closed the automated garage doors. No one would see us together.

She had a beautiful home, very large and nicely decorated.

"I can make us a salad if you would like."

"That will be fine." I said.

"I am going to have a glass of wine, what would you like?'

"Water, is fine for me." I still was not sure this was such a good idea.

"Pleases relax, she said. I will not ask any questions about your relationship with Michael. I can tell you the kind of man Michael was with me and whatever happens after that is up to you."

"Is that what you told Susan?" I asked.

"Not exactly, I became a friend of Susan's after she married Michael. It was shortly after that incident with Michael at the Club. I am sure you know what happened that night."

"Yes, I do and I cannot blame her for never going back."

"He really embarrassed her. She came to me knowing I was a regular at the Club and she wanted me to keep an eye on him, not for his drinking, but for his cheating. She did not trust him and she had every reason not to."

"Was that reason Margaret?" I asked.

"Yes with Margaret, but similar to your reasons, she wanted to know about the relationship I had with Michael."

We sat down and my stomach was turning. This was not going to be good.

"Michael and I were friends for over a year. He would flirt and invite me to dinner but I told him we could only be friends, as I would not let it go any further. He was seeing Margaret, and there was no way I was going to be a third party. When Margaret would go away for vacations and seminars, he would always tell me they were splitting up. But as soon as she came back, they wasted no time, they were back together. One time there was a death in her family and she was going to be gone a month. After a week, he told me they were through. They had a terrible fight before she left. I waited another week and thought well maybe they were. We had a mutual friend who was getting married, so I asked him if he wanted to go to the wedding with me and he said he would. The bride had made reservations for me at a hotel they were staying at, as I was in the wedding party and we were going to have a "girl's breakfast" then get ready for the wedding. The wedding started and Michael was not there. It was only after the wedding I saw him sitting in the back. He told me he was late and apologized. He met my friends and co-workers and made a very good impression and we had a few comments that we made a cute couple. I guess I got caught up in the moment. After the dancing and the champagne and the wedding atmosphere, I invited him up to my room. It was a night I thought I would cherish forever. He was a great lover, very passionate and very gentle. He professed his love for me and he felt I was always the one. He left that morning with a promise we were now a couple and he was happy. We called each other constantly. And when I went to his home, he would send me home with a promise that we would be together soon. He said I could not stay the night with him due to the fact that Jeremy was visiting him from college. I thought he was a good man in that respect. There were a couple of days that I did not hear from him, so I went to see if he was okay, unannounced. He was drunk, so I did not stay long. It was downhill from there. He would call me when he was drinking, he would invite me over when he was drinking, he would profess his love for me when he was drinking. I saw a side of him I did not think I could be a part of. Then one evening I had enough and I called him an alcoholic and he really became angry. I thought for sure he was going to hit me. I walked out and it was a matter of days that I found out he was back with Margaret. He used me and I was devastated. I felt sick and worthless. I could not face my family or my friends, so I told them I had found a job in another city, so I would be moving." She stopped for a minute. The worst of it all was that I was always in love with him. From the first time I met him, I knew he was the one. I waited for the time when we could be together. I had put my life on hold for the day he would realize my feelings for him and it was all for nothing."

I looked at her and I remembered Michael had told me he really did not want to marry Susan, but felt she left him with no choice as he did not want their relationship to end. Was he still seeing Margaret while going out with Susan? Was that the real reason he did not want to marry?"

"You told this to Susan?" I asked.

"Yes, but after a while she changed. Michael had told her the rumors of him having an affair with Margaret came from me. And he said I was jealous because I could not have him and that is why I married a younger man to make him jealous."

"She believed him?"

"What else was she going to do? She was completely dependent upon him."

I suddenly remembered that she quit her job right after they married and then she put him on the deed to her house, the only thing she owned. It started to make sense. So he had control over her. He bought her things to make sure she would stay dependent on her.

"But you are different in a way. I watched him with you at the dinner the other night. Maybe he has finally found love in you." She said.

I got up and asked her if she would call a cab for me, as I still did not think it would be a good idea for us to be seen together. She called and she did not ask me any questions for which I was thankful. I helped her with the dishes and then I heard the cab outside. Before I left I looked at her and she looked at me.

Elizabeth Klein

"I wrote him a letter telling him how much damage he did to me, I kept it for three days before I mailed it. I had to tell him what kind of a horrible man he was and to this day I still cannot forgive him."

"He lied to you and he used you." I said. Sometimes we go with our hearts and take a chance and too many times we lose."

That was all I could say to her. I never wanted to marry Michael and never threatened him, as Susan had done to get him to marry her. Margaret had moved so I did not feel there was infidelity in our marriage for which I was thankful, as that would have ended our marriage immediately. The drinking was bad, but maybe I was fortunate that it was mainly done in the privacy of our home. I had not heard of any recent instances of him being seen drunk elsewhere and I definitely would have from Lesley. He had attempted to get control of me but because I had money saved and he knew it, he could not. There was his health insurance and it helped, but I was not using that as much as I thought. I was just on medication now and it was helping. I did not need the testing that I needed before.

So why was I with him? I felt alone and scared after I was shot. I became weak when so much was happening in my life that I could not control. He touched my heart when he told me he loved me, even though he knew I did not love him. Maybe I was different from the others. Could I be happy with that? For now, I told myself.

I returned home with so much going through my head. It was all in the past, it was years ago. Who do you believe? Susan believed Andrea about Margaret and if it were true, then maybe he was not so much in love with Susan. If there was infidelity, then why did Susan stay? What was I feeling when I was in Susan's room, was there more to finding the real truth? Did it really pertain to me or the past? I had to stop this.

Michael was in a good mood when he came home from work. We went out to dinner. He asked me if the Sauna helped me.

"Yes it did, very relaxing and the heat felt like it did some good." I said.

"I am glad you are feeling better. I promise you I will take care of you."

"Thank you, I said. I have been thinking maybe we should start going out with Ben and Lesley again. How about I invite them out for dinner this weekend?'

"That would be nice." He said.

I was starting to question why he was he so compliant. I became angry at myself. There was no reason other than getting together again.

We made arrangements for dinner the following weekend.

I knew I would be seeing more of Andrea. I just did not know what to say to her. Was it possible that she still was in love with Michael after all this time? He made it clear that he did not care for her at all at the dinner. I admit he led her to believe he loved her at one time. But if she was that secretly in love with him, then it was easy for him to use that word and he got what he wanted. The past, all of this was in the past. Let it go, I told myself. But I couldn't stop myself. He used the word "love", the same word to get to me.

I went back to the spa, always hoping Andrea would be there.

She did come over to talk to me after her workout.

"Another day at the spa?" She asked.

"Yes, this old body needs some therapy and the sauna does help."

"Look maybe we should not have had that conversation the other day. You and Michael seem to be holding it together. He hurt me, but it wasn't meant to be and there are times when I say things that maybe I should not."

"Sometimes you can never get over the deception and I wanted to know about Susan, but now maybe it is better to leave it alone. Whatever happened between them when they were together is irrelevant at this point."

"I agree, but I would like to be friends, secret friends." She said.

"Yes, it would have to be a secret." I smiled.

"If you are up to it after your sauna, we can meet at the juice bar."

"That sounds good, I will see you there."

I was not sure this was a good idea, but I liked her and I never wanted Michael to tell me who I could see and who I could not.

The sauna felt so good, I could use it every day. I wanted to too try the pool next, but will work out the kinks first.

Elizabeth Klein

I met Andrea at the juice bar and we really had a nice time. Michael was not brought up and I think we had come to the same conclusion, for us to be friends, our discussions of Michael and the past needed to be kept at a minimum.

The weekend arrived and we went out to dinner with Ben and Lesley. It was nice being with them again.

"So what have you been doing to keep you busy?" Lesley asked.

"She joined a spa and she has been getting some sauna therapy." Michael said.

"What a good idea, I may try something like that, but I need more like a workout. Ben, I would advise you not to comment on that statement." She said while looking at him.

"Not even that you look beautiful?"

"Wow, what a save." I said.

Our laughter could be heard throughout the restaurant. Then Lesley said she needed to use the lady's room and maybe I should join her.

I got up and followed her. I knew she was dying to hear what had happened when I went to see Andrea.

"I really like Andrea, I told her. We went to her house from the spa and had a nice long talk. And what came out of it, was maybe to keep things from the past in the past. Otherwise, your head swells up with more questions that never have the answers you are looking for. And if you continue on that path, your minor headache turns into a major headache."

"I think I am the one who told you to leave it alone." She smiled.

"Yes, you were the wise one." I laughed.

We talked a little more then went back to the table. It was a good night. When we got home, Michael had another drink. It was his third.

"I had a good time with those two. We should do that more often."

"I agree, I said. Lesley likes to take credit for bringing us together, but she admitted it took way to long"

"You are happy, aren't you? I know I have my moods, but we do get along for the most part. Don't you think?

"For the most part," I answered. Wondering where this conversation was going.

"Well I promised to take care of you and I think I have been doing that."

"You have, but I think we should discuss the part where you say that I will be taken care of forever. There is a part of your life I know very little. I respect your privacy, but it is not you anymore, it is us. You keep telling me I am taken care of, but I have nothing more than your word. You are not telling me anything about your financial affairs. I know talking about these things are uncomfortable, but I would be lost if anything should happen to you." I said.

I felt he opened the door to that conversation with the "taking care of me statement" and I wanted to know how that was going to come about if anything should happen to him.

"You do not have to worry about anything like that. It is all taken care of. I have told you that before."

"But I don't know what to do." I wanted to know.

"It is taken care of." He said, in a voice that told me the discussion was over.

Well, I struck out again on that conversation and I am not happy.

He put his arms around me, a sign that I was not to say anymore. But I needed to pursue this and I started to say something when the phone rang. He answered it," how is my only son doing these days." I blew him a kiss and went to bed. I was not in a mood to talk to his only son or his son's father.

I really enjoyed going to the spa. Andrea and I became good friends.

She talked of her marriage to the younger man and she was hurt by him as well. But she had such a good sense of humor and she would talk of some of the most humorous aspects of that marriage. I laughed more with her than anyone else. She said one time they were getting ready for a romantic evening and they created a scene from a movie they saw. They lit numerous candles in the bedroom and she said it was romance all the way, until they knocked a couple of candles over and their carpet caught fire. She picked up her clothes ran in the bathroom to get dressed, because she did not want to be seen nude when the fire truck arrived. Fortunately, her husband put out the fire, but he could not believe her. Instead of helping him put out the fire she runs in the bathroom!

I told her I would probably do the same thing.

There was another dinner at the Club. For once it was just a get-together for a nice dinner. Michael went right to the bar. He had a drink and brought me a glass of wine. I saw Andrea and she was smiling. I know she wanted to come over and talk, but she did not.

Michael told me there was talk of a seminar in California before the holidays and if I would like to go with him, as many of the other wives were going. I told him I would like to go back to California.

Then Ben and Lesley showed and they sat next to us. Ben and Michael left the table to talk to some of the guys.

"I have some news for you." She said.

"Maybe it is something I do not want to know."

"Maybe not, but as usual I will tell you anyway. Ben told me that Michael and he had a lunch date last week, but Michael said he needed to go to the bank first. He withdrew $80,000 from one his accounts and had it wired to a bank in New Mexico, to his son."

"That is a lot of money. I knew Jeremy called Michael. It was after we went out to eat, last week."

"As his wife, I would think he would talk to you about it." She said.

"I don't know, it is his money he can do what he wants with it, but as his wife, you are right he should have said something to me."

"Well if you pursue the matter, let me know what the hell his son needed that kind of money for." She was serious.

"You are a little nosy, aren't you?"

"Always," she said and laughed.

I thought that was a lot of money. I would never have dreamed any of his kids would ask for that amount money. And how could I bring that up, he could very well tell me it is none of my business.

The rest of the evening was pretty much ruined for me. I should have been angry at Lesley, I did not need to know that, but I know she wants to keep me informed about things that are going on behind my back.

I asked Michael if we could make it an early evening as I was not feeling well. He said no problem and we left a short time after.

Lesley called me the next day.

"Are you feeling better?" She asked.

"Yes, and no I did not ask him about the money. It is hard when you can imagine what the answer would be, that it was none of my business."

"But it is your business, you are his wife. I cannot imagine Ben doing something like that without talking to me first."

"Your marriage is based on love and trust. My marriage is not. Look at what I am doing now. I am talking to a former lover of his behind his back. I am asking questions that maybe I shouldn't."

"How do you manage a marriage like that?" She asked.

"He hides behind his alcoholism and I hide from love. I do try to be a good person. I am not a mean or vindictive person. And yet I cannot seem to get close enough to him for him to trust me with anything of his. He tells me he loves me, but isn't trust a part of love?"

"It is a big part. You trust your partner with your very own life. I would do anything for Ben and I know he feels the same with me. It is also feeling good about your- self. How in the world can Michael feel good, when he hides everything from you?"

"Again, he does not trust me. He has a hard time with an independent woman. He wants the control."

"Listen to me, take care of yourself. If he continues to hide things from you, there may be more in his life he is keeping secret."

"I do not even want to think of that. I am trying so hard to find trust in him and maybe eventually I can receive trust from him. Right now his word is all he has given and the trust issue does not look good."

"They are just words and he is good at that. You know it, with all the speeches he gives to raise funds. He knows the right things to say."

"You are right, I know that. It is a lot to think about and get stressed about. More questions and maybe more lies." I said.

I did not want to talk about this anymore. She knew she upset me and I know she only wants to help me, she cares. I don't want to think of what may happen in the future. I do not know if we even have a future together.

Andrea was not at the spa the next day. I missed my time with her, she makes me laugh and she does not question my life with Michael. I still wanted to ask more of her, but I knew to leave it alone, at least for now.

Michael started to drink more. His son called him a couple of more times and even though the conversations seemed civil, I felt there was something else going on. I seemed to be left out when it came to his kids.

Then suddenly the daughters started to call. Was it all about money? Sometimes he would get mad after the phone calls and I would have to listen how it would be nice if they could start taking care of themselves. I could not keep my mouth shut and would tell him his kids were adults now and maybe he needed to stop the money train. I will never learn to keep my mouth shut.

I started to feel alone and decided maybe it was time that Michael and I went away together. I was hoping that he would not drink as much if we went away for a while. Maybe we could even talk like a married couple should.

When I brought it up, I was surprised he agreed with me. He said that was a good idea and I could pick the place. I asked him if he had ever been to Hawaii. He said only once and it was just a stop coming back from the war.

"Would you like to go there?" I asked.

"If you want to go, we will go. But I only fly first class, I do not like feeling cramped when I fly."

I was excited. First class, that sounded just fine with me.

I contacted the travel agent and we were set to fly out in two weeks.

I think he actually looked forward to the vacation. He needed to get away.

Flying first class was terrific. We were the first ones on the plane and settled in. Also my husband was the first one to get a drink. It was not of convenience that he flew first class, it was he could start drinking, before we even took off. I really had to watch him as I did not want him intoxicated when we got off the plane. Fortunately, he ate a good lunch and that helped.

I was never so relieved when we finally landed and checked into our hotel. I was so stressed worrying about him. I hurt all over. I told him I wanted to lay down for a while and then we could go look for a place to have dinner. He was tired and also laid down. It was dark when we woke, but not too late to eat. We walked along the shops and found a nice restaurant. I had a glass of wine and the food was great. After we ate we just walked some more along the shopping area. Then because the beach was on the other side of the street, we crossed and walked back to our hotel along the beach, holding hands.

Why can't it always be like this I asked myself? Our time is so short. We need to enjoy life more.

When we got to the hotel we went to the lounge area and I had coffee and he had a drink. He was doing well as far as his drinking, since we arrived. I watched the fire in the fireplace. It was a romantic setting and I was saddened, as romance no longer existed between us.

We showered (separately) and watched some TV. I fell asleep before he did. Sometime later I felt his arms around me when he came to bed. If this is all he had to give, then I will be content with being in his arms as I slept.

In the morning we had breakfast in the hotel. We then stopped at a desk that had a tour agent there. We sat with her and planned our daily outings. We were going on a short tour that evening and then go for dinner. We decided to walk again along the shops. He bought something for Jeremy, but not his daughters. He kept asking me what I wanted and I told him when I saw it I would let him know. When we got back to the hotel he said he was going to lay down for a while. I walked onto the balcony and watched the people on the beach. There was a wedding going on next to a large tree. They looked so in love with each other. I hoped they had a long and happy life.

Dinner that evening was great and we had a good time.

The following day we went to a place where they make pearls into jewelry. I found a ring I really liked. It was a beautiful green pearl. I kept looking at it. Then finally found the courage to ask the salesperson if I could try it on. Michael said it was beautiful.

"I think you should have it." He said.

"It is rather expensive, but I do like it. It is a beautiful color. Maybe we should walk around and look some more."

I took it off and gave it back to the salesperson. As I was looking at the other jewelry, I looked around and Michael was gone. I walked around a little more and then he found me.

"You did not find anything else you wanted?" He asked

"We have a couple of more days. I will still look."

The tour at the jewelry store was over and we went to another restaurant for lunch. This was going to be a short day, as tomorrow we were going to travel across the Island.

When we got back to the hotel, the person at the desk waved Michael over to him. Michael held my hand and we went to see what he wanted. The man told him his package had arrived and he handed it to Michael and Michael gave it to me. When I opened it, it was the ring. I could not believe he bought it for me, it was so expensive. He said the look on my face was worth every cent.

Later that evening we walked along the beach again and we saw the sunset. Michael kept lifting my hand looking at the ring.

"You have good taste" He said.

"I have you, don't I?"

He surprised me that day and I thought maybe we should get away more often. He was different, here in this place.

The next couple of days were all day tours. We did not plan anything for the following day and we just lounged at the beach and rested. That was a nice quiet day.

The day tours wore me out. It was on the bus and off the bus all day long. But we did see some beautiful scenery and we visited a pineapple farm and the factory.

The last night we were going out on a boat and have dinner. As we stood along the railing, leaving the harbor, I loved the cool breeze blowing around me. I hated to go inside. It was a fully booked tour and a lot of people were on the boat. I had some wine with dinner and Michael had his drink and then another and then another. After we ate we went outside on the deck again and there were a couple of men playing instruments. The music was nice. Everyone was having a good time. It was a great evening and we had a wonderful time for our last evening there. Tomorrow we go home.

It was a good vacation and much needed by both of us. I think Michael enjoyed himself and he seemed to be able to relax more. I was hoping that I could convince him that we needed to get away more often. We were at an age now that we should be enjoying more of life.

I wish I could honestly say that we grew closer on that trip, but I would only be fooling myself. As soon as we returned everything went back to the way it was before we left. The closeness I felt with him was gone and I still feel a loss, I was never going to convince him to trust me.

I called Lesley when we got back and we made a lunch date for the next day. I had already called my sisters and told them we must plan a sister's vacation to Hawaii, as soon as one of us wins the lottery.

"So you had a good trip?" Lesley asked.

"We did and his drinking was kept to a minimum when we were out. He had packed a bottle of Vodka in his suitcase and he had a few drinks before bed. But all in all he kept his drinking under control and we had a good time and it was so relaxing."

"I see you bought a pearl. It is beautiful."

"I really like this ring, but it was expensive. I often wonder if he buys this jewelry for me or for show."

"Probably for both, but what does it matter? You have some beautiful jewelry that he bought for you. You cannot complain about that one karat diamond ring. Now I can complain, but you have not right to."

"Do you recall seeing Susan with a lot of jewelry?" I asked.

"You know, now that you mention it, she did have a lot of jewelry. She had this diamond bracelet that she wore all the time and rings on every finger. She did like jewelry and she had plenty of it."

"I was afraid of that." I said.

"Well you have the car and you have the jewelry. You never know what is next."

"Death, I said."

"Why would you say something like that?" Lesley asked. She was surprised by what I said.

"Lesley, that just came out. I can't believe I said that."

We sat quietly for a while.

"Now I am scared for you. Death, that was horrible."

"I scared myself. I did not even think of that word. It just came out."

Elizabeth Klein

"If ever you think you are threatened, you get in that car and get out of there. Promise me." She was serious.

"I promise, but I can't imagine anything like that happening. Michael is not capable of that. I have never seen him so angry that he would threaten me. This is just crazy. It was just a word."

"It came from somewhere. You must be careful and I mean it."

It did not matter how many times I promised her I was okay she still seemed concerned. I could not let her see that I was frightened as well.

But it was just a word.

The rest of the day was a nightmare for me. That word was loud and clear in my head and the question "why", always followed it. What made me say that?

As the days passed, I still was questioning that word. I know Lesley was worried so I did call her often to let her know I was okay and not to worry. I did not feel that helped her much.

I saw Andrea at the spa and she had thought I quit going.

"No, Michael and I took a trip to Hawaii and it was fun and relaxing."

"How nice is that. I told you I felt you were different in Michael's eyes. I do not remember a time when Susan and Michael went away together. She had a sister and I know they went to Scotland. I guess Michael was busy at work. Of course that is the universal excuse not to go anywhere." She said.

"Very true, but at least she went with her sister. My sister's and I try to take a vacation every year. Michael was not happy with the last one we took and he let me know about it. He has a problem in controlling me and of course being an, "independent woman.""

"Are you happy with him?" She asked.

"Do you know that is the first question you have asked about my relationship with Michael. Now before I answer that one let me ask you one. What is happiness?" I asked.

"I think it is contentment and enjoying what life has to give."

"Then I can tell you that does not exist. There is no contentment as you always want more. You want more love, more appreciation and more money. It is always more of things, that you think will make you happy, but in reality, it is only temporary.

"You are not happy, you answered my question." She said.

"I guess I am not, in that sense, but I cannot complain."

"You won't. Susan tried to tell me and she could not either."

"I want so much to know Susan, but I can't now. There are other things I need to deal with, then maybe."

"I am here for you anytime you need to talk."

I really wanted to, but it was not the time and I questioned if I could really trust her.

Things started to drastically change at home. Michael seemed more on edge. He would get angry at me for stupid things. I think he felt he needed a reason to drink and I became that reason. His kids called after we got back from our vacation. I could no longer stay in the same room when they called. I guess they felt they needed to keep tabs on their father now, more than ever. He actually spent money on this trip, a trip I convinced him to go on. Now I am the wicked stepmom, I felt that was okay, I could be that.

Michael wanted to go to New Mexico for the weekend. If I told him, I did not want go he would want to know why and yet if I did go I would be miserable. But he did something for me, the Hawaii trip. Maybe I can get through a couple of days with his kids. I told him we were to stay at a hotel, I needed time to rest. He agreed and made the reservations.

On the drive, I asked him if there was a reason he wanted to go see his son.

"Not really, we are staying at a hotel close to Jeremy and hopefully the girls can take some time from their busy lives to visit us.

He was not being truthful with me. There was a reason for this visit.

After we checked in the hotel, Michael called his son and right away he made plans to go over there.

"Does Jeremy still live in an apartment?" I asked

"He used to, he has moved."

When we arrived at Jeremy's house, it was absolutely beautiful. We did the usual greetings and then Michael said he wanted us to see the house. We walked in the side door and when we turned toward the living room, I almost went into shock. The living room was all glass facing a beautiful view of a small lake and trees that outlined the lake. Jeremy walked us to the

Elizabeth Klein

glass doors and there was a deck that went the full length of the house. We walked to the rail and there were steps that lead to a pathway. We followed Jeremy to a boat dock and there was a large boat tied next to the dock.

It was a gorgeous place, quiet and peaceful. But how could Jeremy afford this and then it hit me, his father. I was feeling sick. Michael came here to see what his son had bought with the money he gave him. We walked back to the house and Jeremy had just purchased a new grill and he was going to cook outside. There was also a picnic table outside and we would eat out there so we could enjoy the view. After dinner, out came the alcohol and the toasts were made. I only had one drink and was watching Michael as I had no idea where the hotel was, if I should have to drive back. After his third drink, I asked him if we could get back to the hotel as I was tired from the trip. Fortunately, no resistance to that suggestion, he was tired also and we had the next day to visit.

I was so glad to get back in one piece. It was dark and Michael got lost twice, we had to turn around and find the main highway.

When we were getting ready for bed, Michael asked what I thought of the house. I told him it was absolutely beautiful. To be able to sit in that living room and see the lake and the trees, it was something anyone would dream of. He agreed and he thought Jeremy got it for a good price as it was a foreclosure. He was very lucky to find it.

He was lucky alright. He had a father who would do anything for him.

The next morning, we went back to Jeremy's and stayed all day. The daughters were to drive there in the afternoon, but they never showed. How could you blame them, they knew where the money came from to purchase the home. Why would they add insult to injury? I almost felt sorry for them, almost. The drinking started early afternoon and I was thankful I remembered the way back to the hotel. I enjoyed the outdoors, I took a walk, it was nice and peaceful. Then later we went for a ride in the boat Jeremy just purchased. It was close to evening and we saw a beautiful sunset over the lake. It was a nice day, but I kept thinking at Michael's expense. Jenny was her usual bubbly-self. I suppose she had every reason to be so happy.

I asked her several times about the sisters but she said they had not been in contact with them since they moved. It was Jeremy that called them and told them their father was coming this weekend and if they would drive up there for the afternoon.

"It is their loss, she said. If they want to be so selfish and not take a few hours of their busy lives to see their own father, then it is something they can deal with."

"It is sad and I know it hurts Michael." I said.

"I know it hurts him as well, but they are the most self-centered females I have ever met. It is always the about "me" attitude." And no matter what Jeremy does or has, they will always be jealous of him. He keeps reaching out to them and they slap him down every time. I don't want anything more to do with them."

"I can't blame you, but be careful, because Jeremy will always be in the middle."

"I have already let him know how I feel. There have been too many heated discussions about them in this house."

"It is never easy with family and I have to agree with you, it is out of jealousy."

But I was thinking they had every right to be jealous.

Just then Michael and Jeremy came out on the patio to join us. This time it was Michael who said it had been a long day and wanted to go back to the hotel. We made arrangements to go to breakfast in the morning and then they would drive us around to see the town and the beautiful scenery.

When we got back to the hotel, Michael said he wanted to call his daughters and give them a piece of his mind as he knew there was no reason for them not coming to see him. I told him to call tomorrow. I did not want to hear the heated discussion between them and then the sorrowful shit at the end of the conversation. I had it with all of them and although I liked Jenny, she knew exactly how they were able to get that house. Maybe that was a condition Michael had them make, not to let anyone know where the money came from. Selfish they may be, but stupid they are not.

I did not want to stay another day, we came, we saw and now we can leave. Somehow, someway I had to convince him to leave after breakfast. I decided to tell him I did not feel well, but I would try and make one more day. I was surprised when Michael said he was really tired and agreed with me to head home the next day. He said after breakfast he would tell Jeremy we were going to go back. That would give Michael a day of rest before he had to go back to work.

Jeremy was upset as he wanted to show us around, but Michael said another time.

The drive back home was silent. He knew that I knew there was no way Jeremy could afford that house without his dad's help. But he still was not going to tell me.

I was very glad when we got home. He was going to call his daughters after we got home but decided he was still not in the mood for their excuses.

His drinking started early and that did not make matters any better.

I tried to be the good wife, but I sure was getting tired of it.

After that trip I started questioning the marriage. When I married him I did not know that I would be a step-mom to some grown-up spoiled children and they were children in adult forms. And maybe if we could talk about it sometimes instead of eliminating me from decisions he made, like a husband and wife should, then I could deal with this. But we were not man and wife, we were still just friends. A condition I made from the very beginning and now I was living it in a different phase of our lives. Could I spend the rest of my life with Michael's moods and his drinking and his heartless offspring? That was another question, I could not answer. Every time I told him I wanted to talk, he would blow me off. Finally, I just came out and asked him if our marriage was going to survive. That got his attention.

"What would make you ask me that?"

"We don't talk about things that married people normally talk about."

"If you mean our families, I think we both know where we stand. You seem to have a hard time with my family and I just keep away from your family," he said, sarcastically.

"Why would you say that? I have spent more time with your family than you have with mine. I am not talking about families. I am talking about us."

"Are you telling me you are not happy?" He asked.

"No, I am not saying that." My thoughts were the truth. My words were not. I was not happy.

"This is exactly why we stay away from these discussions. You do not know what you want and I am not going to guess, so there is no reason to continue with this conversation." He turned away.

There again was his way of saying to keep quiet. I was getting angry and because I felt the anger, I knew I would say something that I may regret.

I gave in telling him I was just tired and should make it an early night. He agreed with me, just go to bed.

I went to the spa the next day even though I did not feel well as I did not get much sleep. But I was hoping to see Andrea.

Thankfully she was there. I was going to start asking some questions. It was time.

We went to the juice bar and I told her we just got back from Jeremy's.

"Not a good trip I gather." She was good.

"No it was not. We went to see Jeremy's new home. A home which Michael felt he did not need to talk to me about giving him the money to put the down payment on it. Did Susan ever complain about his kids?"

"There was a big problem when it came to both of their families. Susan thought as long as he pampered his kids, she was going to do the same. She found out that he sent $5,000 to Ellen one time, so Susan went out to the Mall and bought for her daughters and grandchildren. She ran up almost $5,000 on their credit card. That one almost ended the marriage. He took the credit card from her and told her if she thought that much of her family then she could go live with them. She brought up the $5,000 that he gave to Ellen and that is when he told her it was his money and he could use his money for whatever he wanted."

"Those are the words I knew I would get. So what did Susan do?"

"She never would tell me what happened. I guess some pretty harsh words were said. About a week later, she showed me a diamond bracelet that Michael bought her. And that is when our friendship came to an end. I told her she was being bought for a diamond bracelet. That she was to be a good girl and he would reward her. She liked jewelry and he had her. So what did you go through for that diamond ring?"

"His drinking was becoming more than I could deal with. He is not a very nice drunk. Sometimes he would just go to sleep but other times he becomes verbally abusive. I am not sure I can be bought though, I do not care for jewelry and I told him that."

"For Michael that seems like the only thing he can do to keep peace, it worked with Susan so he thinks it will work on you as well."

"Andrea, maybe I should stay out of his financial affairs. I do not care about his money, I never did."

"As his wife, he should have told you. He doesn't trust you."

"I know that, and I also know he won't change."

"Michael will never change nor will the women he attaches himself to. He looks for their weakness and uses it against them."

To hear it finally put in words took me by surprise. I was weak and now I am living with the consequences. I have no one to blame for the life I am living but myself and I am ashamed to admit it to anyone.

I left it at that as I knew I could not say any more to her.

I did not go out much after that day. I guess in looking for answers, there was only one and I was not sure I was ready to make it yet.

After the conversation with Andrea, I knew I could not stay in this marriage much longer. If I did, it would only be a matter of time where my life was no longer mine. Some have the ability to take away everything that matters to you, especially those things that are hard to get back once they are gone, your self-esteem and your self-worth. I was more depressed now than I have ever been and I knew the reason.

But how was I to face my family and friends. I needed some time.

That evening with Michael was the usual. He talked of work and had his drinks. As we watched TV, I would look at him. This is not the man I knew before we married. What changed? Me, I thought, I did not see what was right in front of my face. He was my friend and there was no reason for me to know what he did when he was not with me. I was aware of his drinking but made excuses for it. The truth came after we were married and it was then that I knew he was an alcoholic. I questioned our marriage from the very beginning. So why did I stay? Because of this house, I finally found some security and some comfort. I felt safe here, I can hide from the outside here. No-one has to know of my life within these four walls. I can endure as I did not feel I really had a choice, at least for now. I had to think this out before changing my life again.

My thoughts were interrupted by the phone. I knew it was one of his kids and I got up and went into the bedroom. I changed into my nightgown and went into the bathroom. I looked into the mirror and it was not me looking back. It was a woman who sold out for a home and a man who did not really love her. I went to bed and cried myself to sleep.

The next morning, I called my sister to see if she wanted to go to lunch. I did not want to be alone. She said she had been really busy at work and if she could take a rain check.

I thought I would go shopping, just to get out for a while.

I got in my car and even though my thoughts were the Mall, I was driving towards the old house. I sat in the driveway for a few minutes, wondering if I could conquer my fear of being there. I walked slowly to the front door. I opened the door (I had my own key). I noticed right away the house was not cold but had a warmth to it. I thought Michael had turned the heater off. I walked into the kitchen and I noticed there were glasses on the counter. Michael had been here. I looked in the cabinet and there was a bottle of Vodka. Did he come here often? I wondered. I walked to his bedroom, the door was not locked. I looked in and saw the bed was not made. It looked as if someone had been sleeping in it. I sat on the side of the bed. My only thought was that maybe Michael had someone else. But I remembered Michael saying Margaret had moved. Maybe it was not Margaret. Was it Andrea? No he hurt her too much, it could not be her. Maybe it is better I do not know and why should I care. I got up and walked into the hallway, past Susan's room and into the office. The desk was cleared, the stacks of paper and cards were gone. There were some boxes in corner that I had not seen before. I knew it was wrong but I wanted to see what was in them. The top box I opened had picture albums in it. I looked through one album. There were pictures of Michael and Susan's wedding. The next album had pictures of them together on a vacation. They looked

Elizabeth Klein

like a loving couple. I went through five albums and in every one they looked very happy together.

How well we can pull off the deception of our lives. I did not want to see any more of the albums. If only I could find that box of letters, but they were not in that room.

I turned and went into the room I feared. It still was very cold and I sat on the small couch.

"Did you endure it, Susan? Were you afraid to let others know the truth about your marriage? We are alike Susan, as I am doing the same thing. But our fate is different, although I sometimes feel as if my life is slowly slipping away."

I heard a whisper and then there was a noise in the closet. I got up and opened the closet doors. The rush of cold air went past me. She is here.

"I know you quit your job after your marriage. Is that what you really wanted to do, or was it something Michael convinced you to do?

I felt awkward talking in the air, but I knew I was not alone in that room. I started to get that sick feeling again, but I needed to stay there. "Why do I suddenly feel ill, Susan? Were you sick?"

Maybe she was sick at heart as I am.

"Did you want out of your marriage? Were you afraid of him?

The air became heavy and it was hard to breath. I had to leave the room.

Out in the hallway, I realized I had been touched, but not in a friendly way. It was more of a feeling than anything else. Was this a warning? I had to leave the house and I still do not have any answers, only more questions. And one more thing I did not want to deal with, maybe there was someone else in Michael's life.

I went home and laid down for a while. My thoughts and emotions were not going to let me rest. More lies and more deception.

I heard Michael come home. I was surprised that I had been laying there for almost two hours. I told him I was not feeling well. He told me to rest as he had a meeting that evening, so he would get something to eat there. He changed his clothes and gave me a kiss and he left.

Now the doubt came. Where is he really going?

The next day Lesley called and I was more than happy to accept her invitation for lunch.

"So how is married life? She asked.

She could have asked me a million things, but she started with that.

"Like all marriages, some ups and downs."

"You sound a little depressed. Are you okay?

"Yes, I am fine. Michael has been so busy with work and meetings that sometimes it gets lonely. I have been thinking about visiting my sister Barb for a few days."

"You should do that. It always does a marriage good to have some absence every now and then." She was smiling.

It took all I had not to tell her of how much he may enjoy my absence more than she knows. It must have showed.

"There is more you are not saying. I am your friend you can talk to me."

"You are my friend, but it is nothing, I am still getting adjusted to married life after being single for so long."

"But you seem happy with Michael and your health sure is improving without all the worry you had."

"You are right about that. Like I said it is nothing." I tried to smile.

After lunch, she said to have a nice visit with my sister and to call her when I get back.

I honestly wanted to tell her of my suspensions, but she was not one I could confide in. After all she was so happy that Michael and I finally married. And she reminded me it was her plan all along.

That afternoon I called my sister Barb and told her I may come to visit her for a couple of days. She was thrilled.

Then I talked to Michael that evening, he was not happy.

"Why do you want to go see your sister?"

"I did not think I needed a specific reason Michael, my sisters and I are very close, you know that."

"If you want to go, then go. But there was another function that we were to attend, but I am sure your sister is more important."

I could see he was getting upset so I did not say anymore. I did not back down and I did not want to attend another function.

I wanted to leave the following day, but Michael said he needed to take the car in for service. He wanted me to have a safe trip.

The next day I was packed and ready to go, just as Michael was leaving for work. He surprised me when he said to have a good time and to call as soon as I got there. I guess he changed his mind about me being away for a few days. Either that or someone else convinced him.

My sister left the key to her house under a rock on her patio. She said she would get off work early and we would go out for dinner. I took my things in the spare bedroom and called Michael to let him know I arrived safely. He did not answer so left a message. Then I laid down for a while as it was a half day drive. I must have fallen asleep.

My sister woke me up.

"My, aren't we getting old. You cannot make that drive anymore without getting tired? Maybe I should let you sleep some more you "old" woman."

"You are right behind me in age, so no more comments on being old."

"Well get up, we are going out to dinner."

"I will be ready in a few minutes. I am really hungry and of course you are buying." I laughed.

"The first meal is on me, but the rest of your stay, you are on your own."

She made reservations at her favorite restaurant. I decided to have a glass of wine, as I knew I was going to get the first degree and I did not know how much I could reveal to my sister without her thinking I was a mental case.

"It is nice of you to come for a visit, but there is more to this trip than you are letting on. So start talking."

I just had a drink of my wine and decided to take another gulp.

"I am not so sure this marriage was a good idea. You think you know someone and then you live with them. You find out things that were hidden from you. There is a side to Michael that I do not think I can live with anymore. He is an alcoholic and can be verbally abusive."

"I did not expect that. Have you given him an ultimatum? Maybe he can get help. He does love you."

"Sis we have had alcoholics in our family. It is never them with a problem, it is always you."

"Does he know how you feel?"

"No, I am trying not to make a decision right now. I never want any regrets. But there are other things going on as well. I had this feeling when we first moved into the new house that he was having a hard time adjusting. The first couple of months his drinking increased. I think his comfort zone was at the other house and I took him away from that. I went to his other house a few days ago and he had been there. I saw glasses on the kitchen counter and when I went into his bedroom his bed was not made. There is no intimacy in our marriage, which I have accepted, but now I am wondering if he has found someone else to fulfill his needs."

"Why didn't you tell me about this?" She was surprised.

"I have not even been married a year yet. How could I tell anyone what my life has been like? Everyone thinks we are a perfect couple. I can see now why Susan's and Michael's home life was not known. I have the same feelings and want to keep my problems within the walls of my home. And I feel as if I have failed in the marriage as well, which is something that is hard to deal with."

"You have not failed, you did not know, so don't go blaming yourself. It takes two to make a marriage and alcohol can sure destroy it. But I know you cannot go on like this, you will eventually have to make a decision and you know I will always be there for you. The family will be with you and support you." She smiled.

"I know, but for now I prefer to keep this between us, so please don't say anything."

"You know I won't, but I am worried about you."

"Please don't worry it will work out for the best, it has to for both of us. I do feel better that I was able to confide in someone."

"Well let's try and make your next few days pleasant. I took a couple of days off and we are going to shop, check out the movies and hopefully win some money at the new Casino they have just opened."

"That sounds good to me." I was starting to feel a little better.

Elizabeth Klein

Our dinner was served and we just talked of family and her job. It was a nice evening and for the first time in a long time I slept through the night.

My time with her took me to another place, no worry and no stress. But the days went by quickly and I knew I had to get back home. I had decided I would attempt to make the marriage work. I just wasn't sure how.

I let Michael know I was on my way home and that I would call him as soon as I got there. He seemed happy that I was coming back. I wondered if he had any idea of what has been troubling me. Sometimes I am not very good in hiding my emotions.

I returned home just at dinner time and Michael had bought some take-out. I told him of the things that I had done with my sister and how much fun I had. Then thought I had better tell him I was glad to be home even though the drive back seemed longer than usual. How does one compromise with their life?

We were almost at our one- year anniversary. My only thought was that at least I made the year. There were so many times I thought about leaving, but his "good" personality would always show up. The phone calls were not as frequent from his family. It was almost six months since he had heard from Ellen, but that was just her. Diane was consistent with every other month. I could no longer be in the same room when she called. Jeremy made his usually weekly. They were both enjoying Michael's money.

Then one day, I found a letter in Michael's suit coat, as I was getting it ready to take it to the cleaners. It was from Candy. I read the letter, it was short. She had heard of her father's marriage and she was happy for him, as she knew how he felt after Susan's death. After all she went through the same emotions after her mom died. She hoped he had a happy life with his third marriage and then she signed it "Candy."

I decided I better leave the suit coat in the closet, but I did write the return address down. This was another life that seemed to have been damaged by Michael and one day I would like to talk to her.

Michael wanted to know what I wanted to do for our one- year anniversary. I said get away for the weekend. I liked the cabins, where we spent our honeymoon.

Maybe if we went back to where we started, I would get my nerve back and tell him things were going to have to change.

He thought the cabins were a good idea and he would make the reservations.

The day we were to leave, he told me he had a meeting at the Club that morning and we would leave in the afternoon. I was packed and ready to go. The afternoon passed and I tried to call him and see when he would be home. He did not answer his phone. Of course I was worried about him. It was almost night when the doorbell rang and a man I had seen at the Club before, was helping Michael in the house. He was drunk.

I asked the man what happened. He said they were just having a good time and Michael had one too many. He thought nothing of it.

He left and I turned to look at Michael sitting in the recliner.

"What is wrong with you? Today is our anniversary. We should be on the road going up to the mountains."

"I just need to rest a little then we can go. You can drive." His words were slurred.

He got up and almost fell on his way to the bedroom. I followed him as he staggered into the room then he fell into bed. He looked pathetic. How could he do this? I sat down and cried. I need to leave I told myself. I need to leave him.

When I pulled myself together I called the cabins and told them my husband became ill and we could not make it.

I sat down, my head started to hurt. My heart was broken. This was our anniversary. Why would he do this today? I wondered if he really wanted to go.

I walked around the house, our house. Could I leave, could I just walk out? I went out on the back patio, I needed some time. Calm down I told myself, calm down. I waited and I cried. This has to end, but how?

I took some of my medicine, I was in pain and I wanted it to stop.

If he should come to, what could I possibly say to him to make him understand what he has done to us? Would it honestly make a difference? No, it would not. I just need to get away for a while.

I walked back into the bedroom packed a few things, I did not know where I was going, but it did not matter. Nothing seemed to matter.

Elizabeth Klein

I felt sick and a little light-headed. How much medicine did I take? I could not remember.

I picked up my bag, found the car keys and walked out to my car. I put my bag in the back seat. I was behind the steering wheel. I laid my head on the wheel for a moment. I could not drive unless my head cleared a little. I turned on the ignition. I had put my foot on the gas, but I was not moving. I started laughing and crying at the same time, it was still in park. I stopped, it suddenly became very quiet. There was a voice, a voice I had heard before in my head. "No."

I turned off the ignition and I looked around and no-one was there. I slowly got out of the car. There was no way I could drive. I was not well and I was upset. I did not want my life to end in an auto accident. Death, there was that word again. Was the voice another warning?

I honestly do not remember what happened after that. I woke up in the spare bedroom. I turned on the lamp on the nightstand. It was dark as I walked past the living room and into the kitchen. I did not turn on the light. I was going to the refrigerator. I was so thirsty. I walked to the other entry from the kitchen into the living room. I walked right by Michael in the recliner. He scared me when he spoke as I past him.

The pain of what he did came back at me and I started crying.

"Why? I asked, why of all days?

"I did not want to go. It was just for you. It has always been about you"

"Have we gotten to the point where we cannot even talk with each other anymore? Is that where we are at now?" I was holding back my tears.

"I should have said something, but you wanted to go." His words were slurred.

"It is your damn drinking and you will never stop. You are better off alone, that way you can drink yourself into oblivion any time you want. And maybe the people you say you love will not be hurt by you anymore."

"I am not an alcoholic." He said with anger in his voice.

"You are and you will deny it to your grave.

Unfortunately, that may be your outcome sooner than you think. You do not have control and you never will. That is exactly what an alcoholic is. The alcohol controls you, you do not control it."

He got up and moved so fast, I did not have a chance to move. I felt his fist hit across my face and I fell to the floor. I felt the blood flow from my nose. I was dazed, but covered my head waiting for the next blow.

He said something but I could not hear, there was too much ringing in my ears. He reached for me and I yelled at him, "get away, you get away from me."

I did not see him walk out of the room. I heard him slam the front door, get in the car and he was gone.

I was so frightened he would come back I stumbled to the door and locked it.

I wanted to call the police, but what good would it do. Do I really want this known? Do I want my family to know? I was ashamed, this was my fault. I allowed this to happen.

I knew I promised Lesley I would call her if anything should happen. But I couldn't. I started crying, I could not call anyone. If only I could talk to my sister, she would know what I should do. The harsh reality was I could not let anyone know about tonight, not now. I was still dazed and could hardly walk, but made it into the kitchen to wash my face. I got some ice wrapped it in a towel and put it on my face. I could feel the swelling. I went back in the living room, it was still dark. I just sat in the chair and cried until I could not cry anymore.

I knew where Michael had gone. I knew he would stay away. I had to think this out and carefully. We were done, there was not going to be a "happily ever after." Margaret was right, she knew.

The next couple of days I stayed indoors. I wanted to run, to hide. But the reality was, I had nowhere to go. I was staying.

Fortunately, I did not have a black eye, but the side of my face was still red and swollen. I was sick, sick with worry, sick with the decisions I have to make and sick with the fact that our marriage was over.

Alcoholism destroyed us and yet there was no way I could tell anyone, not now. How could I handle the divorce? He was prominent in the community, if what happened that night became public I am not sure what would become of him and I did not want us to be part of a scandal. I am not out to destroy anyone no matter what the price I may have to pay.

Elizabeth Klein

He would survive and once again I felt I was damaged and this time, I felt beyond repair.

I was grateful he did not call. There was nothing he could say or do at this point to make me feel anything for him. There was nothing left for either of us, except time.

I finally received a letter from him a week after he left. He wanted to talk.

I knew we could not continue this way much longer, we had to make some arrangements. I needed to know where I stood.

I called him and asked that we meet at a restaurant or someplace other than the house. I was afraid of him.

He agreed to the restaurant.

We made arrangements the next day. It was so awkward when we met. I was able to cover some of the bruising on my face with makeup. I still did not want anyone to see me. Except for him, I wanted it to be a reminder of what he did.

We just ordered some coffee. We were not going to stay long.

He did not look well and I was worried about him, the "Mother Teresa" in me again.

"There are no words to express how sorry I am. There is no excuse, for what I did. Even now I get sick to my stomach thinking about it. I love you, that will not end even if this marriage does. I have no right to ask you to hang in there with me for a little a longer. But I can and will try to change for you. You mean that much to me."

"You cannot change. It would be foolish of me to think that you could. I thought with time, I could finally find the love that you needed from me. Maybe things would be so much different. But everything about this marriage has been a lie. And I have no intention of living the rest of my life that way."

"So there is no more that I can do or say to save this marriage?" He asked.

"I think you know the answer." I said with the tears starting. I promised myself I would not cry.

'I needed to hear it from you." He said.

I thought there was no more to be said. I started to get up.

"There are some important things we need to discuss. And there is something I need to ask you, but not here. Can we go to the house?"

I hesitated, could I trust him after what he did? I knew I would make a spectacle of myself if we stayed here any longer, the tears would come.

"Yes, but just to let you know, I am afraid of you, so please don't come close to me."

"I promise, and again I am sorry. I never wanted it to be this way."

I walked ahead of him my hand to my chest. My heart was breaking.

When we arrived at the house, I made another pot of coffee, I needed it.

Nothing was said for a while. I guess it was hard to start when you are trying to end a marriage.

"I love this house and I would like to stay in it until after the holidays. Then we can decide on our living arrangements." I said.

"That is not a problem. I will continue to stay at the other place. This is more house than either one of us needs. But if you want to stay in the house, you can, until we can work some things out."

He stopped and I could see a change in him, he was business now.

"As you can understand this mess is going to be difficult for both of us. I am well known and I do not want the gossip or our business known, to be dirty rumors. We can be civil to each other and you can get what you want and I will keep my standing in the community. That little incident the other night will not be discussed. It did not happen."

"You do not know me at all do you? Do you think for an instant that I would want anyone to know what you did to me? I have to live with the fact that I was so weak you totally demoralized me. And you proclaimed love for me. Do you know what love is? I don't think so."

The hurt was turning into anger.

"At least you never had to worry. And yes, I know what love is and you are a person that is incapable of it. You needed time, remember. You are damaged goods, remember. Your heart is cold and it will always be."

He was telling me it was my fault, I could not find the words to respond to that and I started crying.

"We will keep this marriage intact for a couple of more months. I am going to California in a few weeks and I need you to go with me, for appearances only. Once that is over and we get through Christmas we will start divorce proceedings. Until then we are still married. You will stay here and I will stay at my place. No one will know the difference. Not even our families."

"You think you are going to get your way?" I asked.

"I am confident that you want it this way as much as I do."

He was right about that.

"Who are you? I asked. Where is the man that I married?"

"You accused him of being an alcoholic remember. Did you ever think maybe I was drinking because of you?"

"You did not need an excuse to drink, although you used many." I said.

"This conversation is coming to a close. If you cannot do what I ask, just for a couple of months, then we battle in court and I do not think you are up for that fight."

"I can just walk away. I don't need anything you have." I was angry.

"So living with your son, is that what you want? You will be able to live here with all your things. I want nothing of this house. Think about it, you are not getting any younger. Don't be stupid."

I was numb, and just wanted him to go away.

As he got up to leave he said he would be in contact with me to give me the details of the California trip.

I sat in the chair asking myself what just happened. Did I sell out? I walked around the house, looking in each room. When I decorated the house it was with a part of me. I did love this house and I had to agree with Michael, I did have a cold heart. I could love a house but not him. In order to keep it I would survive the next couple of months. Sometimes I could be a good actress and Michael and I had the same script, he would have to play his part as well. But the joke was on me, he had been doing it all along.

It was hard for me to sleep or eat. I was hurt and hurt bad.

I could no longer avoid seeing my sister Lily. She wanted me to have lunch with her before I was to leave for California.

"What in the world do you do to keep so busy?" My sister asked.

"I have all my Christmas shopping done, that is pretty good." I lied.

"I guess so. I have not even started. You look tired and you have lost weight are you feeling well?" She asked.

"I have some good days some bad days, so the norm for me."

"Do you have to make this trip with Michael? I would think he would want you to stay home if you are not well."

"I am fine. I am taking my medication. This is the first trip that all the men are bringing their wives and I need to be there for show. Anyway he will be in meetings all day, so I can do even more shopping and maybe get some rest in between." I smiled, though I was feeling awful. She would not know the truth, at least for now.

"You need to go back to the Doctor. Maybe get another work up and make sure your head is still intact." She laughed.

"I will after the holidays. Maybe things will calm down more then." I was thinking the calm before the storm.

When she finds out that my marriage was a failure, she will want to play the "Mother Teresa." I know others will feel sorry for me, I hate that the most. I already felt sorry for myself. I did not need help from anyone else feeling sorry for me.

It was time to leave for California. It was going to be a long trip for me.

We were flying first class, which was good as we would not have to talk to each other. I would watch a movie and he could drink. I did notice that Michael did not look well. I guess this was taking a toll on both of us.

After a couple of drinks, he fell asleep. I watched him, he looked tired and he had aged. I felt some sadness at that moment. I could not remember the man that struck me or the man that was so controlling. Sometimes when you hear the truth you become someone you do not want to be. Was that happening to him?

Was I the cold hearted bitch he thought I was?

No, because after everything that has happened between us, I still care. I couldn't help it, we had years together.

When the plane was landing, I woke him up. He still did not look rested. We rented a car and went to the hotel. The clerk looked at us, as Michael wanted to make sure we had the connecting rooms. It must have

Elizabeth Klein

seemed weird for a married couple asking for two separate rooms, but it was a condition that I had made.

After we finished putting our luggage away, Michael said he would take a short nap and then we would go get something to eat. I was hungry, but guess I was going to have to wait. I watched some TV in my room while he slept.

It was starting to get dark outside, when I woke him and asked him if he was hungry. He got up and said he needed to wash up and then we would leave.

We went to the restaurant in the hotel. Michael did not eat much. He said he was still feeling tired. He wanted to make it an early evening so he would be rested for the following day.

We went back to our rooms and he opened the door between them. He said he wanted to take a shower and then maybe we could talk.

I did not want to talk. Nothing more had to be said.

After his shower, he came in my room and sat down next to me on the bed. He reached for my hand.

"I wish I could turn back the clock, so we could be happy again but I know I hurt you and I have to live with that the rest of my life. Just know that I do love you and always will." He gave me a kiss and walked back into his room and went to bed.

How can you pick up the pieces and put them together again? I can't, he is an alcoholic and he will hurt me again, if not physically, then emotionally.

I won't let that happen again.

After a couple of hours, I heard him get up and go into the bathroom. He dropped something. I went in to make sure he was okay. He had dropped his medications and I helped him pick up the pills. When I looked at him again, he looked ill.

"Michael if you are not feeling well, we need to get you to the hospital." I was beginning to worry.

"I am all right, I just feel so very tired."

He went back to bed and I made him promise me, if he got up again and did not feel any better, that we would go to the hospital.

He kissed me on the cheek and said he would be fine.

I watched some more TV and then decided to take a shower. After my shower, I walked quietly in his room to make sure he was okay. He looked a little better.

I went to bed, but I could not sleep. After a while I heard my name being called. I jumped out of bed and ran to him. He was holding his chest and gasping for breath. He was having a heart attack. I sat him up hoping he could breathe better. I called the desk and asked them to call an ambulance and to hurry.

He was losing consciousness. I kept watching his breathing and although it was raspy, he was getting some air. I held his hand and told him everything would be okay. It seemed forever before the attendants arrived. They started doing vitals and asking me about his medical condition and medication that he was taking. They moved him on the gurney and started to leave. I could not go with them. I would have to drive to the hospital. I must have gone into mechanical mode, I dressed and then I called his kids. I only got Diane's answering service, so left her a short message, to call her brother. I gave Jeremy all the information I had and told him I would be at the hospital. I had to ask directions to the hospital as I had no idea where it was. I went in through the emergency room and told them I was the wife of Michael Andrews. They looked up his name and told me I would have to wait a few minutes as they were trying to stabilize him. I sat down not knowing if he was going to make it and blaming myself as I knew he was not feeling good, I should have made him go to the hospital, but I didn't.

I called Lily, I woke her up. I was starting to fall apart and she was having a hard time understanding me.

"It is Michael, he had a heart attack and I am at the hospital."

"Is he okay?

"I am waiting in the emergency room. I cannot see him right now as they are trying to stabilize him. I called his family, they are on their way. Lily, can you come? I really need you here for me."

"I will check on flights and get there as soon as I can. I will call you, take care of yourself, he will be fine."

I could not help it, I started crying. I did not want to lose him this way?

Finally, they came and got me. He was getting ready to be transported to ICU. I talked to the Doctors and they said he was stabilized. They wanted to keep him sedated for now, but I could go with him to ICU.

I was shocked to see how pale he was. He had oxygen and all kinds of IV's and a heart monitor. I watched the heart monitor as we went through the hallways, it was not a good heartbeat.

Once we were in ICU, I had to wait outside of the room, so they could adjust everything. When I finally was able to go in, I moved a chair near his bed and I held his hand. This can't be happening I told myself. We were at the point of ending what we had together. "God" please not this way.

Jeremy was there in four hours, he brought Ellen. And I guess Diane was on her way. Jeremy talked to the Doctors, but there was not much news.

"How are you holding up?" He asked.

"I feel like I am in a nightmare and I will wake up soon."

"What happened?"

"Your father was not feeling well from the time we left to the time we got here. I told him he should go to the hospital, but you know how he is. We both went to bed and I was sleeping when I heard him call out my name and as soon as I saw him, I knew."

I looked at Ellen and she bent down to kiss her father and she was holding his other hand. She was crying.

There was nothing we could do, we just sat there and waited. Jeremy went and got coffee for us. I had been up all night and I knew I could not hang in there much longer. The stress was taking its toll on me. But I was afraid to leave. After another hour, I received a call from Lily. She was waiting for me outside of ICU. They would not let her come in.

I almost ran to her when I saw her.

"How is he?" She asked.

"No improvement as yet. They say he is stable for now."

"Well you don't look good. Why don't we go back to your hotel and you can get some rest."

"I hate to leave him, but Jeremy and Ellen are with him so maybe I should, just for a little while."

I went back to ICU and Jeremy said to go and get some rest they would be there. I bent down and kissed Michaels cheek. I remembered he kissed me on the cheek before he went to bed. Little did I know that would be our last kiss.

As we went to the car, I asked my sister how she got to the hospital.

"I just barely got a flight out and when I arrived here I took a cab to the hospital. Fortunately, there is only one hospital in town."

"Thank you for coming. I needed some support and I felt it was not going to come from his kids."

We drove back to the hotel and went to our rooms.

"Why do you have two rooms?" She asked.

I was not prepared for that and I could not think of anything but the truth. It was time she knew the truth.

"Lily, we were ending our marriage after the first of the year." I started crying and she held me.

"Why didn't you say something."

"I couldn't, we made an agreement not to say anything to our families. Please do not ask me why, I can tell you another time. But now my only concern is for him."

"He will be fine, maybe we both should get some rest and then we will go back to the hospital."

I took a sleeping pill and even then it was a restless sleep. I was not sure I could deal with this. He seemed so healthy and yet since our separation I noticed a change in his health. But I thought maybe it was the drinking. Why didn't he say something, why did he always have to be in control? And why was it so important to make this trip?

More and more questions and I still had no answers.

When we returned to the hospital, Jeremy and Ellen left as they needed to get rooms at the hotel and then they were going to get something to eat. My sister said she would wait for me in the waiting room.

I sat and watched him and wondered if he was going to pull through, he looked so pale. I prayed that he would and I knew then I would stay with him for as long as it took for him to get back on his feet. And I told him that as I held his hand. Please don't go, I said to myself, we can be together again.

After about an hour I went to my sister and we went to the cafeteria to get something to eat

"You don't have to stay here. Why don't you go back to the hotel and I will call you if there is a change."

"You called for me and I will be by your side. I can always catch up on my reading." She smiled.

"Thank you for coming. I wanted to be near him, not with his family."

"His son seems nice." She said.

"It is the first impression he makes on everyone." I remembered when Lesley told me that.

"Well at least they are here in support of their father."

"All but one. I should ask Jeremy where she is and if she is coming?"

We finished eating and I went back to the room. Jeremy and Ellen were there.

"Where is Diane?" I asked.

"She said to keep her updated and she would try and get here as soon as she could. She has to make sure her family is taken care of before she can leave." Jeremy said.

All of us just sat there. They started reminiscing and it was nice to listen to them talk of their father is such a way. I did not say anything. I was carrying a secret that tormented me hour by hour. I knew I could never tell them the truth about their father and myself.

The heart monitor started to go off and the nurses came into the room. We were asked to leave. Jeremy and Ellen wanted to know what was going on. I already knew. I went to my sister and told her his heart rate became erratic.

"I don't think he is coming out of this." I whispered.

Jeremy and Ellen came into the waiting room a short time later. It was silent, we waited.

It wasn't a long wait. The Doctor came out and apologized. Michael had another heart attack and he did not pull through. I honestly think you go into some type of shock when you hear news like that. I watched Ellen run to Jeremy, crying. My sister put her arms around me, but I was numb. Jeremy said he should call Diane and asked me if I was okay.

I said, "yes" what else could I say. Ellen sat in a chair and my sister took me out in the hallway.

"I am so sorry, she said. I will help you make whatever arrangements you need to do. You will need someone to get you through that and then we can go home together.

Home, I thought, that is exactly where I want to be.

We had to make some decisions and fast, as I wanted to take Michael home. They were going to take his body to the mortuary in town and he would be prepared there for the flight home. He would then be picked up by the mortuary that we contacted at home.

Jeremy drove my sister and me to the airport and he said he would turn in the rental car. He would catch a flight home and get Jenny. Then they would fly back for the funeral. I said okay.

The day my sister and I were flying back home, I decided to tell my sister more of my marriage. It did not seem to matter at this point.

I told her we were not married very long before I knew he was an alcoholic. I thought I could live with that and I really tried, until the night he struck me and I knew it was over. We made the agreement to stay together for appearance sake, but we no longer lived together. After the first of the year we would file for divorce and I could stay in the house. I then told her, I sold out.

"Why didn't you say anything?"

"It was part of our agreement. I cannot tell you how many times I wanted to talk to you, but I just couldn't. I was so ashamed. I just want to get through this and try to heal from the past. It is over now and maybe I can."

"You will, you have always been a strong person. Just keep your strength for the days ahead and remember I will be by your side."

"Thank you, I need you there."

We did not say anymore, for which I was grateful.

Before I left I told Jeremy that Diane and Ellen could stay at the other house and he could stay with me until the arrangements could be made for Michael's funeral. Jeremy had been so kind and so strong through all of this, I felt with the support we have from each other, we will get through this.

Elizabeth Klein

Damian picked me and my sister up at the airport and finally I was on my way home. I was exhausted, but that was a good thing, I was too tired to think and to feel. But that night, when I was alone in my room, I finally broke down, it finally hit me. He was gone. And although I had been sleeping in our bed alone for the last few weeks, it was not the same this night. I reached out to his side of the bed and I knew he was gone forever.

I once heard from other widows that their husbands came to them. They knew, because just before they fell asleep, the bed moved as if someone was lying next to them. They felt their husbands were telling them they were okay and at peace. I hoped that was true, as I was tormented about the secret we had.

It was only a couple of days before Jeremy and Jenny arrived. I was surprised at their concern about me. It is sad that it takes something like this to happen to bring a family together. The girls arrived a couple of days later.

I received a call from the Mortuary in town and they told us it would be a couple of more days before Michael's body would get there, but we could come in and make the arrangements for him. Jeremy and I went to the Mortuary and we planned the memorial service. We both agreed that it would be a closed coffin. The Mortuary was also going to make the arrangements for burial in the National cemetery, as Michael had already purchased a plot there. Something Jeremy knew about, but I did not.

It was Jeremy who contacted the newspaper and he wrote out the death announcement and the place and time the memorial service would be.

He answered phone calls that came to the house as there were many. When people came to the house, he would answer the door and talk to them. Many times I did not even know who had stopped by. He started to take control, maybe too much. I had a horrible feeling, he was more like his father, than I first thought.

Flowers started arriving and cards from so many people. I just never realized how much Michael's involvement in this community was and his interaction with so many people and organizations. It was overwhelming.

If I needed to get away and hide for a while, I would go to my bedroom. I had a large comfortable chair I would sit and wonder if this nightmare was ever going to end. It was as if everything was moving in slow motion.

The worst part, I was a grieving widow. In his death, he gave me something I thought I could no longer feel. I felt love for Michael that I thought I was no longer capable of and I felt all the sorrow that came with it.

The day of his funeral, was cloudy with a light rain. Michael and I loved the rain, memories came to me of some of the good times we had. The Mortuary was filled with people. His daughters were sitting behind us. I wished I could reach out to them, I just was not sure of their true feelings. Were they playing the part of the grieving daughters? I guess it did not matter we all had parts to play these last few weeks.

He had many friends that went to the podium and they had such wonderful things to say about him. The veterans called him a man of honor and he was. I listened to all the praise and thought, very few knew this man.

There were numerous cars traveling to the National Cemetery, where he was to be buried. The service was heart wrenching and when they handed me the flag, I cried. When the service was over, my sisters were with me as we followed the casket to the gravesite. More words were spoken and then a prayer. I watched the casket as it was placed in the ground. I was motioned over to the side to throw a hand full of dirt on the coffin and then his kids did the same. People started to come to me and give me their condolences. What do you say, how do I respond? I was relieved when everyone started to leave. It was time to go.

I looked around and saw two women at the edge of the cemetery holding each other. I don't know why but I walked over to them.

They were Susan's daughters. They wanted to come, even though there were hard feelings between them. They felt they should be here. And their mom was buried there. They said they would like to talk to me, when I was ready and they would keep in touch. Then they went off to their mother's grave. I did want to talk to them and maybe finally learn the truth. But I needed some time, I was tired, very tired.

Diane and Ellen went home and Jeremy stayed behind to help me with his dad's investments and accounts. Jeremy spent all day at the bank and when he came back, he told me my name was only on one of his father's

Elizabeth Klein

accounts and that was the checking account he opened for us. A grand total of $263.00 was left in the account. Because he never changed his will after we were married, Jeremy was Executor of the Estate. There was almost half a million dollars put in the Estate and the only thing I got was $263.00. Because the house was in both of our names, the house was mine and so were the enormous payments. The other house he had was also in my name. Why? I do not know, but at one time when he was angry at his kids, he had mentioned they would not get that house. So now I had two properties that had mortgages. The car that he supposedly bought for me was in his name only therefore it was to be taken and put in his estate. I did not own the car, the car that we bought using my car as a trade in. Why would he do that? Why would he give me something and yet he never put it in my name?

I was devastated that Michael left me in such a mess. The promises he made to me. They were just words, words full of deception. My life with him was a lie and his love for me was an emotional ploy and I never had a chance. He was a horrible person playing and destroying the self-esteem of the women he was with. But why, what did he gain from being so cruel?

And now I had to know where I stood with Jeremy. I was waiting for him to say something, as I knew what he was up to. I had heard from Lesley that he had contacted his father's Lawyer.

He just looked at me, and I realized for the first time how much he was like his father.

I had a part to play with him and I had to be careful.

I told him his father promised me I would be taken care of. I never dreamed he would do this to me. I told him I was scared for my future. Being left out of the will, was like being told our life together had no meaning at all. The pain from that lie was more than I could endure.

Jeremy then told me his father had asked him to take care of me if anything should happen to him. He made a promise that he would.

"What right did your father have to turn my life over to you? I screamed at him. I could no longer hide the anger and the deception that had been inflicted on me by the death of his father. Your father was a liar and a drunk. He handed my entire life to you and you expect me to believe you are going to honor your father's wishes. I know you and your sisters have already hired his Lawyer. Did you honestly believe that I would not find out about that? Be very careful Jeremy, I know things about your father that you do not want anyone to know about."

It was all I had to strike back at him.

"Is that a threat? He asked. Do you believe I care what you say about my father? But in all honesty, I do not think you would do it. It is not good to speak ill of the dead, you would not achieve anything by doing so and I think you know it."

"And you know the most important thing that mattered to your father was his name." I screamed at him.

"Like I said, if it is a threat, then I have even more ammunition to use against you. You married my father for what you would gain in the event of his death. When you found out you had nothing, you fabricated lies about him to get revenge. So watch what you do or say.

It is three against one, and you won't win." He smiled

"It was not three against one, you have another sister. Have you forgotten that she is entitled to the same as you?"

"My father did not include her in the will. She disowned this family and it is her loss."

"And you do not think she should be told?' I asked.

"She will find out from some of our father's friends, back East. Like I said, she did not care for him in life, she sure as hell is not going to care much if he is dead."

I remembered I had her address and I made up my mind I would contact her.

"I am going back to New Mexico in the morning, he said.

I have already gone through my father's office in the back room and have taken some things that will help me locate some of his other accounts. My father had more money than the money in the accounts. I am going to be looking for that money and I believe you know where it is. If you try and hide anything from me, I assure you I will find it and I will not have a problem coming after you for withholding information from the Estate."

"Michael you will not stay in my house another minute. Pack your things and get out."

"I did not have any intentions on staying here. Just remember what I have said."

I knew that was a threat.

After he left, I fell into a chair and cried. I was drained because of the emotional conflicts. I thought I had no more tears, but they came.

I don't know if I had what it would take to fight for even a little of Michael's estate. I felt being his wife had to count for something in the law. I had to have some rights. All Michael left me were mortgages and bills. I desperately needed help.

My sisters told me to get a Lawyer, to protect myself. No telling what else they would come after. My account was getting smaller and smaller as the bills piled up. I was using a second vehicle that my sister and her husband had. I felt awful about that. When I went to buy a used car, I was told my credit was bad. There was a charge card that Michael had. I did not know about it and yet it had my name on it and was past due. It was in the Estate and there was nothing I could do about it. Also before I could get the deeds of the two properties I was now responsible for, I had to open an account for direct withdraw, the bank had already reported late payments.

It was hard to concentrate on the bills when your life has been a nightmare. Things were not going to get any better. I did need a Lawyer.

The first Lawyer I saw, told me, Michael's will, which left everything to his kids was valid and I was not going to get anything. The second Lawyer said the same thing.

The third Lawyer said he could help me but wanted $5,000 up front. That was most of my savings, but at least I had some hope. There appeared to be a law that I could get one year's salary to help me through the first year after my husband's death. It was better than nothing.

I was so angry at Michael and I was devastated. I had two properties with mortgages and no credit and very little money. Did his love for me turn into hatred? He had to know that by not updating his will his kids would get everything. Did he want to protect them from me, but why?

Did he honestly believe I held money above all else in this life, when I hated to use the checkbook he got for "us"? There were no answers to any of the questions. But the one that hurt the most, was he gave my life to his son. I was on my own and I was scared.

Andrea came to the house one day. I was actually glad to see her. We went into the kitchen and I made us some coffee.

"How are you doing? She asked.

"Not well, Andrea. With Michael's death came a nightmare that I have yet to come out of. He left everything to his kids. He never changed his will after we were married."

"If he could not control you in life, he does it in death."

"I feel that way. Jeremy transformed into his father and he threatened me just as his father did. You know, Andrea, I no longer care about Michael's reputation. I would like to tell the truth to everyone, but I know I can't."

"What is the truth? You can tell me."

"Yes, I think I can tell you. One night, when Michael was drunk he hit me so hard I fell to the floor. I wanted to call the police, but I couldn't. He moved out that night. Our marriage was over and we were going to end it after the first of the year. He threatened me to keep my mouth shut or else it was going to be a very dirty divorce. There was no way I would have survived that and he knew it."

"He never knew the true meaning of love, he played the part well. Andrea said. He succeeded in controlling you, just like I feel he did with Susan."

"That reminds me, I saw Susan's daughters at the cemetery. They said they would get in touch with me. They wanted to talk to me."

"Finally, we will both know what that man did to Susan."

"I feel so lost. But you know that feeling, don't you?" I asked.

"It is hard for me to think he could do this to women and not have any remorse. He just did not care. But because of him, I met you and I am glad we are friends. We share the loss and the pain of being with him, and no matter how hard I try, I can never forgive him for what he did to me. You would think time would heal, but for me it never did."

"I don't think I can ever forgive him either. I know I should, I am a Christian and we are taught to forgive. But this man I trusted with my life and he gave it to his son. I still have a hard time dealing with that."

"Please, let me know what you learn of Susan when you talk to her daughters. Like you, I need to know for sure if he treated her the same as he did us."

We talked a little more. She offered any financial assistance, if I needed it for the estate battle. She was only a phone call away and she would come over if I needed her. I was so thankful I had her as a friend.

The friends that Michael and I had before his death no longer existed. They slowly went back to their lives. I was no longer a part of their lives without Michael. I had heard from other widows that the same thing happened to them. They were on their own when their husband's died. It was a sad reality but it is life and as a widow it was going to be a long and lonely road ahead. I find even with family, I am fighting this battle alone. It is a battle for my future, for my home and for my sanity.

I still was dealing with a lot of anger and I felt that by getting Michael's things out of the house may bring me some peace. He still had so many clothes in the closet and I packed them and gave them to Goodwill. Things that might mean something to his kids, I packed and put them in the garage. It was just stuff and the more I gave to them, the more they were going to have to find a place to store it. I did not want it.

I had procrastinated cleaning out his office. They were going to deliver boxes of his things from work in a couple of days. But now I had to go through his office here at home.

I walked in with some empty boxes and started going through his desk drawers. I could tell Jeremy went through them, papers were scattered all over. Michael had the paperwork for the insurance on the houses and of course they were due, so another thing to pay for. One side of his desk had some accounts that were already closed and some payments he had made. The other side of the desk had more personal items in the drawers and some folders on the bottom.

I found the police report of Susan's death. There was a lawsuit and it was a large settlement. Michael had to split it with the two daughters. Is that what tore that family apart. Was it money again?

Then I found a checkbook, Jeremy must have missed it. I looked through it, I was shocked. He had written checks to his kids in enormous amounts, $10,000, $30,000 up to $50,000. He really did have to buy their love. The kids had been fed and they were still hungry for those dollar signs.

I found a police report, it was for possession of drugs. Jeremy was arrested. His father paid for that one.

He had a folder for Jeremy that held his degrees and certifications from school. Why didn't Jeremy take these? The dollar signs again.

He had another folder for Susan, their marriage certificate, death certificate and the deed to the other house that had both their names on. He inherited that house. She also had IRA's that he inherited. His name was on everything she owned. Why would she leave it to him and not her own kids?

Suddenly I remembered that he was on the title of my house as well. I am going to have to change that and quick. I wondered if his kids had any right to half of that. I needed to check with my Lawyer.

I started to shred a lot of papers. He made so many copies of items. I did find his military file, which I needed for widow's benefits. I had no clue how to apply for that benefit. Everything was so complicated.

As I was going through these things, I almost wished there was some type of organization that would help widows get through all this paperwork and what a wife's rights were.

It was not easy, but then again it was my fault, I trusted my husband to keep his promise to me.

It was starting to get dark and I had not eaten. I spent all day in his room. I had three boxes packed of his things that I was going to give his kids. I thought I had enough for one day. I was finding too much that confirmed the fact that I did not know who my husband was.

I had one more drawer to go through. I was so tired, mentally and emotionally. I had to get something to eat and go to bed. I decided I would finish in the morning. No, just get it over with, I told myself. I opened the drawer and it was just some more papers to shred. I picked up another folder and found two insurance policies that had my name on them as beneficiary. Between the two it was $27,000, it was a windfall for me as my money was disappearing fast. Any amount may keep me above water. I had to use my credit card to get cash so I could deposit it in the bank before the house payments of both homes were due. Finally, I had something from him, but it was too late to change what I felt, it was the deception I had to deal with.

I could not do any more. I put the folder on top of his desk. I would deal with it in the morning. I turned off the light and turned to go, when

I suddenly felt cold. Not here, not now I said to myself. I looked around and then started laughing. That is all I need, for him to haunt me. I was really getting tired.

I ate and then took a shower. I thought it would relax me so I could get some sleep. I went to bed and was lying on my side. I was almost asleep when I felt the mattress move. It was behind me and I felt some pressure against the back of my body. I was not dreaming, yet I was not awake. In my thoughts, I told him I could not forgive him. That was all I remembered and for the first time in a long time, I slept peaceful.

In his attempt to communicate to me, I felt maybe I was able to hurt him as he hurt me.

After about three weeks, I was finally able to get the $27,000. I was contacted by the family Lawyer, that there might be a claim against that policy. That was a useless attempt as I was the beneficiary.

His life insurance policy from work was one hassle after another. One day I called and was transferred to seven different people. Every time they asked for some more paper work, I would send it. Then they would ask for more.

Everything was so difficult. This was all so new to me. I just did what people kept asking me to do and hoped something good would happen.

I talked to my Lawyer. It was hard for me to comprehend that I was not entitled to anything other than the bills. There had to be something to help me get through this. All he said was he was working on it.

The boxes from Michael's work were delivered. I started going through those.

I wished I could have just taped them and put them away. Inside one box was Susan's picture, some cards that she had sent to him and pictures of her memorial and headstone. It was all of her. Now the truth comes and it hits right in the middle of my chest. Maybe he could not love anyone. He never let go of Susan.

I found more and more of her things, nothing of us. Not even the wedding picture I had seen in his office when I was there.

It was too much for me, more pain and it did not seem to end. I cried.

A few weeks later, I received a call from a friend of mine, she knew of someone who might rent the other house and he needed it furnished for the time being. That is if I was interested.

"That would be such a relief, to get a house payment for that house."

"Well, when can he look at it?" She asked.

"I can show him the house anytime, but need a least a week or two, to clean it, before he moves in"

"I think he will go for tha. I will bring him over about noon."

I thought finally some good news. That house payment would be made. I dreaded going back to the house.

I was going to wait for them in the driveway, but because it had been awhile since I was in the house, I thought I should make sure it was okay to show. It did not look to bad and as I walked through the hallway I did not go into Susan's room but I did open the door. I tried to open the room into Michael's office, but it was locked. I could not find the key and I heard them pull up in the driveway.

He was an older man and he did like the house. I explained to him that I would look for the key to the one room and if I could not find it I would replace the door handle. He did not seem very concerned about it. I let him know that I would work day and night to get the house ready to move in. He said he had some time before he could move in, but he wanted to pay the first month rent in advance plus a cleaning deposit.

It would mean that I would have to be in that house. I had no choice. I needed to rent it.

I did not sleep well that night. I dreaded going back to that house.

The following morning, I felt ill but I had no choice, I needed to start moving things out and cleaning. Damian was going to come over later to help me. I was scared. I did not want anything more to happen, not now. I started in his bedroom. When I opened the closet door, Susan's clothes were still hanging in there. Her shoes were on the top shelf. I put as much as I could in the packing boxes. I then started going through the drawers in the nightstands. Still more of her things and as I was putting those in the boxes, I found a small jewelry box. In it was the diamond bracelet. I looked at it as I held it. This meant a lot to Susan, she deserved it. I thought about it and decided I deserved it as well. I had paid the price.

I found her underclothes in another drawer. More of her things, he did not get rid of much, as I thought he did. Maybe he couldn't, it was his attachment to her. This is where his long nights were spent. He was trying to hold on to her. But it was not because he loved her. I felt maybe it was more his guilt, but then again that meant he cared and I could not convince myself of that.

I thought her reaching out to me maybe was not to warn me. Were they threats? I had taken him from the house and maybe from her. I knew she loved him, but still felt it was not a true love. My mind was racing in the supernatural world.

I packed up six boxes of Michael's things and more boxes of her things. I was tired physically and mentally. It was all so much for me to go through. How much more?

I walked into Susan's sewing room. I had that lost feeling. I was thrown into another life that made no sense to me.

He could not love her. He didn't know how.

"Are you here Susan? Did you get what you wanted? Are you happy with Michael now? Is he forgiven there Susan, with you? He is not forgiven here. Forgiveness comes from the heart and he destroyed mine. His love was a lie. Our marriage was a lie. And he lied to you, Susan."

I was screaming at the closet door.

She was there, the room got colder. I yelled at her again and again, she got what she wanted. Why are you still here? I leaned my head against the door begging her for the truth. I finally had to sit down, I felt as if all my strength was taken from me. It became extremely quiet. I listened and I heard the word "no." Then I heard it again.

"You did not want him? Did he abuse you? Susan what is the truth? Is there more you are trying to tell me? What is it?

I waited, but nothing. I felt like I was losing my mind. I wanted to know if he treated her the same way he treated me. Did she sell out to him, like I did? I knew the answers to those questions and yet I felt there had to be more. I finally had to leave the room.

I walked to the room that was his office. I forgot it was locked and I never did find the key. I decided to break the lock. What difference did it make now?

The cards that I did not see the last time I was in the room, were on her desk. He must have gotten them out. I noticed some of them were not even opened. I started to go through them, maybe I could find something, but they were all condolences. I put them in a box on the floor. They were going in the shredder. I felt no one should go through what I have been going through since the death of Michael. Why did he leave so much for another to find? It was not what a surviving spouse should have to do. But then again, he did not care or else these things would have been destroyed. I still had so much left, I knew I had to go through everything and find out as much as I could about her. I might find something in the things Michael kept of her.

By the time I finished, I had three boxes of hers. He kept everything.

I was so tired and wanted to go back home and get some rest.

Damian finally came and moved some of the boxes in his truck.

I am glad he did not catch me screaming at the closet door. I knew I was losing it, but I had to keep hanging on.

It was really hard on me to get this house ready, but again I had no choice.

Every day caused more and more despair, it was all of Susan, in the bathrooms and in the closets and on the shelves. Time and time again, I had to face there was someone else in Michael's life and I never had a chance.

Then I found a letter in a book of hers. She had written she was no longer happy in the marriage. She did not know what she was going to do. Finally, something substantial, there was no happiness in her marriage. Was he abusive and was it because of his drinking? There was more and I had to find it.

There were times I was glad to be alone in the house. I talked to Susan. If someone was there they would have thought, I was crazy. And I felt that way. I was trying to communicate with a dead person.

The plastic containers that I had seen on the shelves of her room were full of her clothes. I did not go through them. They were going to Good Will. I searched for that box of letters again, but they were gone. I know those held the answers for me.

Elizabeth Klein

I had been in the house four days straight and I needed a break. It was difficult for me to accept that the man I was married to was a stranger and incapable of accepting the truth about his own miserable life.

I did not lie to Margaret, he was with someone else and it was not me.

I finished, what did not go to Goodwill I moved to the garage at my place. The house felt different somehow, I cannot explain it. It was if all the cleaning I did washed away some of the bad feelings.

A few days later I was informed by the renter, it would be another month before he could move in, but he would continue to pay the rent. It was going to be a few more weeks to finish up the sale of his home in another state.

When it was all done, I did not feel well physically and mentally. My home became my sanctuary. There I had some peace, I needed that so much. It would be a week before I even wanted to go outside.

It was early morning and I was getting ready to go to the store.

The doorbell rang. I put my purse and keys down and opened the door. It was one of Susan's daughters, the youngest one. Her name was Mary.

"I would like to talk, if this is not a good time, I can come back."

I held out my hand and thanked her. I told her it was time we talked.

She was small stature and seemed very nervous. I offered her something to drink, but she declined.

"I was the one that called and left a message on your phone, saying that I knew Susan. My sister said I should mind my own business."

"Did you also put that piece of wallpaper on my windshield?"

"Yes I did, it was stupid and I am sorry. It was to warn you."

"Warn me about what?"

"Warn you about the person you were with. I was trying to warn you about Michael."

"Please, I need to know. I feel as my life with Michael has been a lie. I can honestly say I did not know the man I married.

"My mom was really in love with him. She had been on her own for many years. I knew she was lonely and I was actually happy when she met

him. He treated her so good and bought her many gifts. She loved all the attention he was giving her.

But after they were married, things changed, he changed. She realized his drinking was getting out of hand. He had a buddy who lived up the street and he would be with him almost every night after work and get drunk. My mom seemed okay with that because he was not driving. That would scare her the most, she was afraid he would get in an accident and maybe kill someone. Eventually she asked him to stop drinking with his friend. But there were words between them and she did not say anything more. He came home bleeding one night. He had fallen on the way home. There was a terrible fight that night and she went to my sister's house. That is when we first learned of the problems they were having"

"Why did your mom go back?"

"She really loved him and she was enjoying the life he gave her, except for the drinking. But it soon became a trade-off. As long as she had what she wanted, she would put up with his drinking."

"Did he ever abuse her? I mean hit her or threaten her?"

"If he did she would not tell us. After the night she came to my sister's, he did everything he could to keep her away from her family. She changed when she went back to him. She would call, but she did not visit with us much. Of course when we would say something, she would get very defensive and upset."

"He controlled her." I said.

"I figured that was it. We tried to talk to her, but she would make comments like were jealous that she finally found someone and that was not it. We were afraid for her. My oldest sister started to get notices that she had been taken off my mom's accounts. Then we found out she put him on the deed to her house. That house we grew up in. She once told us, we were to have it if anything happened to her. But that did not happen, even when my sister and I asked if we could buy it from him. He gave us an amount that he knew we could not pay."

She put her head down. This had to be hard for her.

"When mom was killed in that auto accident, I did not know if I could ever get my life together again, I loved her so much. Michael took over everything after her death. Do you know we were not allowed to see her at the mortuary? He decided it was going to be a closed coffin. He saw her prior to the service, but he would not allow us. Even after she died, he was still controlling. He planned the memorial and we were not allowed to speak. My sister and I were in shock. This was our mother. It was almost as if he was daring us to do something or say something, but we just sat there. The funeral was awful. It was all about him and not about my mom. I saw him put his head on her coffin, many people came up to comfort him. We were standing in the back. It was to the point, that if he got in my face I would let him have it. But out of respect for our mom we stayed in the back."

"So your mom never said anything to you? She never indicated she might want to get away from him."

"When my mom was angry or hurt, she would write him letters."

I was stunned, when she said that.

"I saw a box of letters in her sewing room, but I cannot find them now."

"If you find those letters, then all of us will know the truth." She hesitated for a few minutes.

"Please do not think of me as a greedy person. Some of the antique furniture, like the buffet's and the pictures, some of the older dishes, these are things that my Grandmother handed down to my mom. They were to be handed down to my sister and me, but Michael kept everything. Once my mom died we were never allowed in the house again. Like I said we grew up there and he shut the door in our faces. My mom kept toys we played with. She even kept some of costumes she made for us when we had stage plays at school. She kept a lot of things as we were growing up. There were family albums that he kept. Is it possible that we may have some of those things? We have waited so long."

"You are more than welcome to have anything you want. I can't believe he would do such a thing. What purpose did it serve? They were not his to keep?"

"It was his way. He had a mean streak and I don't know why. We had just lost our mother and we tried to reach out to him, but it was no use. He was a good man in his portrayal to others, but there was a dark side to him. That is why I was trying to warn you. I felt you had to know the truth."

"There was another who wanted me to know the truth. Your mom tried to tell me. Come with me."

She just stared at me for a while, and I told her I was not crazy.

I drove her to the house. When we walked in, she just stood by the door and I could see the tears.

"It has been such a long time since I have been here. Memories are flooding my mind. The family gatherings we had, they were so much fun. That is until he came into our lives."

"Please come to her sewing room." I said.

She followed me and stopped at the door.

"You changed it, it looks nice."

"She is here, I said. Call out to her."

She looked at me, not understanding what I said.

"I know it is hard to believe, but please call out to her."

She walked in the room.

"Mom, I miss you so much. I love you, mom."

We both felt the cold breeze. She started crying, she said she felt something on her cheek.

I could not hold back my tears. Susan was there and she connected with her daughter.

We both had tears. She felt her mom's love and I felt her betrayal of the man she loved.

I left the room. The daughter stayed in there for a long time.

When she came out she asked permission to see the rest of the house. I told her it was okay. She walked through the rooms trying to hang onto the memories of the good times she had there. She still had tears in her eyes as she said she was ready to leave. She hugged me and thanked me for my kindness. She was going to tell her sister they will finally get their mom's things. And she said she will tell her, their mom is okay. She is at peace now.

It was an emotional day for me. I am told in church to forgive. It will be a long time before I can forgive Michael for all the pain he caused Susan's family and myself and so many others. Can one ever be at peace, even in death? I don't think so.

A couple of days later I called Mary and told her they could come over and pick up some of the furniture they wanted and the boxes of their mother's things that I had packed. They arrived at the house the next morning. I met them there. Mary had her husband with her and they had a truck. After moving what they could in the truck, Mary and her husband left. The older sister, Gail asked me about the storage unit their mom had. I told her I never knew about it and I did not remember Michael ever mentioning it.

"I don't think he would have. He probably took over the storage unit, just like he did everything else that belonged to my mom."

"Do you know where it is?" I asked.

"It was so long ago. I handled a lot of my mom's financial statements and I remember seeing the storage unit on one of her statements, but cannot remember the name of the company."

"Michael kept everything. I wonder if it is in one of the small file cabinets that I put in my garage. I was going to go through those things after I finished cleaning in this house."

"In the storage unit are some of my mom's most valuable possessions. I need to know if they are still there." She said.

"But it has been so long, the storage unit may have been auctioned off by now."

"If Michael took over unit, then Jeremy has to know about it. I am sure if he thinks there is anything of value in it, he would keep up the payments until he could return here, if he has not done so already."

"That is a possibility as we only communicate through lawyers now, so I would not know if he has been there or not. I think we need to go through the papers in file cabinet, maybe it is there." At least I was hoping it was.

We drove back to my place. The small cabinet was locked. We found a hammer and screwdriver and pried one drawer opened. There were a lot of Susan's papers in there, but nothing about a storage unit. I decided to go through one of the boxes that I put some of Michael's files in.

Finally, we found a statement in one of his files and we had the address of the storage company.

"You need to go there now and find out about the unit. Hopefully it was not auctioned off." I said.

Gail left and I was hoping everything was going to turn out for them.

I received a call from Gail, within an hour.

"My mom kept the storage unit in her name and my name. She added Michaels name after they were married. I feel that my mom wanted us to have what was in the storage. The manager told me Jeremy was here about a month ago, claiming the storage unit was his and belonged in the estate of his father. The manager told him about my name on the lease and it would be held for sixty days or until I could claim it. I guess Jeremy became angry and told the man he would hear from his lawyer. I have a problem though, I have no key and the man will not break the lock, it is his policy, at least until an auction. Did Michael keep some keys around the house?'

"Michael kept a lot of keys. They are in a jar somewhere in the garage. Come back over here and I will give you the jar, if I can find it."

I thought I saw it on one of shelves that I put up some of the smaller boxes. It was there, a large jar packed with keys.

When Gail arrived I gave her the jar and wished her luck.

It was a couple of days later, Gail called and asked me to meet her at the storage unit, as there was some things in the unit that belonged to Michael and she wanted nothing that belonged to him. My garage was already packed and I was not sure I wanted anymore of his stuff, but could not just leave it there.

When I got there Gail was inside the unit. I saw some beautiful paintings and more antique furniture, as I entered.

"Who was the painter in your family?"

My mother's sister, she left her paintings to my mom when she passed away."

She walked me to the back of the unit.

"Michael's things are in the corner. There is just a trunk and five more boxes."

She helped me move the things in my car.

"I am so happy you were able to locate the storage unit. You deserve all your mother's things."

"It would not have happened, if you had not helped us. I am sure Jeremy thought something of value was in here, but the only value they had were for us, to finally get my mom's treasures."

"Fortunately Jeremy did not get his hands on these." I said.

Elizabeth Klein

She gave me a hug as I left and thanked me again for helping.

As I put the boxes and trunk in the garage, I looked around and saw the boxes I had packed already. Michael kept so much. Did he ever think that others would have to go through all these things he kept of his life? There was so much of Michael's things and boxes of pictures of his kids and their mom. Would his kids really want these things? Why was money more important than the memories these pictures held?

Michael was obsessed with his son. I was disturbed by all the things he kept of Jeremy. He kept multiple certificates that his son had from the time he was in first grade. Any award or accomplishment throughout Jeremy's schooling, he had. Some were in frames. Some were in notebooks and there were only a few early pictures of the girls, Diane and Ellen. Also I found a few letters the girls wrote to their father while he was overseas. Apparently they had been very young, as it was scribbling and they were very faded. I looked through a few of them and was putting them back, when I saw one that had the name Candy on it.

Candy, I thought. Why did she no longer have any ties with them?

I could understand how dysfunctional that family was. Of course the daughters fought for Michael's attention, but unfortunately they learned early to play the guilt game. Jeremy always got more than they did, so they used the crying game and they were good at that.

It still was not over. I still had boxes in the garage that I just threw things in and did not go through them and now the ones from the storage. I was beginning to feel that the reason Michael never threw anything away was that he was trying to hang onto parts of his life he was most admired for. A lot of boxes were of his time in the service. His certificates, newspaper clippings, everything pertaining to the achievements he had in the service. And photo albums of the men he served with and the places he was stationed. Even the uniforms, the trench coats and other clothing he packed away. It smelled terrible and I had to throw out most of the clothing.

I sorted more boxes of pictures of the family and even more of Jeremy. I kept thinking he was a sick man, a lonely man. He tried so hard to hang onto the past. Maybe he couldn't and that is why the drinking.

Everything was finally packed and it would all go to his family. I wanted nothing more of him. I had my lawyer contact Jeremy's lawyer and ask if they would make arrangements to pick up his things. Jeremy's lawyer sent over a truck a couple of days later to get the boxes. I knew Jeremy would pay the price for that.

For some reason I kept the things from the storage. I was tired and even if I found more of Jeremy or the girls, I would throw it away. I did not think they even wanted what I gave them. They were only after the money. Money they still believed I had.

Then I was notified from Jeremy's lawyer that there was a storage unit that Michael had. Jeremy felt that the things in the storage unit should be put in the estate. I called my lawyer and told him I had no knowledge of a storage unit and I really did not care about it. I smiled, when I thought of his reaction, especially when he found out the storage was emptied.

A couple of weeks went by and I finally decided to get the rest of the stuff out of the garage. I was so frustrated with all the junk and that is all it was. I packed up the rest of it and took it to the dump. At least there it would be buried, forever.

Lesley called, I had not heard from her in a long time.

"How are you doing?" She asked.

I hated that question as I could never tell them the truth.

"I am hanging in there. I have not heard from you in a while. How are you doing?"

"I am unemployed now and enjoying it. I like staying home and collecting a check."

"What happened?"

"They needed to cut back, so they let go all their older employees. But to make it look as if it was not discrimination, they laid off a couple of the younger employees, as well"

"I did not know. I guess I am really out of touch."

"I have been looking for another job, but not seriously. Ben said I needed a break."

"Why didn't you call?"

Elizabeth Klein

"I figured you needed some time to yourself. Ben told me that Michael never changed his will and the spoiled brats got everything. I hope you have a lawyer."

"I do, but it does not look good for me."

"You have the house, don't you?"

"Yes and I have the enormous house payment as well."

"What are you going to do?" She asked.

"I don't know. I will have to wait and see what happens with my claim against the estate."

"Why don't you come over and we can talk. It sounds like you need to talk to someone."

"Maybe later, I am glad you are enjoying unemployment."

"I am always here for you, you know that. So don't wait too long, okay."

When I hung up, I wondered why I did not want to go over and see her.

Was I getting to the point where staying home was better than answering questions that I did not want to? If I did not visit with anyone, then they would never know the truth about my life. Why did I feel I could talk to Andrea about things and no one else, even my family? It was because Andrea is the only one who really knows what I am going through.

I called Andrea to tell her I talked to Susan's daughters.

We decided to meet at the spa. I had not gone back since Michael's death, but it was probably something I should have been doing to release some of the stress that I have been under.

I was feeling a little better after being in the sauna. I need to force myself to get out of the house and take care of myself.

I saw Andrea at the juice bar. She was talking to one of the male instructors. She introduced me to him and then he left.

"Are you getting lonely, Andrea?" I smiled.

"There are times when my sheets get very cold and I think I should warm them up every now and then."

"I never heard that one before." I smiled.

"You have not been out much. You need to get out more often."

"Funny you should say that, as I was thinking the same thing, just for different reasons." I laughed.

"It is good to hear you laugh, you are so solemn."

"It is not like I do not have a reason to be solemn. I keep looking for some light in all this darkness."

"It will come soon and then you will be able to live your life again."

"I keep hoping, I guess that is all I have left."

"Well did you learn anything more about Susan?"

"I learned that Michael treated her the same way he treated us. He was the alcoholic and he was verbally abusive. The physical abuse they are not sure of, as Michael did everything he possible could to keep her from her family. Now that I think about it, that is why he was so angry with me when I was with my sisters. He was trying to isolate me from my family. He almost did it to. I was ashamed at what I had become, weak."

'You are not the only one who was put in that position after being with him." She had some sadness in her voice.

"He had a lot of hatred for her daughters. I said. That is the only word I have for what he did to them. He would not allow them in the house they grew up in and he would not give them anything of their mother's. I cannot figure what value her things had for him, other than trying to keep Susan's memory."

"It was his guilt. He treated her badly and he felt by keeping her things it would take away the guilt. He somehow could convince himself that they did have love." Andrea said.

"At one time I felt the same. With his death, I actually thought I finally found the love I should have had for him. The reality was that he never loved me, he couldn't."

"He could not love anyone. He wasn't shown much love growing up. You can't give what you never had."

"I guess love is learned, you have to know what it is. Maybe that is why I could not give him the love he needed from me. I gave it once and it had a really bad outcome. Maybe I was afraid."

"You were honest with him, just as I was. He was not honest with us."

"The truth does hurt."

"Forever, she said."

It seemed like our good mood was broken. Maybe one day we could talk of something other than the past.

Elizabeth Klein

My lawyer contacted me and we had a court hearing in two days. He asked if I was ready and I told him I was more than ready to end this. Then he called me the morning of the court hearing and told me it had been canceled by the other lawyer. I was sick, I wanted this over. If there was something I was to receive, then tell me and let's end this.

It would be two more months before I received a check from Michael's life insurance. It was the light I was searching for. I was able to pay off my credit cards and still had some left over to put in the bank. I also found out that he had a retirement account as well. I guess I should have been excited, but I learned it had only been put in my name six months prior to his death. In other words, he still had his dead wife as a beneficiary, six months after we were married. How much more? I kept asking myself.

It would be another month before I received his retirement. I took it at a lump sum and put it in an IRA. It was there if I needed it.

I traded the old clunker I had purchased from a private buyer and I bought a newer car. Of course I had to pay cash, but that was okay as I hated payments.

The other house was rented, so I did not worry about that. Even though worrying was an everyday ordeal, I could never feel comfortable.

I never knew what was going to come up, from the past.

I told myself that I should be grateful now, for he did take care of me in some aspects. But I just couldn't forgive him.

I thought maybe if I visited his grave, I could talk to him and tell him what he did to me. Get it out of my system and then maybe I could find the forgiveness. I knew I could not start over with my life until I could forgive him. I got in the car and drove the half hour to the cemetery. I thought I knew where his grave was. I remember the bench that was by the tree. His grave was in the fourth row, or so I thought. After looking for about fifteen minutes, I walked back to the chapel and looked over the cemetery, trying to remember the landmarks. I returned to the bench and walked the entire rows. I finally found his headstone. I walked closer to it. I fell to my knees after what I saw on the headstone. I closed my eyes and opened them again.

The words tore at my soul and the tears came again. I thought there was no more this man could do to me.

Apparently he did not purchase two separate plots, but he bought one and they were both placed in there. I was not prepared for that. I wanted to talk to him, but I could not. Below his name on the head-stone, read his loving wife Susan. They were together, he finally got what he wanted, to be with his wife Susan. I don't know why this felt like the final blow to me, but that day I swore I would never return.

It took me days to recover from that trip. The head-stone was embedded in my mind. The darkness was back and I did not even care.

My sister left phone messages and so did Lesley. The same question over and over again, "How are you doing?"

I was alone and for now that is what I wanted.

Andrea called and left a message for me to meet her at the spa. There was no way I could even talk to her now. I had nothing to say.

I could not let anyone see me. I started having nightmares. It was always Michael laughing at me, from the grave. I was the fool. I believed him. I was sick, but there was no medicine to make me better.

I started to lose track of time and did not know what day it was, nor did I care. I wandered through the house. I saw him in every room. It was his laughter, if only I could shut that out. I always loved his laughter, but this laugh was horrible. Sometimes I would scream, "you won".

He took everything from me. There was nothing left.

Damian came over one day. I had not even answered his phone calls. He had a key and when he saw me in my chair, he called my sister to come over right away. I knew they were there. I just could not communicate with them. I heard a siren. Then some other people were trying to talk to me. I just looked at them. I didn't understand. They were doing things to me. I did not want them to touch me. I told them "no". My sister was trying to calm me, but I told her "no." They tied my arms down, I couldn't move. I was put on a hard stretcher and they took me from my house. I started crying. "Why are you doing this to me?" I was given a shot and I do not remember anything after that.

I woke up in a hospital bed. My sister was there and also Damian.

"Why am I here?" I asked.

Elizabeth Klein

"You suffered from severe dehydration. You looked horrible, why didn't you call?"

"I was not myself and when I get to that point, I just want to be alone."

"Sis, you can't escape into your own world. It does not work. Please get some help, if not for you, then for us."

I saw she was concerned and maybe afraid for me. It was time I thought, I am not well. If I do not get help, then he has won.

"I will, I promise, as soon as I get out of here."

"That is all I want. You cannot do this by yourself anymore."

I looked at my son and I saw he relaxed some. They were worried about me. Unfortunately, I had to come to this to realize that my life did matter.

When I finally returned home, I walked through all the rooms. I wanted to see if maybe I needed to make some more changes, to make this home my home and not so much a place of sorrow and despair. I opened all the blinds, rearranged some furniture, took pictures off the wall that were reminders I held onto. I even decided to paint a couple of rooms a different color and finally replace some carpet. I wanted new life in this house and a new life for me.

I had my first session with the Psychologist before I even left the hospital. He made me realize I was living a past life, a life with Michael. We were going to start working on the present life and I was to focus on all the positive things that have happened to me and not the negative.

I told him I wanted that, I needed that and I was ready.

Damian started dropping by, just for coffee, he would say.

Lesley came over, just to keep me updated on her job search.

My sister came by with some food. She said she always cooked too much.

I did not get upset with them, it was what I needed. The one person I did not hear from was Andrea. I had tried to call her several times and she never answered. I convinced myself she had connected with that cute instructor at the spa.

I decided I was ready to venture out and I went back to the spa. I even swam in the pool for a little while before I hit the sauna. I went to the juice bar and I saw Andrea, sitting by herself.

"Hi, I said. I tried to call you. When you did not answer, I thought perhaps your sheets were warming up."

She laughed, "I found out he was married, something he neglected to tell me. You are looking good. I heard you were in the hospital."

"Brain damage, I said. It happens every now and then."

"I did not know, she said. Why didn't you say something?"

"I couldn't, I was not myself."

"Do you remember when I told you I transferred to another city, after what Michael had done to me? I didn't transfer. I went away because I felt I was having a nervous breakdown."

"He didn't really leave you, did he? He followed you. Not in reality, but in your mind. Did you hear him laughing?"

"How did you know?"

"Same here, I said. But I am no longer living in the past. I want to live in the present and I am doing that, with help."

"I am glad to hear that. I convinced myself I would be better if I came back here and to start over again. When I saw him with Susan, I realized he still had a hold on me. I did marry to make him jealous. It was a foolish thing to do. After Susan died I thought I had another chance with him, but then there was Margaret and then there was you."

"Did your feelings for him end with me?" I asked.

"No, you were temporary and I knew it would only be a matter of time with you. When I said you were different, I really meant, you were not his type."

"And what type would that be?"

"You were not in love with him, as you said. He needed that in order to possess you. It was his way of getting what he wanted."

"And what did he want?"

"Everything you had and more." She said.

"I know Michael was a lot of things, but he did not need money."

"It was not his need, but his want. He is the father of his dependent children and they all have the same want."

"I had nothing he wanted from me. We were married in part because I was ill and he offered his insurance. There was no monetary gain he could have from me. I was on the brink of losing everything I had."

"You had something, she said. There is something you are missing."

I could not think of anything. I had nothing, but a small IRA, the mobile home and my other house. Those were not worth much.

"You are wrong, I said. Granted he told me he loved me and I fell for that, but I am telling you the truth, he had nothing to gain by marrying me."

"I am upsetting you, I am sorry. Just forget I brought that up."

"He did have a lot to gain from Susan though. Especially once he knew he could control her. But again, he never trusted her. He told me after her death, he started receiving beneficiary checks for her. He found out that from her mom's estate, an account was set up which would give each of her remaining children checks every month. Susan never told him that and he was angry, he felt she had no reason to keep that bit of information from him."

"I bet that did not set well. He never trusted anyone and yet he would get upset over someone who did not trust him." She laughed.

"Andrea, did you know he had another daughter named Candy?"

"I only heard her name mentioned a couple of times. He did not talk of her, only that she lived with her mother."

"I have her address and am thinking of writing her. She seems so different from the others."

"You are still searching aren't you? I thought you were on the road of recovery and yet you still have the need to know."

"I feel that I am connected to her in some way. A feeling I cannot shake."

"Why don't you give yourself more time, before you look up more females in Michael's past. The answers you are looking for died with Michael."

"I know the man he was. But just maybe there was someone in his life that knew a side to him that we never saw. I think that is what I am searching for, some part of him that he could never show. I know it sounds crazy, but I cannot believe in my heart that he was always a cruel and selfish person. And either way, I feel contacting Candy and talking with her may end all this turmoil I seem to put myself through."

She said she felt sorry for me as no one knew Michael and if he had a side of him that was good, it would never make up for the broken women he left behind. She got up, she said she had an appointment and left.

I knew what she said was the truth and the reality was that I became one of those women she talked about.

My Lawyer called and said that he had attended the court date. He knew I was in the hospital and that they had told the judge things were moving along. I told him I did not feel that anything had moved along. I felt as if I was stuck in time and I wanted this over. He said that an agreement had been made that I was entitled to something from the estate, but as yet the amount was still being negotiated.

"Negotiated among whom?" I asked.

"Between Jeremy and his Lawyer." He said.

"And you honestly believe that is going to happen any time soon?"

"I will e-mail him in a couple of weeks and let them know, this is not going to be an on-going thing. We have another court date in a couple of months and if not settled by then, we will ask judgment from the court."

"That is what I want. This had to end so I can get on with my life."

I really wanted to end the strings attached to Jeremy. Even though we no longer communicated, he was still there. I remembered the last day I saw him and realized he was so much like his father. I would truly enjoy the day that Jeremy would have to write me a check from his father's estate. That would be a wonderful ending to totally cut off any future contact with him or his family.

When I had finally cleaned out the office that Michael had here at home, I decided to make that room into a den. I called Damian and asked him if he could help me move his desk out. I had purchased a hide-a-bed from a friend of mine and he was going to bring it later that day. The desk was a large desk with shelves on the top. Damian said to put it in his truck, as he thought he could use it. It was heavy and I dropped the side I was carrying and it landed pretty hard on the floor. Finally, we got it to his truck, and my back told me it was a stupid thing for me to do. I walked back in the room and saw two envelopes in the middle of the floor. They had to have been attached to the bottom of a drawer, as I had taken everything

Elizabeth Klein

out of the desk. The first envelope had the letter Andrea had written him, so many years ago. I sat down and read the letter. It was straight from a broken heart and brought back emotions that I wanted to forget. She went into detail of the night they shared together. She had waited so long. He had fulfilled all the dreams she had of having him with her for a night of lovemaking. She would always cherish that night and the many more to come. Then the letter changed as she described what damage he did. How could he deceive her, how could he use the word "love" so despicable? He was a cruel and heartless human being and she wanted him to rot in HELL.

No wonder she could not forgive him after what he did to her. I wondered if there would be a time that I would be able to forgive.

I knew I had to or else I would be stuck in time as she was. She would never be able to find happiness without forgiving.

I did not have the heart to give her the letter. It would only add to the pain she had been carrying all these years. But why did he keep it?

It was another question that would never be answered. The other envelope was old. The writing was faded and it was dated over fifty years ago. The letter was from his first wife, only they were just engaged at the time, she was almost eighteen. She wanted to break off their engagement. She hated to write the letter with him being in the service, but she knew he would be on leave soon and she preferred he did not come and see her. She wrote about the last time they were together. She realized at that time he had a temper and his harsh words toward her were very hurtful. He had misunderstood her, but he would not let her explain before he started yelling at her. Why do things always have to be about you? She asked in her letter. Why are you always right and I am always wrong?

Before she made a terrible mistake in marriage, she wanted to end it now. She said she would take the blame. She would tell everyone she just was not ready for marriage. Which was somewhat the truth, she was afraid of him and his temper. She asked for his forgiveness and said it was for the best. Her letter did not end in love, she just signed her name.

What did he say to her to change her mind? He had to see her when he came back on leave. Were there more spoken words of love that were meaningless? He somehow convinced her to marry him and her life as well, *started with lies. I felt sadness for her, she was so young. I put both letters in a diary that I kept.*

At my next appointment with the Psychologist, I told him of the letters I found.

"He was like this at such a young age. How did he acquire such a personality so young?" I asked.

"You told me once that his mother was an alcoholic and basically did not give either his sister or him any resemblance of love. They probably felt abandoned by their mother. He basically hated his mother and even though his Aunt was there for him, his opinion of women was already instilled. Love did not exist, it was not necessary to get anything he wanted with it. The words were enough, even though they were meaningless to him.

I am sure he even blamed his mother for his sister's suicide."

"I think he did. He told me his sister married very young, just to get away from her mother. Her marriage did not last long and that is when she started taking drugs. Because you were treated badly, does that excuse your behavior toward others?" I asked.

"No, it does not. But we are talking about a very young boy who needed to escape, just like his sister did. He felt she abandoned him and probably blamed her for his sister's suicide. With his marriage at such a young age and his wife already having apprehensions, there was no chance of either one of them really knowing what love was. It was probably more sexual for him and security for her. After they had children it became a responsibility."

"I was foolish to think that love would eventually happen. Although I thought it possible at some point." I said.

"Never look for love from another person. You love yourself first and foremost and sometimes love will find you." He smiled.

"I still cannot forgive, even though you have given me a better understanding of him. I know so many that have been treated badly and because of that they do the opposite, they treat others with kindness and compassion."

"It is a choice." He said.

Elizabeth Klein

I left his office with more insight as to why he did not know how to love. I almost felt sorry for him, maybe he never had a chance. But he did have a choice.

Sometimes when I am alone at home, I wonder how many women have gone through what I have gone through. How do they continue on knowing they were lied to? And at the most tragic time of their lives, the death of their spouse, the person who promised to take care of them. Do they feel the deceit that I carry with me?

As you get older you do want some security, you are no longer able to work like you use to. There have been many times I feel useless because I no longer worked.

I really did not ask much of this marriage. I wanted companionship and some happiness at the end stages of my life. Was that so much to ask for? I told that to Michael many times but I guess I never convinced him it was not about his money. To him everything had a price and I was not worth it. I know I must not think that way as I am trying to keep the past in the past, but these thoughts haunt me continuously.

I hate looking in the mirror. I do not recognize the person looking back at me. I have aged so much through this ordeal and I am so tired.

These thoughts are not good. Am I ever going to get through this?

A couple of weeks later, I decided to write Candy. It had been on my mind for a long time. I told her who I was and the reason for the letter. I wanted to know more about her father and her life with him.

I thought I might as well be honest, if she did not want to talk of her father, I would not hear from her and I really could not blame her for that.

The following week I was surprised when I received a letter from her. But it was not a letter at all, it was a piece of paper with her phone number.

I wanted to call her that evening, but thought I had better wait. Now that I had the opportunity to talk to her I was not sure what to say.

I thought about it and decided to call her the next evening.

"Candy, this is Beth. I wrote you the letter."

"I know who you are. I cannot tell you how hurt I was that I learned of my father's death from relatives here and not one person in my family."

"I had asked Jeremy to call you, but he said you would not care. I think he was more concerned about the will at that time. I think you could have contested that." I said.

"There was nothing my dad had that I wanted and as far as Jeremy is concerned you can tell him I have no interest in my dad's will."

"I do not think that is possible as we both have Lawyers. But am sure he would breathe a sigh of relief."

"What is it that you want from me?" She asked.

"I am not sure Candy. I am searching for answers to so many questions. I thought I knew your dad, but in reality I did not know him at all."

"Maybe you do not really want to know and what purpose would it serve, he is dead. He cannot destroy any more lives."

It was a statement that I have heard so many times.

"You are right, but the suffering he has left behind still continues and I am not just talking about me."

"I know, she said. She was silent for a while.

I waited and then I asked if I could come and visit with her. I wanted to meet with her face to face. The voice I heard at the other end had a lot of sorrow and to hear it was heartbreaking.

"You would come here?" She asked.

"Yes, I will fly out to meet with you, if that is okay."

She agreed and I told her as soon as I could make the arrangements I would let her know.

I called my sister and told her I would be gone for a few days. She wanted to know where I was going and to avoid the cross examination I told her to see a friend of mine, whom I just had contact from.

"So you are not going to tell me who this someone is?" She asked.

"No, not right now, maybe when I get back."

"You can be so stubborn at times, just be careful okay? You have made a lot of progress. I don't want to see you slide back."

"It is not like that. I may be helpful to someone else and it is something I need to do."

Elizabeth Klein

"Have a good trip, sis. And take care." She said.

As I was on the plane, more questions arose and I wondered what did I really want from Candy? It did not matter. I was on my way to meet her.

She was at the airport to meet me. I was surprised to see that she did not look like anyone in the family, but then again I never saw a picture of her mother. She was my height, and had curly blond hair and was really pretty. When she approached me she smiled.

"It is good to finally meet you. I hope you had a nice flight?"

"I cannot tell you how glad I am I made this trip to meet you. Thank you for letting me come." I said.

"As we discussed you will stay with me. I have a small home but it is comfortable. I can take you there now unless you would like to go get something to eat."

"No, I am fine. I would like to go to your home."

Everything seemed so awkward and I am sure we both felt that way. She was not sure why I came, but I am glad I did.

The drive was long and I felt she really went out of her way to pick me up. When we arrived at her home, it was in a small and old subdivision. She had a picket fence around her yard and a nice big porch that had some rocking chairs on it.

After she showed me my room, I put my things away. She went in the kitchen to make something for us to eat. She was so different than I expected, so very pleasant to be with and to talk to. She said she took time off work to spend with me. She needed a vacation anyway.

The way she looked me in the eyes, I could tell she was still trying to figure out why I was there. But then again, so was I.

"I am hoping maybe we can help each other with this visit. I want to return home a little different than I left and I honestly think this visit with you will make that difference." I said.

"I do not know what you want from me?"

"I know the others, the brother and the sisters. They are their father's children. But you are not, so I want to find out about you. I want to know your childhood with your parents. That is only if you want to tell me."

"I am sure you know more than you think you do now. It was impossible for my dad to change. He was his own person, selfish and always in control. He could not be anything other, he was heartless."

I saw some sadness in her eyes. This is going to be painful for both of us.

She said dinner was ready. While we ate we just made small talk. After dinner, she poured us both a glass of wine and we went out on the porch and sat in the rockers.

"I know very little of your mother. Michael did not talk much of his first marriage."

"I can understand that, the marriage itself was almost nonexistent. I saw very little of love or even physical contact between my parents. No holding hands and no hugs or kisses. I was happy when he finally made the decision to end it. My mother was too weak to make the decision and of course she settled for the financial settlement made in return to give up her rights to Jeremy."

"In going through Michael's things, it was more than obvious his obsession with his son. It almost made me ill." I said.

"It was obvious to everyone. Diane and Ellen did not stick around much after he became old enough to start school. That is when dad really kept Jeremy at his side."

"And what about you? I asked. Jeremy's wife said you two were close at one time."

"I was still older than him, but my other two sisters were teenagers when he was born. So they had no interest in him, especially when dad bragged so much of finally having a son. I helped Jeremy say his first words and I helped him walk. We played a lot together and I will always remember his laughter." She smiled.

When she said that I was taken back to a time where I loved to hear Michael's laughter.

"When did Michael take over the care of Jeremy?"

"It was when Jeremy was about four. Dad wanted to put him in pre-school, so he would be ready to be a scholar in kindergarten. My mom was pushed aside and so was I. Dad took total control of Jeremy's life from then on. When the divorce came about I had just graduated from high school and I was more than ready to leave and come back here where my mom grew up and her family lived here. But when we returned here I stayed with my Grandma. My mom said she had to visit with someone in another town, but she would not tell me who.

It did not take me long to get it out of my Grandma, that my mom went to see a man. What I learned that night started my road to decline."

She was silent for a while.

"If this is difficult for you, I understand. There are things in our past that are painful."

"You traveled all this way to know my side of the story and maybe it is time. For some reason I feel safe with you, I trust you and that is a difficult thing for me to do."

"I am not a threat to you in any way. I said. I think we both want the same thing. To put this all behind us, so we can start moving forward in our lives."

"You are right. It has been a long time, holding this inside and trying to pretend that I was okay. I have had two failed marriages trying to pretend I could give to someone something I knew nothing about and that was love. Maybe if I had found the right man, I could have learned to love, but the ones I chose had the same characteristics as my dad. I wondered how could I have fallen for men like that, when I had so much hatred toward my dad."

"Maybe, because deep down you really did not hate your dad." I wanted to help her so much. I knew this was hard for her.

"I felt that lost love the night my Grandma told me the truth about my mom. My dad was overseas serving in the war and my mom was on her own raising Diane and Ellen. My mom met a man and I guess they were carrying on an affair. My dad was on leave and he kept it a secret when he was coming home, so no one knew. He wanted to surprise us. But he came home to an empty house. My Grandma was taking care of Diane and Ellen and my mom was in a bar with this other man. My dad called my Grandma's house and my mother's sister answered the phone. She was mad at my mom for what she was doing and she told my dad where he would find my mom. It was an awful scene when dad confronted the man and my mom. Fortunately, dad was still in his uniform and there were men there that held him back from going after the man my mom was with. He could have faced some serious charges being in the service.

My dad went to a friend of his to cool off and stay the night. My mom stayed at Grandma's. After a couple of days Grandma told my mom to go talk to my dad and beg him for forgiveness, otherwise she was going to be left alone with two small girls to care for. My mom did and for the sake of the girls they got back together. Only this time dad was taking the family to California, away from her lover. After the move to California, I was born in less than nine months. Needless to say my dad had doubts about me being his child. That is when the marriage no longer became a marriage, it was for us they stayed together. Dad started to have affairs. I guess he was looking for something my mom could no longer give him. Mom put up with it because every time she would visit Grandma, she would visit this man as well."

"Did Michael start drinking then?" I asked.

"My dad always drank, but I guess it increased tremendously as time went by. I grew up knowing my dad was an alcoholic and I hated him for that as well as I was being treated differently from the other two girls. I did not get the praise or the attention that was given to them. But we all paid the price for his drinking as we could not even invite our friends for meals or sleepovers, unless he was gone for the night."

"Because you were born after the move to California, when did you find about the infidelity of your mom?

On one of my mom's trips back home, she brought me with her. I stayed with Grandma. I told her that my dad had a drinking problem and mom and dad were always fighting. I guess she thought I was old enough to know the truth of what my mom did before I was born. It was a shock to me. I always blamed my dad for their bad marriage.

"Did you ever talk to your dad about it?" I asked.

"I did, I told him I understood why their relationship was not of a loving couple and I was sorry. I asked him if we could start over and maybe keep communication opened between us. He seemed like he was ready to give it a try. But things never changed and then the divorce. Mom and I moved back here and there was little contact with my dad. But then for some reason he did let me know about his marriage with Susan. We did start talking on the phone every now and then. But that stopped.

Elizabeth Klein

"After Michael died, I started to go through a lot of his things. He kept all the letters you and the other two wrote to him when he had to go overseas. He was trying to hold onto you, even then." I said.

"He really kept my letters?" She asked.

"Yes, he did, after all those years."

There was something more I wanted to ask her, but wanted her to hang onto her thoughts of those letters for a while. I got up and went into the house and brought the bottle of wine out and poured us both another glass of wine.

"Candy, when you moved back here with your mom, did she ever discuss any of the affairs your dad had with the other woman?"

"She was hurt by that and I think it was pay back to him, when she went back home to see this other man. She was afraid to end the marriage, because Jeremy was so young."

"Why did she leave Jeremy for Michael to raise? How does a mother leave a young child?" I asked

"She was threatened. He would hire the best Lawyers and he would degrade her in court, claiming she was mentally ill and not fit to raise him. And then there was the money. She sold out and I was angry about that. It was hard for me to forgive her for leaving him."

I saw the tears in her eyes. The pain she had from both her mom and dad.

"It is getting late Candy. Maybe a good night's sleep will do us both good. I still have a couple of days here for us to catch up and I want to know."

"I am so sorry. I am sure you are tired. We do have time and I enjoy your company so much. I was very apprehensive about you, but now I see there was no reason to be that way. Thank you so much for coming."

"I should say thanks to you. I know how difficult it is to bring up the past and I appreciate that you have done that."

She came to me and gave me a hug. She reached out and I was grateful.

She made sure I was comfortable in my room and said she would have coffee ready for me in the morning.

I was not sure I would be able to sleep as so much was going through my head. She was so different, maybe she was not Michael's daughter. Maybe Michael blamed her for her mother's infidelity and that is why it was easier *for him to let her go. No, that wasn't it, by then he had been too wrapped up in his son to care for anyone. Tomorrow, we would talk some more and I slowly drifted off to sleep.*

Candy was true to her word. I could smell the coffee when I woke up. I put my robe on and went into the kitchen.

"Good morning," she said, as she handed me a cup of coffee.

"I am sorry I slept late, I must have been tired. Is it okay if I get a shower and then maybe you know a nice café, where can have some breakfast?"

"You do not have to buy breakfast, I can make it."

"I would like to see some of the town, while I am here and I have heard the food is pretty good in some of these small towns." I smiled.

"Well it is good ole home cooking and I would like to show you around."

When I was ready, she said we could walk. A couple of blocks from her house was a nice, cozy café and the food was delicious.

I enjoyed the walk so much. I love visiting the east, as so many of these older areas of town, have the quaint homes with the big porches. Something that is rare in the west. And I live in the desert, so not a lot of these big trees around.

"I can't imagine living anywhere else. I have always been comfortable here and the people are so friendly. The house that I live in was my grandmother's. My mother passed away before my grandma. I was surprised that my grandma left the house to me. There are a lot of good memories in this house and it was one place that I felt some love." She said.

"Did your relationship with your mom change, when your grandmother told you of her affair?"

"I was angry for a long time. Like I said, I had blamed my dad for the problems in their marriage. It was always his fault for the affairs and treating my mom the way he did. I thought if I could have just talked to him about things, after I learned the truth. Maybe I could make our relationship better. But there was Jeremy and for a long time he did not need anyone else in his life, even the women he became involved with were only temporary. Jeremy was already finishing up college when dad met Susan, so maybe he was ready to settle down. Did you know her?

Elizabeth Klein

"No, I did not. I met a couple of women who knew her through Michael, but they were not close friends of hers. I met her two daughters after Michael's death and they were very nice."

"My dad did write me and tell me of her death. He seemed devastated. I asked him if he wanted me to come out and he said "no.""

"He may have been reaching out to you then. Did you keep in touch?"

"I did try, but after writing him a couple of times, it would be months before I would hear from him again. So I just sent him cards every now and then."

"Candy, what was your relationship with Diane and Ellen when you were with them?"

"We were sisters in name only, because there was such a difference in our ages, we did not have the same things in common. I was the quiet one and did not care for the partying scene. Diane and Ellen were the wild ones or the partying type. I remember they were always in trouble when they were in high school. Dad was always bailing them out of one scrape after another. I think my dad blamed mom for that as well. Both girls married right out of high school and dad was more than happy to pay for their weddings and see them off. But that did not happen, one marriage did not even last a year and the other one, having two kids within eighteen months of each other, ended shortly after. I heard from relative's that dad continued to support them, or bail them out. I think he really wanted to keep them away from Jeremy, his perfect child."

"Well he wasn't that perfect. Michael had kept copies of a couple of his traffic tickets and even a drug arrest."

"So the perfect one was flawed." She said with a smile. But why would he keep copies of those?"

"Going through his things, I could not believe all he kept. All the papers of his time in the service, he had evaluations, not only of himself, but the people that worked for him. Reports, travel papers, assignments, etc. I honestly believed he kept everything because his past was always better than his present."

"I do remember our garages always being filled with boxes of his things. I can't believe he kept them so long. Did you find any pictures or anything of me?" She asked.

"Some of the boxes were so old and broken. The ones with the family albums in them, especially when all of you were young, had water damage. The pictures were stuck together and warped so much, I could not save those. I am sorry."

"No, don't be. My grandmother had a couple of small photo albums and I have those."

I told her I would like to see them later. We decided to walk some more as we had a big breakfast. Later that afternoon we went shopping and before returning home she stopped at a floral shop and bought some flowers.

She drove to the cemetery and we placed flowers on her mother's and grandmother's grave. As we stood by her mom's grave I reached over and held her hand, she held onto mine for some time before we turned to leave.

I was back on the porch, sitting in a rocker and she brought some coffee out.

"Thanks for a nice day. I can see why you like it here, so nice and quiet."

"I don't think I could ever move, like I said, I find peace here."

"Candy, do you have children?"

"No, I had two miscarriages and never was able to get pregnant after the last miscarriage. I felt it was just as well, dysfunctional families run high in my family circle. She laughed. I do have someone special in my life now. I am active in my church and a man that I have known for some time, asked me out. We have been dating for almost a year now and we enjoy our time together. He does make me happy and we talk of marriage one day."

"I am so happy for you. You have such a wonderful personality. You would make anyone happy."

"And you, do you think there could ever be someone in your life?" She asked.

"I will never, say never. But for now I am enjoying my friends and family."

"Well I am happy and I am sure you will be as well. I will pray for you."

"I will need a lot of prayers, I am sure. But know God's plan is not always our plan." I said

There was a silence for a while. I was enjoying the cool breeze and just relaxing in a different time and a different place.

"Did dad do a lot of damage to you?" She asked.

"I guess I was different from Susan. I had a property and some money that kept me going, even after our marriage. Your dad was very controlling and I was not the person he thought he could dominate. His drinking increased after we purchased the new house. He did not want to leave the comfort of his old house, so it was a difficult transition for him. Of course he really did not need much of an excuse to drink. I did convince him, we both needed some time away. We did go to Hawaii and I would like to think he had a nice time. But after that, I would try to get him away for other trips and he would enjoy himself the first few days but then he always wanted to get back home. We usually would have disagreements on most of our trips. Just stupid things, but he never realized how it affected me, I would enjoy the first couple of days and then he would get an attitude toward the end of the trip. It would basically ruin the trip for me. So at times when he would ask if there was anywhere I wanted to go, I would just say no. It wasn't worth it."

I felt that was enough to tell her.

"He was controlling and at times he could be cruel with his words. I was not going to be put down and that is one reason I decided to go with my mom." She said.

"You are so fortunate to get away from him. I really tried to give him what he needed, but I don't think it was ever enough for him. I don't think he could ever be happy with anyone. I told her.

"It is sad because he really had a lot to give, but he could not let it out. There are so many that search for something that is right in front of their eyes and yet they cannot see it. He passed away empty and lost. But God is forgiving more so than us." She said.

"Have you forgiven him?" I asked

"Sometimes I think I have. The negativity and anger I had for both my mom and dad is gone. I want to be at peace and will try to continue to be that way for the rest of my life."

"I think my time will come. There is still so much hurt, I cannot seem to get beyond it right now. But this visit with you has given me a good perspective of another life he had and of course you turned out just fine. Something good that once was a part of him." I said.

"You will find your peace. You are on a journey and as much we have shared during your time here, I think you can find your way. I want you to be in my life, if you will have me."

I got up from my chair and went to her. She got up and we hugged each other tight. I was not going to lose her. She would forever be in my life. As the tears filled in my eyes I knew going back home, I would be a different person and I will find forgiveness for Michael, as I have found my peace with her. I found what he could not see, a part of him that was feeling, caring and loving, his daughter Candy.

The following day went by quickly. We drove to the mountains and had lunch at a nice chalet. When we returned to her house, we sat by the fireplace and she showed me the family albums her grandmother had saved. She would laugh when she saw some of the pictures and it was nice to hear her laughter. She had moved on and I felt she would have a future, no matter what she decided to do. I went to bed early as I would be flying back the next day. I wanted to stay, but knew I had unfinished business back home. But sleep was not going to happen.

She came in my room at 2:00 am.

"I have been praying on something a lot since you have been here. I think tonight I received the answer to that prayer. I was with my mom as she was dying. She held my hand and told me she needed to tell me something and asked me to keep it to myself, as it would only cause more pain to the son she had to leave behind. That decision was one she had to live with the rest of her life and she regretted it every day. She told me Jeremy was not Michael's son.

I could not believe what she was saying.

"What did you say?" I asked.

"I know, I had a hard time trying to understand what she was telling me. She said one time Michael had gotten an apartment for her. Some of his friends were coming for a visit and he literally did not want her around. So he rented a place for her. My mom said she would not leave, but eventually she did, he had his ways of persuasion and threats. He was going to tell his friends that she was with her mom because her mom was ill. She was only suppose to be in the apartment for a month, but it was a time when he started thinking of a divorce. He felt she should stay in the apartment

Elizabeth Klein

a little longer. During that time mom slept with a man who was in the apartment across from her. When Michael came to talk to her about the divorce a few weeks later, she told him she was pregnant. He had no reason to believe it was not his. And when it was verified through an Ultrasound that it was a boy, he changed. He started to take care of mom. He made sure she rested and he even hired a housekeeper to help mom. Mom was sick most of the pregnancy. She was terrified he would find out. But it never entered his mind, he was having a son and everything else did not matter. When she delivered, she knew she could never tell him. The first couple of years were great, but after that he took charge of Jeremy and no one else seemed to matter."

"Do you know what that means? Jeremy is not entitled to anything. The sisters would be next in line, including you. Why didn't you say anything?" I asked.

"Out of respect for my mom, she had a lot of problems in her life. She carried the guilt she had of leaving Jeremy behind. But she knew he would have a better life staying with Michael. I did not care for anything Michael left and after hearing about the threats Jeremy made to you, I have come to the conclusion even though Jeremy had another father, he is Michael's son."

"I don't know what to say." I was shocked.

"I would ask of you to respect my wish to keep this to yourself. But I know you have the ability now to make his life miserable, so I would understand if you feel you need to expose this." She said, as she as she turned her head around not facing me.

"Please look at me, I would never do anything to hurt you and I know what the consequences are if he found out about this. He would call you a liar. And the girls would request a DNA test, so they could have everything they could get their hands on. I do like the thought of revenge, but my faith is stronger than trying to get even.

We talked for about two hours more. She really did have a hard time telling me everything, but she did say she was glad that I was the one person she could tell. Many times she wanted to reveal the truth to Michael, but she figured that they all did a pretty good job in destroying themselves so she decided just to keep her distance. They were never close to begin with and in all honesty she was better off.

I tried so hard to get some sleep but it wasn't happening. This family had its dark secrets, all of them had. Especially the mother and Michael and it all came down to lies, self- esteem and money. Candy was different and I guess she escaped, thanks to her Grandmother.

I was finally able to get some sleep. But woke up late and only had a couple of hours to get packed and ready to leave. Candy and I did not say much.

When we arrived at the airport, she parked her car and came in with me. It was hard to leave, as we had bonded in those couple of days. I told her I would expect her to visit with me as well. It was not goodbye, but only until we saw each other again. After more tears and hugging, she looked at me and asked if I was her step-mom now. I told her now and forever.

I was a different person going back. I was afraid I would revert back to my miserable self, but I did not. I made a lunch date with Lesley and one with my sister. Damian came over for dinner and we laughed and talked of the future. I had a lot of work for him around the house, so I was going to keep him busy.

When I had lunch with Lesley, she noticed a change in me.

"I found what I was looking for in my visit with Candy. She is the total opposite of Michael and the others. She chose to go with her mom after the divorce. She learned a lot of truth when she went back and she felt hurt from the things she learned of her mom. She stayed with her grandmother and she turned out to be a beautiful woman, inside and out."

"I was worried when you told me what you were going to do. Sometimes when we go looking for something, it does not turn out well. But in your case maybe it was just what you needed and I am happy for you."

"Well, I now have a step-daughter, so finding her was worth the trip."

"Michael never talked of her, how sad is that." She said.

"Very sad, but I am sure there was always that doubt that she was not his. But she said she put that behind her as he was the only father she knew."

"And the others never kept in contact with her?"

"I think there was an attempt on her part. But she was so distant and of course their dad was their main concern as he had the money." I said.

Elizabeth Klein

"He sure was not the man I thought I knew. I saw through Jeremy right away, but not Michael. He did well in hiding his true self."

"He was good at what he did, in his business and in his organizations, but he just could not give his relationships the same effort and time. He is gone now and I feel I can finally move on. I would say he has taken enough from me, but I am still working hard on the forgiveness." I smiled.

"So we are right back where we started. Only this time I will not be a matchmaker, I have learned my lesson." She said.

"I had some good times with Michael and those are the times I try to remember. I think my time for finding that special person has pretty much run out, so I will keep with my family, my friends and my new step-daughter."

"You will be fine, I have faith." She said.

"Faith is important and it has gotten me through some of the hard times. I feel stronger now and I intend to enjoy life, time goes by so quickly."

"Speaking of time, I have to get going. I have a new puppy and it is not a good idea leaving him alone for long periods of time." She smiled.

"I must come over and meet this new addition of yours."

"You are welcomed anytime. We have a new look in the house, it is called potty pads decor on the floor. He is still having trouble getting through his thick head to go to the door and let us know when he has to go out."

"Well you trained your husband to obey you." I laughed.

She laughed and we said our goodbyes and I told her I would see her again soon.

My lunch with my sister pretty much went the same way, only my sister seemed more relaxed that I came back ready to start over. She had been so worried about me.

"I think the nightmare is over, I said. Out of Michael's death, I gained something more important than his possessions or his money. I met someone whom he did not have any influence over and even though her life has been difficult, she made it through without ever asking him for anything. Except she wanted to love him, but he never saw that. I guess he couldn't, love for him was paid for. It was the only way he could get even a resemblance of love from his other kids."

"It is a sad life to lead, never being able to accept love. But you know so much more about him now. His childhood was not that happy."

"Sis, very few of us have had a happy childhood. Even though we struggled through life, we turned out pretty good. More than anything we wanted to be loved and give love. There were no price tags attached to that. I know I married for the wrong reasons, but I would never hurt Michael. I gave him what I could and with time I was hoping it would have been more. I tried, I really did, but it became obvious after only a few months that the marriage was not going to last."

"I know you had a hard time dealing with his drinking, but was there more to it than you are telling me?" She asked.

She knew, but how? I could never hide anything from her.

"It is all in the past now." I said.

"You say things without the words. I wish you would have come to me."

"I couldn't, it would not have turned out well for anyone and by then our marriage was already over. There was no "happily ever after" for me."

"You are going to start anew. Just remember you have family for the difficult times." She smiled.

"I am hoping the difficult times are starting to dwindle, but I always know you are near."

"This is getting a little emotional. I already feel tears coming, so let's eat before I have to ask for more napkins" She started to eat.

It was a good lunch and I am feeling so much better, I have changed.

It was the following week that I received a call from the office Michael had worked. It was a person I became acquainted with at the parties Michael had for his employees.

She told me of a Lawyer who called and asked for Michael. She said she told him that Michael had passed away. He then asked if there was a way he could get in touch with me. She took his name and number and told him she would call and relay his message to me.

"Did he say what he wanted?" I asked.

"He did not say much to me, only that he was a Lawyer from Las Vegas and he had been in communication with Michael."

"I will give him a call and thanks for calling me first, I appreciate that."

Elizabeth Klein

I have to admit I was afraid to talk to this Lawyer as I did not have a clue what he wanted. But I had to find out.

I called his phone number and he did not answer so left a message for him to call me.

When he finally called, he said he was so glad to hear from me. He told me how sorry he was to hear that Michael had passed away. It had been awhile since he had contact with Michael. Michael had denied the first offer and he was working on another offer.

"I do not know what you are talking about, when you say offer."

"Michael had been explicit to only talk to him. He told me you were in no condition to discuss this matter."

"I do not understand. What matter are we talking about?"

What he had to talk to me about had to be in person. So he asked me if it would be okay for him to come to my home.

"Can you give me an idea of what it is you have to talk to me about?"

"Only that it is good news." He answered.

We set up an appointment the next day and of course I was worried, as when I always thought something good was going to happen to me, it was the opposite. But he did specify it was good news.

I asked my sister if she could come over when he came and she said she would. She was also questioning as to what this was about and why he had to see me in person.

When he arrived, he introduced himself and asked me if I remembered him.

"You do look familiar, but I do not know why."

"I was at the hospital to talk to you about a lawsuit that had been filed on behalf of the victims that suffered on that New Year's evening. Your husband said you were not well and suffered some brain damage. He then handed me his card and said it would be best to communicate with him, as he did not feel you would understand what was happening concerning the lawsuit. He later sent me paperwork that was signed and notarized by you indicating that he was to be your legal guardian over the lawsuit. I was so sorry to hear about the loss of your husband, you have suffered so much. But you seem to have recovered immensely from the brain damage that you suffered."

I looked at my sister and she put her finger to her mouth, indicating I should not say anything.

"And what is this all about?" I asked.

"Well your husband would not accept the first offer of the settlement. He said you would be in recovery for a long period of time. He instructed me on your behalf to turn the offer down. I thought it was a good offer, but he insisted that your suffering was worth more. So I turned the offer down, against the wishes of the other defendants. It was awhile before they gave us another offer. I was trying to get in touch with your husband to see if he would agree to the new offer, as the others wanted to settle. I met him at the address of another home, to see if he would approve and I told him that the others were not going with this any further. He finally approved the new offer and would accept the settlement on your behalf. Of course it took more time to work some things out. I wanted to go to his home and let him know everything was settled. There was someone else there and it was then that I learned he passed away. I had his card from his office and I went there to see if there was a way that they could help me get in contact with you. A woman there said if I left my card, she would give you a call to contact me. I was not sure how well you recovered from your head injury. Your husband never gave me another person to talk to on your behalf."

"The head injury was not as bad as the Doctors originally told my husband and I am doing much better. So what happens now?"

"I will write the offer on a piece of paper, as it has to be confidential. If you agree to this amount, then we can finish the paperwork."

He wrote something on a piece of paper and handed it to me.

I had to look at the amount a couple of times to make sure I was actually seeing the dollar amount. I could not believe it and I was shaking as I handed the paper back to him.

It was all I could do, to answer him without choking.

"It is more than enough, I answered. You could tell them I agree to it."

"Thank-you so much, he said. The others will be relieved that you agree to that amount."

"No, thank-you, for all you have done in this matter." I said.

Elizabeth Klein

"I will keep you informed of the process, but like I said it should not be very long and I will bring your check to you personally, as you will have to sign some papers."

"I will wait for your call. I said."

He got up to leave and again stated how well I had recovered from the brain damage that I had suffered. Then said he would be in touch and left.

My sister looked at me and I honestly did not know what to say.

"He told that man that he was your legal guardian. How did he get that paperwork? And to think he never told you anything about the lawsuit. How was he going to hide that from you?" She asked.

"The only thing I can think of, is after we were married, he took over my hospital bills and put his name on my other home. I signed papers for him to do that, he must have put the legal guardian papers in with those, so I had no idea I signed it. My whole existence with Michael was a lie. But it just never seems to end. There is always one more lie to be told. And how was he going to keep the money from me? Another lie, he was so good at that."

"Well from the look on your face, you will not have to worry about finances for a while."

"For a long, long time, I said. I will need to get a financial advisor and create an estate. I am also going to notify my Lawyer, that I want nothing from Michael's estate, so we can finish with that and as soon as possible."

"If you need help with anything, you know where to reach me. But I have a feeling you will be able to hire your own office staff once that check arrives." She laughed.

"No-one in this family will ever have to worry about finances again and that is a promise. Through this whole ordeal you and the rest of the family have been there for me. I feel this is a gift, and I intend to share it. I would always tell myself to leave my worries to God and he will take care of them. God has been true to his word."

"You take care of yourself first, if anyone deserves this gift it is you. The suffering you have had endured has been a nightmare for you and it is finally over."

"I hope so, that is all I really wanted was for this to end, so I could start over."

"Well I better get home. You know where I live." She smiled at me and gave me a hug.

The thoughts going through my head, after my sister left, were coming in waves.

The Lawyer had been talking to Michael the whole time and I never knew. Michael had convinced me that his Lawyer was taking care of everything, so there really was no reason to question him about it. But then I learned that he was the beneficiary of that settlement in case anything was to happen to me. Not my family, but him.

Another blow, how many more? I want the truth, but what kind of a man would do this? Again the same question I had asked myself so many times before. He had to know one day that I would find out about this. What was his motive? Was he hoping that he would be able to control me to the point that I would sign over that settlement to him? He was able to do that with Susan's investments. Why, I asked myself, why won't he just go away, why is he still haunting me with his lies and deceptions?

This is the end, for my sake, I will make sure of it. I must start a new life. I have so much to be thank-full for.

The following days were so hectic. I had so many things I wanted to do and now that I could afford it, there was nothing that was so important anymore. I found myself laughing more, the burdens were lifted. I was happy and I kept thinking of Candy. It did start with finding her. I called her. I needed to talk to her.

"How are you doing?" I asked.

"I am fine, but I have to admit I miss you. We just did not have enough time."

"I will come to visit again soon. I must tell you I have stopped trying to get anything from Michael's estate, as I have come into some money. I wanted to end any and all communication with his family, All but you of course"

"I had some doubts about seeing you again. At first I thought you just needed to know more of Michael. But when you left, I made up my mind

that I would be the first to make the attempt to keep you in my life. I am so happy you called." She said.

"Candy, I am your step-mom, remember? I want to always be a part of your life."

"Then step-mom, I have some good news for you. I am getting married and I would be honored if you were at my side."

I had to catch my breath. I thought another gift from God.

"I am so happy for you and you know I will be there. I would not miss that for the world."

"Well it is not going to be a big wedding. We would rather save for a honeymoon, but we haven't decided where to go yet."

"What is the name of your husband-to-be?" I asked.

"His name is John and I love him so much. I think I knew it from the start, but was afraid. I don't have a good track record with men."

"Sometimes you have to go through the hardships, so when you find that right person, you do know it. When is all this to take place?"

"We are thinking maybe this summer. We will both have vacation time by then, so will not miss much work. I will let you know the date as soon as we make up our minds. I am so happy. I have found you and now the love of my life."

"I can hear the happiness in your voice."

We talked for almost an hour. We were both moving on.

I heard from my Lawyer that he still wanted to keep the court date. I told him absolutely not. I was finished and because I withdrew there was nothing to make me go to court. My Lawyer argued with me and said I could still get money that was due to me from the estate and I should continue to fight for it.

"Why is it so hard to get through to you and Jeremy that I want nothing. This ends and it ends now."

He said he would tell them and I was right. I did not have to go to court.

A couple of days later as I was checking my e-mail, I saw one from Jeremy. I opened it, as I knew it would be the last time. I had every intention of blocking any further communication from him.

He was angry and he wanted to know where the rest of his father's money was. He was sure now, since I no longer wanted to pursue any settlement, that I had the money.

I was only waiting for the right time to bring out the truth, but then again maybe I will wait. He threatened me with a lawsuit.

I had to laugh. Now the shoe was on the other foot. He would spend years thinking I had his father's money and there was nothing he could do about. I would let him think that, it was a lie and it was my lie. After all the lies I had been through, now it was my turn. I would let him continue with his Lawyer to try to get to me, because now I have a new Lawyer and he was highly recommended. I told him to continue letting Jeremy file charges against me. What a better way for him to spend his father's money!

I did e-mail him back. I wrote "have a nice life", then I blocked his name. It was over, at least for me.

The Lawyer from Vegas called and he would come to see me the following day and he had the check.

The first thing I intended to do was to write a check to Candy. I wanted her to have what her father did not even provide in his estate. Almost as if she did not even exist. She had every right to get part of his estate, but she wanted nothing from him. Maybe I could give her the wedding she really deserved.

I spent most of one day with the financial advisor and I started a trust. I then spent a couple of hours at the bank. I needed cashier checks for the investments and also one for Candy.

I mailed her a check and wrote her a letter. I wanted to let her know that I felt she was cheated out of her share of Michael's estate. I understood why she did not pursue it and it was probably for the best. The money was hers and I wanted no discussion as why she could not take it.

I went back to the spa. I wanted to talk to Andrea. She had been right, there was something more that Michael had wanted from me.

I met her at the juice bar.

"I have not seen you in a while, I was worried."

Elizabeth Klein

"I went to see Candy and I now have a wonderful step-daughter, who managed to keep her distance from the others. We talked of her life and the life she had with Michael. She really opened up to me. I think she needed to talk as much as I wanted to know more about Michael."

"I am glad it turned out well for you. I guess you have to go with your gut on some matters. "She smiled.

"There is more. Remember when you said Michael wanted more from me. There had to be something I was missing? You were right. The accidental shooting in Las Vegas, involved a lawsuit. Michael told the Lawyer he was my husband and I had suffered from some brain damage because of the gunshot wound. Michael would be my representative as far as the Lawyer was concerned. Just prior to Michael's death a settlement was offered and Michael refused it. He was holding out for more money on my behalf. The Lawyer contacted me a few weeks ago. The final settlement was more than I ever dreamed of."

"You never knew any of this?" She asked.

"I did not have any idea this was going on. After the Lawyer left, I almost went crazy with all the questions. Michael would have to tell me at some point. Did he think he could honestly cash a check at that amount and with my name on it? When and how was he going to tell me? But after a while, it no longer mattered. I am at peace for the first time in a long time. None of the past matters now."

"I felt there had to be something. Sometimes I could not even know how you must have felt with so many questions and no answers. How do you move on when you learn of the betrayal and you were used?"

"You have to or else he wins." I said.

"I wish I had your strength, I just cannot find the forgiveness."

"You have to Andrea. You are only hurting yourself, by not letting him go. The pain has to end and you will find the peace that I now have."

"Then I need to be with you more. If anyone can help me, it would be you. You know my pain and I do want it to end."

"I am always here for you and you know that."

I wanted to help her. I know how hard it is to forgive.

I told her more of my visit with Candy and also of her wedding. She wanted me to be there with her and it really touched my heart. I was looking forward to seeing her again and on such a joyous occasion.

We both got ready to leave and as I stood up, Andrea hugged me.

I was hoping that I could help her. Maybe, with God's grace.

It was evening when I received a call from Candy. She had been crying and I could not understand much of what she said. I thought perhaps the wedding was called off. But I heard the words "thank you" and I realized that she had received the check.

"Candy, please calm down so I can understand what you are saying."

"I cannot think of the words. Thank-you just does not seem to be enough. I called John and he is coming over. I cannot seem to stop crying and I am shaking. I feel like this is a dream, but I am holding the check, it is real."

"Yes it is real. You and John can start your lives together with some financial security. And if you want a big wedding, you can have it. You deserve it and more."

"There are just no words. This will help us so much."

She started crying again and I told her to talk with John and start making plans and I will look forward to hearing from her again soon.

I had to laugh, she was so very emotional.

A few days later I received an early morning call. I hate those calls, it is never good news and I was right.

"Mom, my son Daniel said, Shea is in the emergency room. I did not want to say anything to you right now, but I am really worried about her. She is pregnant, mom. She started bleeding last night and I brought her here."

"Daniel, you should have told me. How far along is she?"

"We think about two months, just not sure."

"Sometimes there is some early bleeding. It does not necessarily mean she is having a miscarriage." I said.

"She really wants this baby, mom. It would be devastating for her to lose it."

"And how about you? Do you want this baby?"

Elizabeth Klein

"If you could have seen how excited she was when she knew she was pregnant. I got caught up in it and I realized how important this baby is for both of us. Now we may lose it."

"Don't think that way. Have you heard from the Doctor yet?"

"I am in the room by myself. They took her to have an Ultrasound. Will the Ultrasound let us know if the baby is going to be okay?" He asked.

"Yes it will, but either way you be strong for her. Do you want me to come?"

"No, not yet, better find out what is happening first. I will call you as soon as we know something"

"Daniel, I know you to well. You will not call, but you have to promise me this time, after all this will be my first grandchild."

"I promise, mom, as soon as I know something."

"Hang in there kid, it is not always bad news. I love you."

After he hung up I got on my knees and prayed for the life of this baby.

Two hours later, he called me back.

"She is okay mom, you were right, the baby is fine. The Doctor said the baby had a good heartbeat. She can't stop crying, so I better take care of her and I will call you later."

I could tell he was chocked up, so I told him to give her my love and I would talk to them later.

I am going to be a grandmother, wow.

I called my whole family the next day and of course Lesley. I know my son was annoyed with me as I called him three times that day. I talked to Shea and I could hear the excitement in her voice. She said she did a lot of praying in that hospital room. I told her she had plenty of company in that respect. I asked her if she wanted me to come and she said no. She was enjoying being waited on hand and foot from my son.

After a few weeks I decided to go see them. It was going to be more than a visit. Shea gave me a big hug and I could feel her joy. My son gave me a hug and told me it was not necessary for me to come.

"I know you had another Ultrasound, but no one called to let me know the results. So I made this trip to make sure everything is okay. Seeing as a certain son of mine cannot pick up a phone,"

"I will make sure that son of yours, who will be a father soon, to call his mom more often." She said.

We both looked at Daniel and laughed.

"The baby is doing well, everything is fine. Also the father is okay." She went over to him and gave him a kiss.

A few minutes later a truck parked out front.

"Well they are finally here. We better move some things so they can get in."

"Mom what did you do?" He asked.

"Come and see."

The men opened up the truck, and there was a crib, a changing table, a stroller and so much more for the baby. I also bought boxes of diapers and clothing.

"Now, Daniel, if you can show the men where to put these things."

Shea started crying and gave me a big hug.

I stayed for a couple days and I really enjoyed helping Shea decorate the nursery.

I was ready to leave and Shea started crying again. I told her I was going to be a Grandma now and I wanted to hear more from them. I gave my son a hug and put an envelope in his hand.

"Take care of her, I said to him. She needs you more than ever now."

"Mom, you have done enough, I don't need this, we will be okay."

"You do not argue with your mom. Please call once in a while."

I hugged them both and left. I gave my son the deed to the house and a check to help them out.

Just before I left to go to Candy's wedding. My son did call. Shea had another Ultrasound and the baby is a boy. I actually heard the excitement in his voice.

"Well I am glad you did call. And be prepared to receive some boxes of boy outfits."

"Mom, if you buy anymore, Shea and I will be sleeping in the garage."

Elizabeth Klein

"I will be a Grandma, it is my right and you do not argue with your mom remember?

"You are impossible, but I love you,"

"It is nice to hear those words a little more. Take care of Shea, I love you both.

I feel so blessed. I thought of Michael, the first time in a long time. If only he knew what it felt like to give, of your-self. The happiness and love you feel in return. There is no amount of money that can be placed on that. It is such a shame. He missed out, not knowing.

Candy and John were waiting for me when I arrived. He was such a nice man and you could tell he really loved Candy. He was always holding her hand and looking at her. We had dinner and had a nice time, we laughed so much. It was nice to hear laughter again. John dropped us off at her house and I went to the room I had before. I told Candy I was exhausted and I wanted to turn in early. I also told her she better get some rest as tomorrow she will be a bride.

The wedding was held in her friend's back yard. It was beautiful, lots of flowers and wedding decorations. There were only a few of us, but it did not really matter. I watched as they said their vows and I remembered my vows to Michael. It was a combination of sadness and happiness.

After she tossed her bouquet, Candy and John danced and there was love. We had something to eat, as Candy had hired a caterer. I met her friends and they were so much fun to be with. After a couple of hours we left. John dropped Candy and I off at her house. She needed to change and get packed for her honeymoon.

"I feel so bad that we decided to leave right after we were married." She said.

"It is fine. I knew I could not stay long, so everything worked out. I am so happy for you and John, I wish you both the best marriage has to offer."

"I love him so much. I did not think I could ever find true love. But I did." She smiled.

When John came to pick her up, she kissed me good-bye and John gave me a hug and said "thank-you for being here for her."

"I love her just as much as you do and I will always be here for both of you."

After they left I did not realize how tired I was. I slept soundly that night, with a smile on my face.

The next day I called a cab and went to the airport. I was looking forward to going home. Short trips really take a lot out of me, but I have a beautiful memory that will be with me forever.

When I returned, I started to go the spa more often.

One day when Andrea and I were at the juice bar, I decided to bring up an idea I had been thinking about for some time.

"Andrea, how about you and I go away for a while?"

"What do you mean, like a vacation?"

"Yes, a fun trip, for the both of us"

"And what have you been thinking, about this fun trip?" She smiled.

"I was thinking about a cruise. I have always wanted to go to Alaska."

"Alaska sounds good. And when would you want to take this fun trip?

"As soon as I can get the information, so that means soon."

"You get the information and I will make the reservations. No arguments about the financing of this trip."

"Wow, I will not make any hassle about that statement." I laughed.

We were on the ship, within five weeks, after I first made the suggestion. I had to admit Andrea liked to go first class. We had first class flights and a Luxury Suite on the ship. I was impressed. We spent most of the day just unpacking and getting settled. We chose the late dinner hour and when we arrived at our table, there were two gentlemen, who were sharing our table. I looked at Andrea and thought, did she set this up? When we started introducing ourselves, it became obvious that Andrea did know one of the men. I looked at her and could not believe she did this, but then again this was Andrea. I had to smile.

The man that knew Andrea was Doug and he introduced his friend Nick. I have to admit we had a nice evening, talking and laughing. We decided to go to the lounge after dinner. There was a piano player there and I loved the music he was playing. We had a few drinks and then went *on the deck. It was beautiful, the ocean below and stars above. Andrea and Doug walked away as I was leaning against the banister, just taking it all in. Nick was standing beside me.*

"Is this your first cruise?" He asked.

"Yes, and I hope it will not be my last."

I looked around and realized Andrea and Doug had disappeared.

"Where did they go?" I asked Nick.

"I doubt very seriously if they will be returning any time soon. Doug and Andrea have known each other for some time. She told Doug about this cruise and asked him to join her and bring a friend. When he asked me I thought it was a good idea, but when I learned Andrea would be there, I told him we definitely needed separate rooms." He laughed.

"I hope that this situation will not become complicated for both of us." I said,

"Not at all, but I sure am happy to have met you. I guess we are going to be on a lot of excursions on this trip and maybe if you are agreeable we can stick together on those trips. I doubt seriously if our "friends" will be much of our companions." He laughed again.

"I think you are right and I am very happy to have met you. I just wish Andrea would have given me a heads up, but I should have known she would have something else up her sleeve."

"That is Andrea for you." He smiled.

"Well if you don't mind, I feel rather tired and I would like to return to my room, but I feel rather lost on this ship and was wondering if you could help me find it."

"These ships are always confusing the first couple of days. But after time you will know your way around."

He held my arm and it was no time at all before we came to the room. I had forgotten we were in the Luxury Suites.

"Thank you so much. I guess we will see each other again tomorrow."

"Yes, we will. We are scheduled to go on a whale watching boat tomorrow afternoon. Have a good night." With that, he turned and walked away.

I stood there watching him for a while. I should be angry at Andrea, but I was not. This is going to be a fun trip.

When Andrea finally came to the room, I had been asleep. I woke up and looked at the clock. It was 3:00 am.

"Sorry, I did not mean to wake you up. But if I am going to get a lecture, I might as well have it now."

"I really should be angry, but I like Doug and I like Nick. You are so unpredictable." I laughed.

"This was your idea and I just added some amenities. It sounds like the one I planned for you was enjoyable."

"Maybe not as enjoyable as the one you gave yourself. Time will tell, I said. But maybe you can tell me more about Doug, like how did you two meet."

"We dated in high school. He went off to college and I started working in a Public Defenders Office, in the same town we grew up in. For some unknown reason, we always kept in touch. He married and had a couple of kids and I married a Lawyer in town. After my marriage ended, with a wonderful monthly allotment, we found each other again.

His marriage ended after his kids left home. Doug is also a Lawyer and Nick works in his Law Firm, which is in New York."

"So does that mean we have the Law on our side." I smiled.

"That is really funny. Too bad they live so far away."

"Maybe not, sometimes it is just nice to have the communication with someone. Not the complications of a relationship." I was serious with that statement.

"Well the complications I had this evening, I can deal with." She smiled.

We talked for about an hour more. She told me he was one man she could really enjoy herself with, but love always seemed out of the question for both of them. Although time will tell and hopefully we had a lot of that.

We finally went to sleep. It was apparently going to be a long day tomorrow.

I really have to admit that I had fun. Nick made me laugh. He was fun to be with. Most days we were all together, most nights we were not. Nick and I would walk around the deck in the evenings and just talk.

He told me he never married. Every time he thought he found the right one, she would screw it up.

"She would screw it up and it never had anything to do with you?"

Elizabeth Klein

"Yep, that is how it went." He smiled.

"Well it seems more like you were looking for something really special or maybe your high expectations just could not be met."

"I do not think I had high expectations. Beautiful, charming and rich, that was it."

"Well that answers why you are still single." I laughed.

We would talk for hours and I realized how comfortable I felt with him. I was not going to question things, as I was here to have fun and so far I laughed more than I had in a very long time.

We had a formal evening for dinner one night. We would meet the Captain of the ship and then have dinner. Nick and Doug were waiting for us by the dining room. We greeted the Captain and all four of us stood together, for a picture. Nick and I danced most of the evening and I felt as if I were in a fairy tale. When we returned to the table after a dance, Doug and Andrea had disappeared.

"I was surprised they waited this long." Nick said.

"I feel like taking a walk anyway, I smiled. Let's go on the deck."

When we started walking, we saw Doug and Andrea at the end of the deck. He had his arm around her. It was romantic.

I did not want to disturb them, so we turned and walked the other way.

"I have to tell you something, Nick said. I think I will just go with two out of three. When you walked toward me while we were waiting to meet the Captain, I thought you were the most beautiful and charming woman on the whole ship."

"Well thank you very much. A woman my age does not hear that very often."

"Age is only a number." He said.

"Yes a number, but unfortunately it increases with time and I decrease with time." I was hoping he would take it as a joke. He did not laugh.

Instead he pulled me toward him and kissed me. For me, time stopped.

I thought I was dead inside, damaged goods with a cold heart. But I felt something, a yearning perhaps to live again and maybe to love.

"I am sorry. I told myself I would not do anything that would make you uncomfortable." He smiled.

"Don't be sorry. In all honesty, I never wanted another man in my life. I always thought family and friends would be enough to keep me going. Now being with Doug and Andrea and you, I feel I am alive again. I can laugh again and I have opened my eyes and my heart. We may never meet again after this cruise and that is okay. I feel as if I have something now that I had lost, that was taken away from me, and that was my self-worth. Thank you for that."

He did not say anything, but held me tight. We kissed again and this time I kissed him back. We stayed on the deck to the early morning. We talked of our lives, our struggles, our relationships and families. He was so easy to confide in and he still made me laugh. Even though I was tired, I did not want to go back to my room. But he saw that I needed to get some rest, so he took me back to my room and kissed me goodnight.

The days that followed went by fast. It was time for our departure. Doug and Andrea were in each other arms and kissing. I told Nick I had a wonderful time and I would never forget it.

"This is not our last time together. We will be talking and maybe there will be another cruise in the future."

He held me again and we kissed. I thought it would be my last kiss.

I was not sad leaving, I had a very memorable and fun trip.

Time has passed so fast. My family is here celebrating the fourth of July with me. Candy and her husband John are here. John invested some money in a small computer business and it is doing very well. They are still so much in love. Daniel and Shea are here, they married right after the baby was born. They did not tell me, as they wanted a nice quiet wedding. Damion is here with his new girlfriend. I think she just might be the one for him.

My sisters and brother are here. Lesley and Ben are giving my son Damion some hints on how to bar-b-que and they are laughing. And my dearest companion Andrea is setting the table.

We are planning our next cruise, with our favorite male traveler's.

And I am in my rocking chair, holding my bundle of joy, my grandson, little Conway.

Life is good.

Printed in the United States
By Bookmasters